DUNES
OF *Fire*

A.J.GOODRUM

PAGE PUBLISHING, INC.
Conneaut Lake, PA

First originally published by Page Publishing 2019

ISBN 978-1-64462-724-2 (pbk)
ISBN 978-1-64628-022-3 (hc)
ISBN 978-1-64462-725-9 (digital)

Printed in the United States of America

Thank you, Dennis, for all your support on the *Dunes of Fire* book.

This book is dedicated to my lovely wife of 27 years, Pamela Goodrum. Without our love, I would not have written this book.

PROLOGUE

KING ARUMET WALKED out and stood peacefully on the balcony of his palace, watching as the glowing sun rose above the horizon in the far distance. Wrapping his robe around him, he tilted his head and closed his eyes, taking a deep breath of fresh air. The scents on the air mixed with the smell of his morning meal the servants had prepared. Glancing over, he saw them patiently standing to the side, awaiting his needs. The meager yet growing light glistened on the surface of the flowing river, bouncing and dancing as the water moved to the great sea to the north. The wave of new sunlight slowly pushed away the night shadows, highlighting the city around him.

Looking below, hundreds of his citizens scurried up and down the main avenue in their daily rituals, preparing themselves for what was to come that day. Columns of smoke rose everywhere as fires burned from families preparing meals. Sounds of voices, animals, and laughter rose in the breeze, indicating his city was beginning to wake from the night's slumber. Taking another long breath of the sweet air, he turned to sit and eat his meal.

Noticing his approach, one of the servants pulled the chair from the table. Before he could reach it, there was a loud noise from the other room that caused him to stop. Looking, the noise came from the chamber doors that had suddenly slammed open. A guard was rushing toward him and slid to a stop, bowing and completely out of breath. The king walked over to him and produced a grunt, indicating his displeasure at being disturbed.

"What is the urgency that you should interrupt my morning?"

"My…my king…" His words did not come out as no air filled his lungs.

"Be quick," he grumbled.

The king could see beads of sweat running down his forehead, and a light sheen covered his bare skin. He waited patiently for him to speak, allowing him to gather himself. His run must have been from a great distance to be this out of breath. During his morning, no one was to disturb him unless it was of great importance. After a moment, the guard lifted his head.

"My king"—he paused again—"the gods have come to the hills."

The king could tell from his now-trembling body and voice that the man did not know how to pass on the news of what he had seen. He walked over and placed his hand on his shoulder to try and calm him.

"Tell me slowly…where did this happen and who witnessed the event?"

"A herder said they came to him while tending his flock of sheep out on the western slopes. He then ran to us and we went out to investigate. When we arrived at the slopes, we saw six golden figures standing beside a glowing white flame."

"What were they doing?"

"Just…they were just standing there, my king, barely moving."

There was now only silence as the king contemplated his words.

"Guards," he then commanded, walking swiftly past him, "prepare my horse! I must go and see this wondrous sight immediately."

The guard led the king and his entourage to the spot he indicated. As they approached, he could see that several hundred people had gathered and were held back from the spot by his troops. Just beyond them, near a small outcropping of rocks, was the glowing flame that highlighted the figures. Pressing through the parting crowd of people, he stopped on the other side and got off his horse.

It was indeed a truly wondrous sight. Two golden figures stood and seemed to gaze out at the people that had gathered. Their skin shimmered like the flesh of fish pulled from the river. The other four figures behind them gathered and arranged objects that mysteriously appeared from the now-pulsing flame. They appeared to be human yet, by their appearance, not. Slowly, he walked up to them, cautiously stopping several feet away.

"I am King Arument, ruler of all this land and the people that reside here," he said, waving his hand. "You are trespassing on this place… What is your purpose and why have you come?"

"We mean no harm to you or your people and did not intend to make such a commotion with our coming," one of the figures said.

"Still, your presence here creates great fear in my people," he said with caution. "Again, I ask of you…why have you come to us? My people think of you as God's by your coming to us in this manner. If you are not gods as you say, I can only assume it for some demonic reason."

Not knowing their true intention or who they were, the king had instructed his guards before he approached them to be prepared to kill the intruders and protect him if needed. With a glance, he saw that they awaited his command.

"We are not God's as you say, and there is no demonic intention for being here," the figure said. "Our people are peaceful and simply wish to be…teachers if you will. Our current appearance is nothing more than protection against the, well, harsh weather in this area."

"But your appearance is not the same as those we know."

"Be not afraid. Over a short time, it will become normal and we will be as you."

"How can that be?" the king asked, unsure of the answer.

They then stood in silence for several minutes. As the being indicated, after a few minutes that they spoke, the king could see that the golden color surrounding them was slowly fading away. Several parts of their arms and face were turning to a shade very similar to his. The change in appearance swept away part of his fear, but some still remained. The figure now looked similar to him but wore strange clothing.

He turned around and told his guards to break up the gathering of people that had grown behind them and send them back to their homes. As the people obeyed and returned to their tasks and their homes, he turned back again to the figure.

"By appearing in this manner, no simple change in appearance will calm the fear in their hearts that witnessing this event has created. You appear to have...abilities beyond those at our disposal and could easily harm all of us. If this is to continue, in peace as you say, may I ask what you really want and if you have a name?"

"My name is unimportant, but for now, you can call me...Miah."

"Very well...Miah. And what is it that you want from us?"

"I will take some time, but we came because you are the future of these lands and we want to help you get there. There has to be a strong foundation for your son's future."

"My...for my son's? I have no sons."

"No sons...yet," Miah said with a grin.

"We welcome those that are friends but take no pity on those that are enemies. I will hear what you have to say. But tell me now which of these are you?"

"We are friends and will try to prove our intentions. Our group has traveled a great distance to meet you and to help your people."

"I am honored, Miah. You will be my guest within my house so we may discuss your intentions further."

"We would be honored. I also come bearing a gift, one of gratitude in humbly allowing us in your presence. If I may be so allowed?"

"A tribute...to me? It is allowed."

"Thank you," Miah said, turning. The other figure stepped forward and handed him a small object. When he turned and handed it to the king, his eyes widened. Before he could reach for it, an arrow sailed over the king's shoulder toward the figure. As the lethal object came closer to strike its intended target, it suddenly stopped in mid-air between them, held by an unseen force in the air, and after a moment, it then fell harmlessly to the ground.

"Is this...magic," the king gasped, watching the arrow.

"We have certain abilities that you could not understand."

Not able to comprehend what had happened, the king quickly spun around.

"Seize that man," he voiced angrily, pointing to the guards. Several of them quickly grabbed a man in the front by the arms and, holding him, pressed him to his knees until he could approach. King Arumet was angry at his subject and began to shout.

"I am your king! How dare you disobey my commands!"

Miah and the other figure did not move and surveyed the event. As the king continued to rant at the man, the figures showed no emotional display. King Arumet was tired of screaming and grabbed the sword from the hip of a guard. Hovering before the trembling man, he stared down at the man.

The king must not hurt this man on our account, Miah thought. Before he could move or speak, he saw it was too late.

King Arumet then yelled loudly and raised the sword above him. The blade came down and struck the man's arm near his shoulder. With a loud cry, the man then collapsed *against the guard still holding him. The other guard stood beside him, now holding his bleeding arm in his hand. The king then tossed the bloody blade to the ground.*

"This is my kingdom and I deal out all punishment."

"Stop," Miah yelled, raising his hand. The king and the others turned around and looked at Miah. "Please do not harm this man further on our behalf. We come here as your friends and in peace. This man has done nothing. Let me help him and, in doing so, show our intentions."

"Let him be his insolence so others may know."

"I cannot allow that to happen," Miah said.

He then walked over to the bleeding man and, kneeling, gently held his face and gave him a smile. Looking at the one guard holding the bleeding arm, he stretched out his hand to him. The guard looked at him and then back to the king. King Arumet produced a shrug and nodded. Handing him the severed arm, Miah pressed it back in place and held it together with both hands. A white glow appeared that hid both the man's shoulder and the tight binding hands. The flow of blood from his body immediately stopped, and the man gasped loudly. Blinking his eyes, the man stared up at Miah and produced a sigh. Standing up, he helped the man to his feet and watched as he moved his arm around, amazed that it was as if nothing had ever happened.

"Thank you, lord…thank you," the man said continuously. Kissing Miah's hand several times, he then ran through the crowd and into the distance, happily screaming his miraculous recovery.

What strange power of healing do these people possess? King Arumet thought after watching the impossible scene unfold before him. Even though they said they were not gods, he knew that they were what they said they were, a friend. They may be a source of power that he could use. He then moved toward both of them and spoke.

"I am a man of my word, and from this day, I and my people will consider you as friends and that you have come here in peace. Because of your power and wish to teach us a better way, I will temper my anger."

The words coming from the king took the guards by surprise and gestured to the remaining peasants out from before them. From past experiences, they knew that he could change his mind in an instance even after saying what he did.

"Everything starts slowly, and it should start here and now."

"Because of our new friendship, I will throw a great festival tonight for you and your teachers. Please come and be my guests."

"We happily accept and will be honored."

"Good."

The king went back and picked up the gift that Miah had given him and placed it in his robes. He then motioned for his people to bring several mounts that would transport Miah and the other teacher to his palace. As the king mounted his horse and rode off with his guards, the horses were brought over, and they climbed up onto them. Looking around, they noticed that the guards that escorted them continued to look back at the pillar of fire still visible against the cliffs. It was a silent sentry to guard the spot.

After about an hour of slow travel, they came over a rise and into a long, wide valley near the western edge of the river. There were huge golden fields of wheat and orchards of various fruits. The light of the fires coming from the city grew before them. It was a stark change from the desolation of the desert they had come from earlier.

The main street curving through the city leading up to the palace was lined with simple mud dwellings. Some of them were several stories high with citizens laughing and talking from the open windows. The group traveled unnoticed as people passing them barely gave them much of a glance even with the guards surrounding them. Other people roamed casually in and out of the market areas, buying staples. The smell of food cooking on the fires filled the air.

The buildings ended and opened into a vast open area leading to a large palace. A large wooden gate was set into the smooth stone walls. Fires burned above the edge, creating light. Miah was surprised that they were able to build such a structure. He would have to inquire as to its origin. Several guards peered over the edge as they approached and yelled down to others behind the walls that they had arrived. The door slowly swung to the side, allowing the group to go inside.

Once inside the walls and dismounted, they were ushered to a large interior where they were asked to wait. They watched as the servants of the house scrambled about in their tasks in preparing for the evening. In about twenty minutes, a woman with several servants approached them.

"I am Enna, first consort of King Arumet. Please follow me."

Leading them down a hallway, several guards stood beside a door and bowed as they approached. Reaching over, one of them opened it and stood back. Entering, the room appeared very luxurious with many amenities. Fruits and drink were arranged on a table in the middle of the room. A large bathing area was off to one side, and delicate linens fluttered in the breeze from the balcony opening. Off to each side, several women stood awaiting instructions.

"These will be your quarters until the festivities begin. Here, no harm will come of you. The servants," she said, sweeping her hands around to them, "will attend to your every need as you may desire and make you comfortable. Clothes that you may be part of us have been prepared for you."

"Please thank the king for all his hospitality, and we are at his disposal."

"Until later."

Enna bowed slightly to them and left with her servants. Once they were in the hallway, the guard closed the door to the room. Miah was not sure of this ritual and felt he could not break with their local customs. Once the door closed, three of the servants came over to him, and the others went over to the other teacher.

"Please, lord, if you will allow us," one of the woman asked.

"Perform your tasks as commanded."

With a slight bow, the woman slowly surrounded him and the other teacher and began to delicately remove their clothing. Once removed, they folded each article. Once they were naked, they guided them over to the bathing pool and led them into the water. Each servant removed their clothing before entering. For some time, the three woman washed them, pouring warm water and scented oils across their skin. Now that they were clean, they ushered them from the pool and began to dry them. Finally, one of the women spoke.

"Did this please my lord?"

"It did," Miah said, enjoying the attention. While standing, a small breeze came from outside and swept across his bare skin. "It was wonderful."

"Then as a man, there must be other pleasures or needs that we may attend to. Do you wish for this? It is our main purpose in life to fill the needs of man."

"I…" Miah began before feeling the woman's warm hands touch him softly.

The other two women kneeling beside him began to stroke his body from behind and down the length of his thighs. He didn't know if he should interact with these people in such a manner but knew if he refused it would certainly offend the king and might have consequences for the servants. He turned and, seeing the other three women crouched beside the other teacher, knew that he could not refuse. He then nodded and turned back to the woman.

"And your wish, my lord," she inquired, waiting. "Do we not please you?"

"You and the others do please me," he said, relenting to their custom. "I will allow you in your task."

With a smile, the women stood, and they guided him over to the bed while the other teacher was taken to another room by the other servants. As he lay down on the cool material and became comfortable, he watched as the women arranged themselves beside him. This act was something that was not normal among his people. It was more of an animalistic and demeaning behavior.

Am I breaking my societal laws by doing this? he thought.

Before he could think about it further, the woman leaned over and began to kiss him with a purposeful passion as the multitude of hands and wet lips began to massage him. The tenderness of their touch began to arouse him. He had already committed to this course of action and could not turn back. Reaching up, he pulled the woman close to his chest and returned her kiss. His resistance slipped away as the world around him merged into a sea of unbridled desire.

The sharp knock at the door served as notice that the festival was about to begin. Miah and the other teacher had dressed and were ready as it opened. Entering the room, she noticed that the robes they wore made them look like any other citizen. Pausing, she looked around at the servants.

"Have you been well cared for?" she asked.

"All of our needs have been well cared for," Miah said, looking at the servants.

"Excellent… Please, if you will follow me. The king is waiting."

They followed Enna back down the hallway to a large open hall. When they entered, they could see that it was already filled with many people from the town. Several tables near the king indicated they were of high standing within the culture. Musicians played from a small alcove to the side, and servants had filled the tables with plates of food. Everyone turned as they began to walk over to the king's table. Several spots at his table were open beside him and, raising his hand, motioned for them to come over and sit. Once seated, the king dismissed Enna.

"Were your accommodations to your liking?" the king asked them.

"You have been more than generous with your hospitality."

"That is excellent," the king said with glee at Miah's pleasure. "Let us then eat and drink. We will have time to talk later."

"As you wish," Miah said.

For hours, the festival was dominated with food of all kinds, drinks, and all manners of entertainment. Women danced to music, and men fought for their enjoyment in a small area before them. During intermissions, high-ranking dignitaries from the city would come forward to the front of the king's table and introduced themselves. Finally, when the night had worn on, the king stood and commanded that the evening was completed. While the hall emptied, the king leaned back on several pillows and looked at Miah. In his hand, he produced the gift that Miah had given him earlier in the day.

"What is this gift you have given me?"

"It is a special healing serum."

"We have such things. What is so special about this?"

"May I demonstrate it to you?"

"Please."

Holding his hand out, Miah took the jar from the king and, looking around, found a small knife on the table. Opening the jar, he placed it on the table and, holding his hand out, used the knife to cut a large gash in the palm of his hand. The king's eyes widened, noticing the blood running from the wound. Placing two fingers into the jar, he applied some of the serum onto the wound and rubbed it. Within minutes, the blood had stopped flowing, and wiping the mixed layers away, he held his hand out for the king. He watched as the cut slowly closed and disappeared, leaving no visible mark.

"That was amazing," the king gasped, taking the jar back.

"It will help in healing simple wounds."

"Now," the king said, taking a sip of wine, "let us discuss your arrival."

"We come to save your society."

"Save it?" the king said, astonished. "Save us from what?"

"From the coming world."

"Impossible, I do not believe this."

"What do you know of the far northern area?"

"What is in the north is the edge of the world. Those that go there die or fall off the cliff in their ignorance."

"No…the north holds the destiny of your civilization. Without a change, you will be destroyed as it develops."

"And you have come to us to save us?"

"We wish only for you to survive as you, and your heirs are the future of the world."

"And how would you do that?"

"It is only a simple request. We wish that you to bring us twelve of your smartest people of who we will pick those that are capable of teaching our very special abilities. From those that we choose, they will then teach others and so on for years to come. In that way, you will be prepared for what is to come."

"Why would you come here and offer us these abilities?"

"The world that you know will disappear, and the great desert to your west will engulf the land. All of this lush land will shrink to nothing without our help. Let us teach your people, and if it is not what is expected, we will leave you as we came."

The king did not say a word and contemplated Miah's words. It could not hurt to have abilities beyond those of any of the other cities around him. If something could give him an advantage over them, he could use it. Here was a person willing to provide something without his asking. He could not see why he shouldn't allow it.

"Very well," he said. "In the morning, the people you ask for will be brought to you. How long will this task take?"

"Less than a day, and after our choosing, we will begin immediately."

"It shall be so. The men will be brought to your quarters in the morning as you have asked. Tonight, relax and enjoy all we have to offer you."

"By your command," Miah said, rising.

They returned to their room and were met by the same servants as earlier. Miah walked past them and out onto the balcony. Looking out, there were only a few fires burning on the other side of the river. The view was calming. It seemed a peace was now occurring over the city and the inhabitants. He then felt a tug on his arm. Turning, he saw it was the servant woman.

"Please, lord, come to bed and rest," she urged.

"Would that please you?"

"It would give me and the others great pleasure to ensure your rest."

"Very well," he sighed, "we will go and rest."

"If…if that is your pleasure," she said softly, leading him toward the bed.

"I will be mud in your talented hands," he laughed. "You may please me as you wish that you can satisfy your task."

The woman unexpectedly produced a laugh at his comment as she and the others began to remove his clothing. He was sure that whatever they had in store for him would be just as wondrous as before. They were very skilled in their actions. As he prepared himself, he closed his eyes as they came beside him. The cool of the night disappeared with the warmth of their bodies.

In the morning, the king brought twelve men he had handpicked to their chamber as Miah had instructed. Taking them into the other room, the king waited for Miah to pick those he would teach. The king was not use to waiting and became impatient. Before his curiosity overcame him, Miah returned. Then several of the men came out of the other room and walked past the king, leaving. Six men came out and stood near Miah.

"We have chosen these men for our task."

"And now what must be done?"

"The training must be done in a special place over the next few days."

"I have such a place, come."

The king took Miah and the others to a chamber off the main palace. It had several rooms and was probably a guesthouse of some sort. It was sparse in furnishings but had all the basic things that would satisfy someone's needs. Miah looked around and, then turning, expressed his approval of the area.

"In this place and in complete solitude, these men will be trained over the course of two days. All the normal needs during this time will be brought at specific times and only to the attending servants. This main room," Miah said, pointing around, "must be changed to include not one object, and that room over there will house the six men. They will never be separated and must remain together. We will need several more servants to attend to their needs. After this time, we will begin in the real world and supervise their work."

"I will command it and will be interested in their work," the king expressed.

"Thank you," Miah said. "Progress will be seen after three moon cycles."

"I will wait your unveiling."

"At the end of this teaching, we will leave another gift. It will be of more importance and guide your people into the future."

"Whatever it is, I will accept it with honor."

Over the next two days, Miah and the other teacher would go from their room in the early morning to the quarters where the men resided. They would stay isolated within the room until late evening when they would come out and leave. Several guards were positioned outside the door and kept anyone from entering or leaving.

On the morning of the third day, they each took three men and moved out into the streets of the city. The king did not interfere with them and gave them full run of the city and its citizens. Miah took his men down to the northern part of the city while the other took his men to the river area.

The king sat in his chamber and looked over the city. He wondered what was happening and what abilities the teachers were imparting to the men he gave them. As he looked up into the sky, he knew that the three cycles were almost completed. After all this time, he would know all in the morning.

When the sun began to rise, the king had the guards take him to the first area the men were working on. To his surprise, it was a towering temple with figures carved from blocks of stone. Men were on ladders everywhere and were carefully chiseling stone into *meticulous figures. There was even strange writing filled with odd figures in precise lines across the smooth stone. One imposing figure, large and in the middle of the temple, he noticed was that of him. Walking closer, he was amazed at the striking similarity. Every portion of the new temple held wonders he could only imagine. He was very pleased.*

Tracking down the other group, he found them in a building with many furnaces. They were creating items he could not recognize. There were piles of various ores taken from the mountains everywhere. Walking over to one of the men, the king's soldier held out an object. It was a sword, but when he took it, it felt heavier than he expected. Twisting it in his hands, he could see that the main weight of it was covered in a shiny material. The man nodded and, taking it from him, swung it swiftly, striking a piece of timber near him. It buried deep into the fibers yet did not break. He smiled as the man struggled to remove it. He then turned and looked around.

"Where are the teachers so that I may thank them for these things?"

"We do not know, my king," the man said. "We have not seen them in several days."

"Guards, go, search them out and bring them to me."

While they left and searched for the teachers, the king went back to the new temple to inspect the creation in closer detail. After several hours of wandering through the structure and talking to the men, inspecting the construction, a single guard came back to inform him of their progress.

"My king...we are unable to locate them. They are nowhere to be found."

"I said they were to be found," he said angrily. "Question the servants."

"The servants of the teachers have also disappeared. There is also no sign of them."

"What?"

"There is also something else, my king. A thing you must see yourself located outside of the city to the north. It suddenly appeared from nowhere."

"Show me then," he commanded.

Stepping outside, the guards had brought his horse. Following the guard for several miles, an object began to grow larger in the distance. He could not believe that such a structure could appear from nothing and without anyone noticing. When they were close, he stopped and got off his animal. He stood in complete awe at the structure. Was this the gift the teachers had spoken of?

Before him was the largest stone structure he had ever seen and was shaped in the form of a lying beast with the head of a strange bird. The beak protruded out from the face and hooked at the end. Deeply set eyes that stared off into the distance. He could not see any doorway that would lead them into the structure. It appeared solid. Between the paws was a large tablet with more of the strange writing he had seen in the temple. Walking up to it, he placed his hand against the surface. His mind became cloudy and a specific thought suddenly appeared in his mind.

We will always be watching. Take care of the gifts we have provided you.

The king instantly stepped back and fell to his knees, staring up at the face on the structure. Seeing the king fall, the guards quickly rushed over to him. He quickly began to swing his arms, keeping them back and then slowly rose to his feet. Looking up at the face on the structure, he began to tremble.

"I will…I will," he mumbled.

CHAPTER 1

WESTERN EGYPTIAN DESERT,
NORTHEAST OF THE CITY OF LUXOR

WITH A TOWEL in both hands, he wiped his face of water after his shower. He walked out into the bedroom and, looking outside, saw that it was still dark. In a few short hours, he knew the sun would rise on another hot day. Getting dressed, he then began to gather his belongings. Picking the last of his things, he then heard a soft moan coming from the bed. With the growing moans, he sat his bag down and came around, sitting down on the edge of the mattress. Stroking her face gently as she turned, she looked up at him.

"Do you have to leave already?" she begged, trying to pull him down.

"Yes," he said, kissing her. "I have things that must be done."

"Do not stay late. We have to have more time together."

"I'll try," he said, pulling the sheets across her. "Go back to sleep."

Standing, he saw her turn to her side and curl the sheets up around her neck. With a stroke of her thigh, he picked up his remaining things and left. Within an hour, he would be back at the dig site and ready to pick up where he left off.

The sun was now beginning to rise above the horizon, and Dr. Manny Cortez knew that, within a few short hours, the temperature would be almost unbearable. They had to get the main digging done before that time. Standing on a small hill, he watched as his helpers moved into the designated spots.

"Jorge, please have the diggers move to the west side of the main dig. We have about five more feet of material to remove before we might be finished in that section," he shouted.

"Yes, sir," he said, turning around. "Let's go, men. We are almost to the end."

The digging commenced and, even with the heat, went well into the night. Jorge, the dig supervisor, was excited to finally unearth the main wall. They had only seen parts of it before, and excitement began to grow. With over four feet of sand and dirt gone, there was less than one foot to go. Looking around, he knew that it was very late, and the men were exhausted. With no moon to help illuminate the area, it was becoming too dark even with the lights to dig any more. He signaled Jorge to have them stop.

"Men, we break until morning."

As the men slowly disbanded and went to their homes, Dr. Cortez went back to his tent and sat down at his desk. Pulling his paperwork out, he looked at it and wondered if what he surmised was truly here. If it was actually the spot he searched for, then everything people knew of this area would change forever. He had to find the chamber the writings spoke of and the clue for the great treasure. Standing up, he stepped back outside and looked around the dig site. With a yawn, he stretched and decided he would return to his room. Tomorrow would be another day.

Entering the tent to grab his stuff, he froze, seeing two figures inside. One of the men was sitting at his desk going through the papers. He slowly looked up from the table and toward him, leaning back in the chair.

"Ah, Dr. Cortez," the man said, "I hope I haven't disturbed you?"

"No, not at all, Mr. Widdal," he said, moving over to the table. "I was just closing up for the night."

"And so, my dear doctor, I've come to see what you have for me today," he asked, looking at a sheet of paper he held in his hands.

Widdal was the man that was financing this dig, and for that, he expected a return on his money. He was a businessman in the area and had great influence and could change things to his will. The man was tall and slender. He was well groomed and had bling on his wrist and gold around his neck. Behind him was a man that went with him everywhere. His imposing figure told all that he was his personal bodyguard and took his job seriously.

He had financed his dig in hopes of finding what Manny had indicated was the greatest treasure for mankind— a portal to another world found by the ancients. Any treasure would keep the search going, but Widdal was a man of power and he constantly wanted more power at every opportunity.

"You might be surprised of our finds," he commented, moving over to another table. On it was several wooden boxes. "In fact, I was going to bring these to you tonight, but since you are now here. These were found today."

Digging around inside one of the boxes, he produced an object and, turning, held it out to him. Even in the dim light, he could tell what it was considering the shimmer. Widdal produced a gasp as he took it from him, noticing how heavy it was. It was a small yet simple statue about a foot in length of an ancient unknown deity and completely made of gold.

"Ah, excellent," he said, turning it over in his hands. "This is more like it. Do you think there might be hidden others like this?"

"You mean like this?"

He produced another piece from a second box. This time it looked like a wide flat plate also made of gold but had what looked like jewels embedded around the edge. Delicate pictures of animals adorned the surface. Seeing the plate, Widdal then looked at the doctor and produced a suspicious face.

"Of course you were going to bring these to me, right?"

"That is the reason for the crates."

"These will go a long way in calming the fears of my creditors. You will have objections of us taking these with us when we leave, do you?"

"No, all the items have been catalogued and photographed."

"Then," Widdal said, standing up, "I guess our business is concluded for the night. You will have these crates placed into my vehicle, yes?"

"I'll have Jorge and some of the men place them in the back for you."

"Excellent…till tomorrow."

Dr. Cortez followed them outside and, calling for Jorge, had him get several men to load the crates into Widdal's vehicle. Watching the men load the crates, he saw Widdal tip his hat and get into the back of the vehicle. As the lights dimmed into the distance, he returned to the tent and collapsed into the chair.

I must be cautious with him, he thought. *He must not be allowed to interfere.*

With his visitor now gone, it was probably time to gather his things and go back to the city. It would be another long day tomorrow, and deep down in his bones, he knew it would bring out something wonderful. He had not been down into the dig site all day and thought a quick inspection would help his thoughts.

Walking down into the dig site, he searched around the exposed stone wall with his flashlight. He tried to determine where they would proceed and see if there might be any inscriptions. Stepping along the length of the wall surface, he would pause and slowly examine different spots. While looking at some different type of stones in the structure near the bottom of the wall, his movement caused the sand to begin to disappear beneath his feet.

There has to be a hidden chamber beneath me, he thought with excitement.

Placing the flashlight down, he began digging frantically. After several minutes, the corner of an opening appeared that was covered by only a small slab of stone. Surveying the opening, he could tell that it was small but could allow a person to crawl though. Seeing the darkness beyond only increased his excitement.

Grabbing his flashlight, he squeezed through the tight opening. He slowly made his way down through the darkness. The rough passage scrapped and tore at his clothes and bare skin. Finally, the passage opened into a chamber where he could stand up. Brushing himself off, he panned the light around the room. Everything the light touched glimmered. He gasped as he realized what was before him.

Damn, it's a treasure room, he thought.

The room was smaller than he expected and only about twenty feet on each side, and the ceiling was about ten foot. He knew from the size it couldn't be a burial chamber but a hidden room to hide the riches of the kingdom. It was filled almost to the ceiling with golden statues of every size and shape, along with huge piles of gold and baskets of jewels. He could barely breathe or move as he looked around at the extraordinary sight.

"Oh my god," he finally said in astonishment.

There was an absolute fortune in the chamber. Even with all the treasure, one thing that did surprise him was on the back wall was a large carving covering it almost entirely. Walking forward, he tried to make out the writing down the sides and who the large figure might be that they had created in great detail. Inching his way along the wall beside it, his flashlight shined over every item. The style of the carving was clearly made during the time of King Arumet, and it looked like it depicted the god Anubis. In small detail, there were two other figures unlike the large one.

Could this all really be that old?

Dr. Cortez slowly flashed the light around the room before moving back to the carving on the wall. Standing in front of it, he tried to read the writing. Starting at the top, he moved slowly down to the floor of the room. At the bottom was a plate, and he noticed that the edge of it was pulled back slightly. Kneeling, he tried to pry the heavy stone plate away. When it finally came loose and fell into the sand, he looked inside. The light caused whatever was inside to brighten, and he could see the side of a metal box. A scary feeling came over him as he shined his light down both sides to look in the back.

The coffin was made of what looked like aluminum but really rough. It was about three feet on a side with a lid. Even being a rough metal, he was surprised how smooth and shiny the surface was. On the corners were edges where he could get his fingers on and slowly pulled it out of the hiding spot. Sitting in front of it, he looked around each side. His mind raced, trying to think of what it might contain. Grasping the top, he lifted and pulled until he heard a hidden seal from below the edge create a pop and let go. Air from inside immediately rushed out.

Damn, that really stinks, he thought, knowing it had been trapped for thousands of years.

Holding his breath until the pungent air dissipated with the room air, he then saw that a gold foil covered the opening to hide the contents. Using his finger, he slowly peeled the edge away until he could look inside. Looking inside his eyes began to widen as he saw what the box contained. Before he could get a feeling of the total contents, he suddenly realized that the chamber might be more than it seemed. Knowing he had been down there too long and others might stumble upon the opening, he dug through the contents before stopping.

"What the hell," he said, examining the object.

He knew that this one item was probably more important to the people that built this chamber from the way they had hidden it. Knowing he had to preserve it from falling into the wrong hands, he grabbed his pack and delicately placed the item into it. Seeing how it had left a space in the box, he had to add something to replace it. Reaching over, he added some of the gems from a basket nearby to replace it.

Picking up his pack, he looked around the room, knowing his time was up. Most of this would have to wait until tomorrow. All this treasure was sure to make Mr. Widdal happy to say the least. Climbing up to the opening, he cautiously looked around the area to see if anyone was around. Not seeing anyone, he quickly moved through the opening to the surface. He hurriedly covered up the opening and marked it.

There was no way that he could hold onto his prize but had to keep it safe. Getting into his Jeep, he headed back to town. On the way, he tried to call his son, but he didn't answer, and he had to leave a voice message. Back at his room, he wrote a quick note and, placing it inside, sealed it up and marked it with the delivery address. The whole time he felt he was rushing, and his heart raced as he took it to the postal office down the street. He wanted to get it away quickly but not so fast as to create suspicion. On the way back, he finally felt he could relax and produced a sigh.

I guess we'll see what happens tomorrow, he thought.

CHAPTER 2

"GOD...THIS PIECE IS absolutely beautiful."

The New York Museum of History had hired Professor Johnny Cortez to authenticate a piece before they paid for it. It would be a very important addition to their display. Holding a fellowship for the University of Egypt, they had reached out and arranged for him to come from his dig in northeastern Jordon and examine it. The fee was something he couldn't turn down and jumped at the opportunity. It was an old cuneiform tablet in hardened but still-delicate clay that had come from a private collector. His first thought upon seeing it was that it was perhaps from the period of the Assyrian Empire and over the last few days had confirmed it. The script was unmistakable and from all the tests had not been forged.

I thought so, he thought, looking down in satisfaction.

They had given him only a few days to make his determination. His fingers slid carefully over the surface and the indentations as he looked through the magnifying piece. He was trying to see if he could feel the energy within the material. For several minutes, he surveyed his fingers' reactions as they transited each small valley and peek. Leaning closer with his magnifier, he noticed that a small line within the text when translated hailed the king at the time.

"There it is...King Sennacherib," he mumbled with a grin.

From the other lines of text, it was simply a tablet noting some minor legislation and the action it would cover. That would put the creation of the tablet somewhere in the range of 700 to 650 BC. With that timeframe, it would have been set within the royal library, which made it very important since not many pieces remained from that period of time. He stood up and smiled, knowing that he was absolutely correct. It was always the little victories that gave him the most pleasure. The payday he was going to receive wasn't bad either.

Opening the office door, Carol had come to see what progress Johnny had made on the tablet. He was leaning over the work table, concentrating on the piece and hadn't heard her come in. Standing for a moment, she watched him.

Johnny was wearing Wrangler jeans and wearing light brown boots. He had a white button-down collar, long-sleeve shirt, and a black kangol hat. His beard was light and trimmed, and his black silky hair was slicked back under his hat. He didn't appear dirty or cheap, but even in his work clothes, he was a chick magnet.

Realizing she was standing with her mouth open and feeling the unexpected rush of emotion fill her, she gritted her teeth and silently chastised herself. With her anger, the door handle was still in her hand and quickly slung the door behind her. The sound of the door suddenly slamming shut behind him startled him.

"I thought you might still be in here."

When he turned, he saw the question had come from Carol. She was the secretary of the museum director. Dressed perfectly to the status of her position, she marched proudly over to him before stopping to survey the table behind him.

He guessed that she was probably in her mid-fifties but didn't appear that old. Her matronly appearance, with her black hair bundled high on her head and the suit-like dress along with the modest shoes, told him she liked her position, and nothing about her would interfere with that view of her. Even the makeup she wore was modest and not overly applied down to the light-colored pink lipstick.

She has to be a complete prude inside.

"And where else would I be?" he then said with a smirk, turning toward her.

"You should be getting ready for the dinner tonight. It is scheduled to start in about two hours. With you still here, working, it indicates that you might not be going tonight."

"Well, I really hadn't decided yet," he said, leaning back against the table.

"You know that you have no choice, right?"

"And if I don't go?"

"Then maybe you should have read your contract closer. The director is giving a gala to honor the museum's opening of our new west wing. All the major donors that made this possible will be there, and he wants to introduce you as a special consultant," she said, turning and heading for the door. Before she reached it, she stopped and looked back at him. "There is a car outside that will take you to your hotel to change and then to the event. They will make sure you are on time."

"Yes, ma'am," he said, giving her a salute.

"You have about thirty minutes," she grunted before leaving the office.

"God, I hate these events," he said, turning to the table before letting out a laugh. "I guess I really need to read those contracts closer."

It was already getting dark when he got outside to the front of the museum. He stopped and saw a long black limousine was waiting at the curb just as she said it would be. Staring at it, he shook his head. He was so used to taking cabs everywhere, and this type of treatment seemed over the top. As he began to approach, the driver leaning against the side stepped over and opened the back door.

"Mr. Cortez," he said, waiting for him to get inside.

"Yes," he said softly.

Once he was in the back, the driver closed the door and also got inside. As the driver headed for the hotel, he surveyed the back. There was a television that had the stock market results on. Next to it was a full bar with just about anything he might want. Wondering how long it would take to get there, he leaned forward.

"How long will it take to get to the hotel?" he asked, hoping he would hear him.

"It shouldn't be more than about thirty minutes," the driver said.

"Good," he said, reaching over and grabbing a glass from the rack. Picking up one of the decanters, he poured out what he thought was some whiskey. Settling back, he drank the liquor and watched the people and cars going by.

Taking the last sip from his glass, the car pulled over to the curb and stopped. Looking at his watch, the driver was right as he saw it took thirty-two minutes. He was obviously very familiar at the streets of the city. The back door opened, and stepping out, the driver nodded to him.

"I'll be waiting until you've changed," he said.

"It shouldn't take all that long," he said, adjusting his pack.

Heading to his room, he wondered what the dinner would be like and if there would be any good food. Opening his room door, he stepped in and, stopping, started to laugh. There was a pressed tuxedo lying across the bed. Placing his pack on the table, he pulled out a few things and then the package his father sent him. He still hadn't had a chance to open it since he received several days ago. Placing it back in the pack, he placed it in the closet, knowing he would have to open it later.

Walking past the bed, he couldn't help but shake his head. *That evil woman thought of everything,* he thought, beginning to strip out of his clothes.

Finished dressing, he headed down to the waiting car. Standing in the elevator, it stopped on the floor below his, and two women stepped in. Sliding next to him, they both produced a smile, giving him a pleasurable eye, acknowledging how good he looked in the tuxedo. Feeling a touch out of place compared to the others in the elevator, he would produce a small smile back at them and a quick nod his head. It seemed like an eternity as the elevator appeared to stop on every floor. Looking at his watch, he couldn't wait to get to the limousine.

When he got to the ground floor, he walked quickly outside and looked for his ride. Just up the street beside the curb, he saw the limousine with the driver standing beside it. He looked to be a young man in his late twenties or early thirties. Bouncing on his toes, he appeared anxious and scanned the street but focused on cute girls passing by him. With a sigh of relief that there was at least a ride, he headed for it.

The driver was tipping his hat at a couple of very young girls walking by him and, when he turned, saw him approaching. He straightened up and, stepping to the back, opened the door for him. Dressed in the black tuxedo, he stood out in the crowd, making it obvious that Johnny was going to be his passenger. Nearing him, the driver greeted him with a smile.

"Good evening, sir," he commented.

"Cute girls," Johnny said, bending to get in the back.

"Yes, they were, sir," he said, closing the door.

The drive to the event was slow as traffic was terrible. At this time of night, everyone was out and about seeing the sights or going to dinner. He watched out the window as the crowds on the street moved and blended as they headed in all directions. The car got in a long line of other vehicles that were dropping off guests at the front entrance. Just before it was their turn to stop, the driver turned to Johnny.

"Sir, when the dinner is done and you're ready to leave, just come out to the front and have the front attendant call limousine Charlie 22. I'll be parked just down the street with the other drivers. I'll come get you."

"Thanks," he said as they stopped. Seeing the mass of people all dressed up heading up the stairs, he laughed. "It might be sooner than you think."

"I can be here in less than five minutes," he grinned.

"That comforting," Johnny said as the door opened. "Wish me luck."

"You won't need it, sir, I'm sure of it."

Johnny could hear the driver laughing as he stepped out of the back.

Once he was inside, there were huge signs pointing the way to the dinner. It was easy to find since there was a string of people heading for a dining area near the back of the building. Near the doors, the line slowed as there was a desk where several women were checking people in and pointing them to their table. Finally getting to the table, one of the women looked up at him.

"And you are?" she asked, holding her pen.

"Johnny Cortez," he told her, smiling.

Running her pen down the list of names on the clipboard, she then stopped and checked his name off. "Yes, Mr. Cortez. You are seated at table 17."

Reaching over, she pointed to a table on the main arrangement sheet and then pointed out onto the floor. When he looked to where her hand was indicating, he could see Carol standing next to the table talking to someone that was seated.

"Thanks," he said, "I see some of my party already there."

People were still mulling around the tables and getting organized when he got to the table. Carol saw him approached and turned, looking at him. It wasn't so much the way she looked, but it was a survey and in obvious detail from head to foot. As her eyes came back to his face, she smiled with obvious approval.

"So…I see that you do clean up nicely." She grinned, placing her hand on her hip.

"Thanks and so do you."

She was not dressed in the stuffy business outfit he had seen her wear over the last few days. Instead, she wore a long evening gown that was light and flowed around her body. It was an elegant blue strapped dress cut low in the front with a corset look in the middle.

"This is Mr. Simmons, CEO of Arrow Industries and his wife, Janet," she said, stepping back. "Kyle, this is Professor Johnny Cortez."

The man stood up and shook his hand. "Glad to meet you, Johnny."

"And you also, sir," he told him before greeting his wife.

Carol then slowly went around the table, introducing him to each one of the six couples already there. When she was done playing the table hostess, she pointed to a chair where she wanted him to sit. Of course it was right next to her chair. With a smile, he pulled the chair out and began to sit down as Carol moved back to Janet to finish her conversation.

I could really use a drink, he thought, adjusting his chair. As if on cue, a waiter came up beside him.

"Can I get you something from the bar?" he asked him while filling his glass with some water.

"Jack and Coke, tall please and easy on the ice," he told him.

"Yes, sir."

When the waiter turned and left, he looked at the bottles of mineral water near each place setting along with three bottles of champagne chilling next to the table. Those would not do the trick and numb his nerves. Carol had given him a look, hearing him give his order to the water but never even missed a beat as she talked.

The waiter brought his drink back just as the director came up to the table. Greeting them, the lights dimmed slightly, and a host came onto the stage and indicated the usual greetings, telling them about the dinner and the evening's agenda. As he spoke, he rolled his eyes and, tipping his glass up, quickly drank almost half the glass.

While the speaker was talking, a waiter came to the table and began taking orders for dinner. He picked up the menu sheet and saw that it was the standard items, wide ranging and probably lacking any taste. They were nothing that he would probably write home about saying how wonder it was. There was the grilled chicken, steamed salmon, and a small sirloin steak. Picking his dressing for the salad, he decided he would take the steak option. The waiter slowly went around, taking orders and two more came out bringing bread and making sure that they had something to drink. He picked up his glass and shook it at the one waiter and he smiled to him, nodding.

The whole evening went just about as he expected…long and boring. It was nice that the director had invited him but he could do with something that wasn't so formal. He thought about an event he could attend later that he could let loose and have some fun. From all the people's faces, this was definitely not that type of event. It dragged on for almost two hours until it finally came to an end and the speaker thanked everyone for coming.

Needing another drink, he stood up and excusing himself, walked over to the bar. It seemed at least the people in that area were laughing and might have had the same feeling as he was having. Edging up to the bar, it opened up and he sat down at the free stool. He ordered another drink and as he waited, scanned the people at the bar. When the bartender brought his drink back, he felt a soft nudge into his back. Turning to look, a woman was standing behind him.

"Hi there." She grinned. "So are you having any fun?"

"Well, not until right now," he said, returning a smile.

"I'm Sara."

"I'm Johnny."

"So can I join you, or are you here with someone?"

"Nope, I'm all here by myself. Please have a seat," he said, making room for her as he gave up the stool.

"Thank you," she said wiping the hair away from her face.

She was really quite stunning and stood beside him. His eyes glanced behind her and didn't seem to see anyone coming after her. He didn't quite understand why she would be attending an event like this unaccompanied. His eyes couldn't help but watch as she slowly slid up onto the stool.

The pure white evening gown was simple yet fit her body perfectly with the color bringing out her sun-tanned bronze skin. Before she could turn to him, he could see the back was very low cut, almost down below the line of her waist, exposing the delicate curve of her back. Turning on the stool, she crossed her legs and leaned on the edge of the bar. The long slit in the front of the dress slid to either side, allowing her crossed legs to become exposed. From the dirty blonde hair, he could guess she spent many an hour at the salon to keep it that way.

Where they were standing there wasn't a lot of room, making for a very close setting. The cozy tightness allowed her to brace the side of her knee against him. Between using him and his knee to keep her position, it appeared she was comfortable. Her movement had trapped him between the bar and her legs. With little talk while she adjusted herself, the time allowed him time to examine her which appeared to be her goal. Taking a breath, she twisted her head and looked over at him.

Looking over at the table, he could see Carol staring over at him. I was obvious by her facial expression that his action was not sitting well with her. He couldn't understand why she would be feeling that way since she had been a pain in his side for the last few days. She should have realized a change in clothing wouldn't change his current view about her. He then focused back on Sara.

"What did you think of the dinner?" he asked.

"I don't usually come to these things for the food." She grinned. "The dinner part is so over the top and doesn't interest me. I only come for the people. Why did you come to this thing?"

"I only came because I was dragged here," Johnny commented, "not because I like these things."

"Dragged huh?"

"My boss, the museum director, invited me."

"So running with the big dogs it seems."

"I don't know about 'big' dogs…I'm a puppy. Let me go over and excuse myself with the people at the table," he told her. "You won't leave while I'm gone, will you?"

"Only if you don't say please, really nice like," she said, leaning over to him and twisting his collar with her finger.

"Sure, I can do that," he said, leaning over to the side of her face. Placing his mouth beside her ear, he blew across it softly. "Please?"

His action created a shiver in her body, and she looked at him as he backed away.

"I'll wait," she smiled.

Figuring that Sara would probably consume all his time, he had to go back and make his apologies to Carol and the director. Excusing himself, he walked back over to the table. When he stepped up, Carol looked at him with a scowl. He wondered the reason for her attitude.

"What's the matter?" he asked, looking for the director.

"Do all the women you meet for the first time just naturally throw themselves at you?" she asked, looking over at Sara. "What is it about you?"

"Most of the time." He grinned. "I don't know why, but over the years, I haven't bothered to fight it. It also saves me a whole lot of time…and all that talking."

"I'm sure it does," she said with a huff, leaning back in her seat.

"I'm going to have to leave as you might have guessed," he told her. "Since I don't see him, can you tell the director when he comes back that I had a really great time and appreciate his invitation? I'll probably see him tomorrow."

"I'll tell him," she indicated, matter-of-factly.

"I'll see you tomorrow also…right?"

"I work there remember?"

"Of course, Carol."

He didn't know how to take her comment but figured he would worry about that later. Walking back to Sara, he could tell that she was getting anxious sitting all by herself for the last few minutes. She slid off the stool and met him before he could reach her. As she took his arm and directed him to the doors, she grinned and dipped her head.

"I think we need to go," she indicated.

"Whatever you want to do."

Outside the museum, he paused, remembering what the driver told him. As the attendant came up to him, he told him the limousine number. Disappearing, they stepped down to the curb and waited. Sara was not a talkative woman, but her body movements spoke loudly exactly what was on her mind. Holding his arm, the limousine pulled up to them, and another attendant opened the door. Sliding into the back, the door closed, and the driver turned and looked at them.

"Where are we going?" the driver asked. Johnny just looked at her.

"Take us to 1763 Arvin Avenue," Sara told him, smiling. Before he could turn and shut the separation window, she yelled out and asked him a question. "Wait! How long before we get there?"

"Oh," the driver said then thought, "I don't think it'll be more than about ten minutes—fifteen at the most, ma'am."

"Thanks," she said, looking at Johnny, "that'll be plenty of time."

As she started to slide back into the seat, her hands abruptly reached over and began to loosen his belt before opening his pants wide. Feeling her hands reach in and take hold of him, she then produced a wink as her head bent over into the middle of his lap. The wet warmth of her mouth made him shiver, and he produced a soft gasp. Looking up, he could see the driver glancing back at them in his mirror. With a smile, he swirled her hair in one hand and reached under her blouse with the other to cup her breast. Gripping her tightly, he closed his eyes to enjoy as she began.

The ten minutes seemed much shorter as the limousine began to slow down and Johnny's moans were closing down. The taxi came to a stop at the address she had told him. Hurriedly, he closed his pants and tucked in his shirt. Sara was leaned against the other door, straightening out her blouse and hair. The limousine was stopped for a moment before the window opened and the driver turned his head around to them. He could see the big smile on Johnny's face as he spoke.

Getting out, Johnny walked over and leaned through the passenger window.

"I think I can take it from here," he told him, looking back at Sara. "You can take the rest of the night off. I don't know how long this might last."

"Thanks," he said with a glance into the mirror. "You might have your hands full with that one, sir."

"I hope so," he laughed. Slapping the side of the door, he waved to him and walked back to Sara who was waiting patiently for him.

Looking up, the apartment building was several floors high. It was a very modern building, and it had a doorman stationed at the front doors, monitoring the people who entered. When they came up, he stepped over to the doors and, tipping his hat, opened the front door.

"Good evening, ma'am," he said. "Hope you had a good evening."

"Yes, Ted," she said, glancing at Johnny, "a wonderful evening with more to come."

"Excellent, ma'am," he commented, winking at Johnny.

Passing him, they went up to her apartment on the third floor. She unlocked the door and, stepping inside, waited for him to move past her. He looked around and saw it was very contemporary with pictures and plants all around. Turning, Sara was standing by the closed door, and he saw her gown hit the floor around her feet. She was now only wearing her underwear and heels as she took a step out of the crumpled gown. She wrapped her arms around his neck and kissed him. Leaning away, she slowly took his tie off and unbuttoned his shirt.

"I've been waiting for this moment all night," she told him.

"Me too," he said, kissing her.

Sweeping her up in his arms, he carried her into the back bedroom. Placing her on the bed, he stared at her as he stripped her underwear off, tossing them to the floor. She lay and watched, using his hands to stroke her body until he was done.

Kneeling onto the edge of the bed, he crawled up between her legs. She obliged, spreading her legs to the side. Pausing, his hand came up to her stomach and moved down slowly until his fingers slid under the edge of her inner thigh. With a quick tug, her eyes widened, and he pulled them down her legs until they were free. Tossing them to the floor, he leaned his face down and traced his wet tongue along the top of her leg, moving ever higher. While he moved, her hands grabbed the top of his head, trying to guide him to where she wanted him to go. As she guided him to the spot, she let out a quiet but audible moan of passion. As Johnny put pressure on the spot, the moans became a controlled scream until she lost control and gripped his hair tighter and tighter. Her body and muscles were tense, and she let a scream for the last time, and her body rested on the bed at peace from the ecstasy.

Johnny grabbed her hand and put it over his shoulder and kissed her passionately. She wanted to stop and rest, but her feelings were so strong for him. Johnny picked up her legs and put his arm under her back and moved her across the bed closer to him. He laid over the top of her and kissed her some more. He moved his lips from hers and started licking her neck. She began to moan again. And her back began to move up and down. Johnny could feel her chest on his, moving up and down from each lick and suck. She reached for Johnny's manhood and projected it into her love canal. Johnny started his perpendicular movement like a jackhammer on a sidewalk, moving as a rabbit in heat, and she went crazy with convulsions and loud screams.

After what seemed like hours, Johnny was finally spent and rolled over to his back, trying to retain what strength remained and suck in his air. She was also gasping and slid over beside him, cuddling up under his arm. A soft moan of pleasure vibrated from her throat as she stoked his sweaty chest. Placing her face against him, she listened to his racing heart as she tried to get closer to him. He swept his arm tighter around her shoulder and, moving her hair to the side, kissed her forehead. Neither of them said anything more or could they as they both closed their eyes, reveling in their recent pleasure before drifting off to asleep.

CHAPTER 3

WHERE THE HELL am I?

He couldn't understand where he was walking. The sky didn't have one cloud and was a bright blue. Beneath his feet was sand, causing his feet to sink in with every step. It made his walk difficult, and he struggled. There were no hills, and all around him was so barren. In front of him was a small outcrop of rocks, barely rising above the surface of the sand. It appeared he was walking toward it.

As he neared the rocks, the sand before him seemed to come alive and glisten. Near the edge, flames jumped into the sky and caused him to stop. He stood staring as it twisted and turned in the air. A hand came out of the sand and appeared to struggle but no form followed it. Slowly, it disappeared back into the sand.

What was that?

Watching the flames dance before him, it became mesmerizing. Without realizing it, the flames began to grow larger and slowly moved out toward him. When he tried to back away, he noticed that his feet were stuck in the sand. Not taking his eyes from the flame, he reached down and tried to dig the sand away. The sand appeared fused, sealing his feet where they were. He stood up and wondered what was happening.

Still watching, there appeared to be a figure forming within the burning flame. Slowly, as the fire moved closer, the figure became clearer. Out to each side appeared spreading wings that didn't burn but simply moved the fire away. Now almost upon him, the face of the figure was almost in front of him but paused. It looked like the face of a woman, but he couldn't make out distinctive features.

Trying to make out who or what it was, it changed into something hideous and swooped upon him. When the creature's wings wrapped around him, he could instantly feel the flame beginning to burn his flesh away. Losing his eyes, he opened his mouth and began to scream out in pain.

Bolting upright in the bed, he quickly looked around and saw that the fire was nothing more than a dream. Rubbing his face, he could feel that he was covered in cold, dripping sweat. Swinging his legs off the edge of the bed, he leaned over onto his knees. He could hear that his breathing was quick, and he tried to calm himself down. Leaning over on his legs, he then felt a hand slowly slid up his back to his shoulder.

"Are you all right?"

Turning, he could see that his sudden movement in the bed had woken Sara from her sleep. She had slowly twisted over toward him in the sheets and was smiling. As she stroked his back, a soft series of moans escaped her lips.

"It was just a bad dream…I'm fine." He smiled back to her.

"Good, I thought it might be because of me."

"Not even…last night was great."

"I'll have to say it was much better than I expected," she moaned.

"I…" he began, watching her sweep the long hair from her face. "I'm sorry, girl, but I think I have to leave."

"That's all right and I understand… Here," she said, rolling over and grabbing something from the top of the nightstand. When she turned back, she held her hand out to him as he began to stand up.

"And what's this?" he asked, reaching out to her hand.

"Well, it's my number, silly." She then laughed, rolling over among the sheets. Propping her head onto her hand, she flashed him a devilish grin. "It's in case you ever find yourself feeling lonely the next time you're in town."

"I'll do that." He grinned, looking at the slip.

"I'll be waiting for the call," she stressed.

Leaning over, he kissed her deeply once more. Before he could move away, she wrapped her arms around his neck, holding him down against her. As he peeled himself away, he placed the slip of paper in his pants and finished dressing. Standing beside the bed, she watched, allowing her feet to twist in the air behind her.

"So…how about once more before you leave?" she asked, digging her fingers into the top of his pants, trying to pull him back toward her. With her other hand fumbling with the zipper, she then laughed. "It shouldn't take that long."

"Really, I have to go."

She then began to mope and, in silence, watched until he had finished. Giving her another quick kiss, he walked away toward the door. With a last look back at her, he saw her roll onto her back, pulling the sheets up around her chin. Her knees rocked back and forth, but she never said anything. Still looking at him, he shook his head and opened the door.

Back at his hotel, he didn't feel tired and knew he would need to go back to the museum in a few hours. He fixed a drink and, pulling out his pack, decided to go through some paperwork. The certification of the tablet would have to be done, and then he could get paid and could leave. Emptying the files out, the package his father sent him tumbled out onto the table. He sat back on the couch and stared over at the crinkled brown box.

What did he send me?

Staring over at the package on the table, he wondered what could be inside. It wasn't often that his father would go out of his way and send him something, except perhaps on a special occasion. Since he had other things to do, he would open it later. Picking up his cell phone, he looked and saw that there was a voice message. He looked at the number and didn't recognize it. Figuring it was nothing more than one of those irritating "robo" computer calls, he hit the Play button and began to listen. As the message began to play, his eyes widened, instantly recognizing the voice.

"Son, this is your dad. Sorry to make this short, but I don't have much time. When you hear this, you have to listen to me very carefully. I found the most wondrous thing in the desert, and it must be protected at all costs. Whatever you do… just don't open that package I sent you until I tell you. I'll have to explain all this later, but in the meantime, just guard it. Anyway, I have to go so… I love you and we'll talk later."

When the message stopped playing, he then noticed that the message was dated almost two days ago. With the work, he had been so busy he never checked. He dropped the phone between his legs and stared over at the brown package lying on the table once again. This time when he looked at it, he felt a rising inquisitiveness. It was a feeling about the contents that wasn't there previously.

So what the hell did he find out there? he thought.

Before he could think about it any further, there was a knock at his door. Walking over, he thought it might be one of the hotel staff, and when he opened it, he found two men standing on the other side. They were dressed in very stylish black suits with straight ties and seemed to be executives.

"Can I help you?" Johnny asked.

"Are you John Cortez?" one of the men asked.

"Yes. Is there a problem?"

"This is Detective Arnold and I'm Detective Simmons," he began, showing Johnny their badges. "We're from the New York Police Department. Do you mind if we come in and talk to you?"

"Sure, come on in," he said, opening the door wider.

"Thanks."

As they entered the room and moved past him, he wondered why the police would be coming to see him. Searching through his mind, he couldn't think of any reason. When they had both entered, he shut the door and, walking over to the couch as they stopped in the middle of the room, picked up his glass.

"So…what can I do for you, Officers?"

"We have a reciprocal arrangement with the Egyptian police department," he said, looking in his notepad. "They contacted us earlier from their Cairo division to try and locate you."

"In Cairo?"

"We don't know how to tell you this, but it appears that your father has disappeared while in Egypt," he began, pulling a folded slip of paper from his jacket. He handed it to Johnny and, unfolding it, began to read. "That is a fax report from their missing persons' department with all the information concerning the situation. There is also the local contact information you might need if you go in-country."

"I just don't understand this," he said, still reading each line on the paper.

"They indicated when they reached out to us they're hoping that you might be able to shed some light on this matter, help them in any way. Your name and contact details were on his work visa."

"You don't think it was a terrorist act of some kind, do you?" It was a farfetched question that had suddenly popped into his mind. Being in that part of the world, one would never know. He thought he would ask.

"No, they did rule that out in the beginning since most of the other people he worked with are there, and after interviewing them, it didn't indicated that scenario."

"That's something," he commented, wondering what to do next.

"If there is anything we can do to help, please call me," he said, handing him his business card. "We're so sorry for your loss."

"Thank you, Officers, for letting me know," he said, standing up.

Shaking their hands in appreciation, he ushered them to the door. Once they had left, he slowly looked around the room, trying to figure out what to do next. There was a long list, but the most pressing was that he knew he had to get to Egypt, immediately. With so many unanswered questions, he would only find those answers there.

CHAPTER 4

LUCKILY, JOHNNY HAD brought his passport with him. Checking, his work visa was still valid for Egypt from the last time he visited. He let out a sigh of relief, knowing that would save him a few days of red tape. Calling around to a few airlines, most of the direct flights were booked solid, and they couldn't give him a seat. Finally, he spoke to Qantas Airlines, which had an open seat, but it was only in very back of the plane. It was also scheduled to depart JFK airport in a few hours. Knowing he didn't have a choice, he confirmed the reservation and gave him his information. Now he had to clean up his business first.

When he reached the museum and met with the director, he was very accommodating after he told him about the situation. Pulling out the certification file from the file, he signed the last sheet and handed it over to him. Carol was standing beside him and took the file after he examined it and handed it to her.

"I know you are on a tight schedule, Mr. Cortez," he said, thanking him for all his work for them. "Carol will arrange for our driver to take you to the airport. I'll feel better knowing you are in good hands."

"Thank you, sir, I really appreciate it."

"If you'll follow me," Carol said, ushering him out to her desk.

Shutting the director's door, she walked around her desk and sat down. Looking at her computer for a moment, she then turned to him.

"The contract funds will be wired to your account today."

"Thank you." He smiled.

Reaching up, she pulled her glasses down the length of her nose to the end with her finger and leaned over on her desk. "So…next time you're in town, maybe we can have a drink together?"

"I would like that," Johnny said, noticing her look.

She smiled at his answer and leaned back in her chair. He then noticed that the top of her blouse was now open more than he had seen in the last few days. That was then he noticed her hair was not up in the usual bun but draped around her face and shoulders. She didn't seem so stuffy and had shown she could let her guard down. This was definitely not the same woman he had tried to interact with for the last few days.

"Call me," she said, picking up the phone with the same smile. "The limousine and driver will be waiting when you get outside."

"Thank you again," he said, turning and leaving.

Downstairs, the car was waiting just like they promised, and when he came out, the driver opened the back door. The driver took his suitcase, and as he placed it into the trunk, he stepped into the back. After the door closed and he settled into the seat, he checked through his stuff to make sure he hadn't forgotten anything as they headed for the airport. Knowing he couldn't do anything else, he leaned back and let out a sigh. It wouldn't be long before he could see about getting his answers.

I could probably get used to this, he thought, looking around the limousine.

Before he knew, it they were pulling up to the airline gate at the airport. Grabbing his bag and thanking the driver, he went inside and headed for the counter. The ladies behind the counter were very nice, and checking his bag and getting his ticket, he headed to go through security and then to the gate.

Finally reaching the gate, there was already a crowd waiting to get on, and he moved through them to sit down in an open seat. Leaning back, he closed his eyes and took a long breath. After this morning, it had definitely been a whirlwind day, and he needed to try to settle down his growing nerves and relax. It would be a long flight.

The lady behind the podium came on the speaker and announced that they were beginning the boarding process. Watching as the first-class passengers entered the plane, he stood up and gathered his stuff to wait his turn. After several minutes, his section was called, and he entered the line and proceeded with all the others inside.

From the look of the seats, it didn't seem as if the plane would be full. Only about half the seats had passengers, and when he reached his seat in the back, he found there were only about a dozen people surrounding him. His row of three seats didn't have anyone in them, and he smiled, thinking he wouldn't have to fight for an armrest. Taking a book out, he placed his pack in the overhead and slid in to move beside the window seat.

It took several minutes before all the passengers settled into their seats and the stewardesses roamed the isles, making sure everything was put away. The ones that would probably be serving the back compartment were very cute he noticed as they would stroll by, checking things and beaming a huge smile. The airline was known for the service, and since it was a long flight, he would have a chance to find out.

They had been in the air for several hours, and after drinks and serving dinner, he could see the lights down the cabin beginning to go off. Slowly, people went to sleep, and with a dark cabin, it became very quiet. It appeared that the whole back third of the plane where he was sitting was asleep. The calm and silence was nice. Reaching up, he adjusted his reading light and opened his book.

"Sir, can I get you something to drink?" a voice asked.

Looking up, a young stewardess in a serving apron was standing near the outer seat, leaning in toward him. She was displaying a delicious smile and, with a twisting of her head, waited for him to answer.

"I'll have a rum and Coke please." He smiled back.

"Yes, sir," she beamed and disappeared into the back. In a few moments, she returned with a glass of ice, a bottle or rum, and a Coke on a serving tray. One by one she placed them on the tray beside him. "There you go. Let me know if you need anything else."

"I'll do that," he said, fixing his drink.

Looking up, he noticed that she didn't really leave but hovered for a moment before going into the back. As he sipped his drink and read, she would come by for what seemed like very few minutes and glance at him. She never went very far up the isle to check on any of the other passengers before turning around and walking back past him.

She definitely wants something, Johnny thought as she passed by him.

Over the course of the next half hour, she had served him several drinks before she disappeared for a while. Each time she paused, he would flash a smile to her. Finally, she came back and stood next to his seat, but this time, he could see that there was no apron. She had only her white blouse and blue skirt and seemed to be trying to be comfortable.

"Do you mind if I join you?" she said, looking down at the seat beside him.

"Please have a seat," he said, pointing over to it.

"Thanks." She smiled, sitting down. Crossing her leg toward him, she slipped off her shoe with one hand and began to rub her toes with the other. "At this time of the flight, it's really boring with all the passengers sleeping."

"Oh, I can only imagine," he said, continuing to focus on her action as she would slowly caress her foot and toes. When she had crossed her leg, the hem of her skirt slid higher up her thigh just above the edge of her nylon. He could see the delicate white skin of her leg between the dark skirt and matching nylon. The small bit of exposure was pleasant, and he didn't know if she realized how far the skirt had risen. There was no way he would mention it and enjoyed the scene.

"I'm not bothering you, am I?" she then suddenly turned and asked him.

"Are you kidding? Not at all," he said, breaking his stare to look up at her.

Now sitting this close, he could tell that she was probably only in her mid-twenties and was as cute as he first thought. Her blonde hair had to be fairly long to make the large bun on the top of her head. There were small lengths of hair that curled wildly about the side of her face. The deep green eyes, surrounded by perfectly blended mascara, burned into his skin when she would look at him. He then noticed the way her pink lips curled and moved as she breathed that excited him. When his eyes lowered, he could see the open blouse and watched as the material moved against her breast. The simple bits of bareness between the edges of the blouse showed that her body to be extremely fit and trim yet didn't seem overly athletic. She then started to twist in the seat as if uncomfortable yet still focused on rubbing her foot. From the way she wouldn't look up at him since she sat down, it was as if she wanted for him to examine her. If that was the case, he would take full advantage of it.

Oh yeah, she wants something besides a person to talk to.

"Uh…I'm Johnny, Johnny Cortez," he finally said, holding out his hand.

"I'm Amanda," she responded, looking up and taking his hand. "It's nice to meet you, Johnny. That's a really nice name."

"My parents seemed to think so," he laughed.

They both laughed at his comment and then sat and talked for some time, but mostly the conversation was about nothing in particular. When he would finish his drink, she would take his empty glass and, getting up, bring him another. While they talked, she would turn sideways in the seat and tuck her feet up under her, leaning against the seat back to look at him. Her intent stare at him while he was talking brought up deep feelings. Finishing his drink, her feet quickly slid out to the floor.

"Maybe one more?" she asked him.

"Well, might as well since they're small."

"I'll see what I can do," she said.

Smiling, she disappeared before returning a moment later. The glass she brought back was much larger, about twice the size of the other one and already mixed. As she began to hand his drink to him, the glass oddly slipped from her hand and fell into the middle of his lap. The liquid and ice covered his clothes, causing him to instantly lift up to keep it from soaking his butt. Using his hand, he made a quick swipe and raked the ice to the floor.

"Oh my god, I am so sorry," she said, embarrassed. "I've never done that before."

"It's fine, really," he told her, grabbing some napkins.

"No, please let me fix this if I can."

"Really, I can just—"

"Please come with me," she said, grabbing his hand. "I have some stuff in the back."

The back of the plane was separated into two sections by a wall. In the forward section was the main serving portion with counters on both sides, and behind it were the storage and a row of bathrooms. As they passed by the serving section, several of the other stewardesses were standing against the counter, drinking coffee and talking. They barely noticed as they went by into the other section.

Taking a towel from the cabinet, she turned back and knelt down in front of him. It was like she had never tried to wipe the wetness from a man's pants. Each time she would wipe, it was hesitant, and he could see her eyes glance up at him. Finally, her hand stopped. Still pressed against him, her head dropped.

"I'm so very sorry," she then moaned softly.

"Maybe this will make up for it," he said.

Reaching down, he took her face in his hands and slowly pulled her to her feet. Twisting her face up to look at him, he stared into her eyes before leaning over and kissing her deeply. He could feel her trembling as their lips met. Closing her eyes, she parted her lips, allowing his tongue to probe deeply into her mouth, accepting his advance.

With their lips pressed in a delicate tangle, he felt her body slowly press up tightly against his chest. His hands wrapped around her back to keep her from moving as her trapped hands between them began to massage the front of his pants, trying to urge the mass she felt beneath to come to life.

Urging her back against the cabinets, their kiss continued as his hand came around from her back and slid up her side and between the opening of her blouse, caressing her heaving breast trapped beneath her bra. His fingers pressed under the edge until he had it slid up toward her neck. As he massaged the quivering mass in his hand, he could hear small moans of pleasure begin to come from her throat. Breaking their kiss, he looked at her as she then slowly opened her eyes.

"So do you do this sort of thing often and in the open?" he casually asked her.

"Never," she said as her eyes widened at the suggestion. "It was just that—"

"Since we're going down this road, shall we go ahead and join the club?"

"What do you mean? What club?" she asked suddenly confused.

"The mile-high club," he indicated, looking at the bathrooms behind him.

She then began to snicker with excitement. "Sure, why not."

Running his finger down over her lips, he gave her a wink. Picking one of the handicap stalls since it was wider, they stepped inside and, with a quick glance to see if anyone had seen them, disappeared and locked the door.

After the first time and over the course of the next few hours, she would come down the aisle and, pausing, wave her hand to him and point. Tilting her head to the side and with a large smile, she seductively indicated that she wanted him to come with her. She was at least taking his mind from the long flight time. It was obvious that she liked being part of the "club" and wanted to take full advantage of the opportunity while she could. Who was he to keep that from happening for her, and he grinned each time she stopped and looked at him. They had now gone into the back bathrooms several times until the other passengers began to wake up and begin to come to use the bathrooms.

For the remainder of the flight, she went about performing her task to cater to the other passengers. Even so, she would always stop and pay particular attention to him to make sure that his needs were taken care of. For the most part, he thought, she had done an excellent job of that pressing need.

Each time he would turn and look to the back, he would see the other stewardesses that were standing near the entrance laughing and looking at him. Amanda would not be with them, but it was obvious from their attitude that their interlude was not a secret between them. He would smile and turn back around.

I really like this airline, he thought.

The plane finally landed, and he checked his ticket to see where he would get to his connecting flight. It would be at least another two hours before he reached Cairo. Pulling up to the gate, the people began to rise from their seats and gather their belongings. It would be at least several minutes before he could actually leave, and he waited, sitting in his seat patiently waiting as they began to file out.

As the passengers slowly thinned out, he finally stood up and pulled his stuff from the overhead compartment. He could see the other stewardesses moved up the other aisle across from him checking the seats. When he turned the other way, Amanda was standing beside him with a big smile.

"I hope you had a comfortable flight, sir, and will fly with us again," she told him.

"I can honestly say that I had a fantastic flight," he said, giving her a large smile, "and I'll definitely fly with you again."

"We're only here to please."

She slowly moved closer and, glancing behind him toward the front of the plane, quickly leaned over and kissed him. Moving away, she looked down at her feet as if waiting for him to respond. Taking his jacket from the seat, she handed it to him.

"Maybe we can get together on another flight soon."

"I would like that," she commented.

Taking the jacket from her, he flashed her one last smile and, turning, made his way to the front and the exit. Reaching the door, there was a row of stewardesses along with the flight crew greeting the passengers as they left. He could see the girls smiling at him as he approached them. The captain tipped his hat to him when he came up.

"We hope you had a good flight," he said to him.

"I had a great flight," he told him. Turning, he could see Amanda in the back with a few of the other girls. They were talking to each other while they stared down the row at him. "One I'll remember for a while."

With a nod to acknowledge them, he saw them giggle as he left the plane and headed for his next flight.

It couldn't be as good as this one, he thought pleasingly, walking down the exit.

CHAPTER 5

T HE FINAL LEG of his flight was crowded and was miserable. He was so glad when the plane finally landed and stopped. Exiting the cabin, Johnny saw where their luggage was due to come out and followed the airport arrows on the signs toward the basement. From his several drinks, he had to stop at the nearest restroom. Feeling much better, he wanted to just get his bag and go to the hotel.

Along the way, he had paused and, looking at the video monitor, made sure which carrousel he could pick up his luggage. It still indicated baggage claim 5. Walking to the area, he saw that most of the people had already come and claimed their bags and his bag was circling the carriage. Picking it up, he noticed that his bag appeared dented and scratched as if someone had lazily thrown it on the ground.

Shrugging his shoulders, he paid it no mind as he was tired from the trip and wanted to just get to his hotel and rest. It had been a long trip from New York. He stacked the carry-on to the top of the other and headed back upstairs to the exit and taxis.

As he came up the escalator and saw the glass doors of the exit, he happened to notice a currency exchange office off to his left. Cursing to himself, he quickly realized he didn't have any local currency and needed to change his American dollars. Entering the small shop, he saw that there were several other travelers who had waited until the last minute changing their cash. Once in line, he looked and saw several armed guards inside the door, watching the people entering and exiting, making sure of the transactions. Patiently waiting in line, he slowly moved along and up to the counter. After several minutes, he finally reached the girl behind the counter.

"Yes, sir," she said.

"I need to exchange five hundred American," he told her, digging into his pocket.

"No problem," she told him while calculating the exchange total. "At the current rate, that will come to $ 4,439.50 Egyptian pounds, sir. Can I see your passport?"

"Certainly," he said, handing it to her.

After she typed his information into the computer for the transaction, she slid it back to him and continued to type. With a smile, she then turned and looked at him.

"How would you like your currency?"

"Uh…" he said, not sure of what he wanted. It was obvious from his expression he didn't remember the sizes of bills. "How about giving me bills that are…well, change-friendly as I go around. Perhaps bills in denominations that normal people would use."

"That's no problem, sir." She smiled. "Most travelers don't know that question either."

"It's been a very long time since I've traveled overseas, especially here…sorry."

"Here you go," she said, counting out his money. When she had counted it all out, she reached over and handed him a computer sheet. "And this is your transaction receipt."

Stuffing the wad of bills in his pocket, he thanked the girl and, folding the receipt, placed it in his bag.

Once outside and as he approached the curb, he could see that there were tons of cabs parked and waiting on patrons to come out needing a ride. Before he could think about anything, a cab driver jumped out of the mulling crowd and tried to grab his luggage from his hand.

"Sir...sir, would you like a cab, a clean cab?"

"Uh...sure," Johnny said, scrutinizing him.

"And where do you want to go?"

I'd like to go to bed, he instantly thought.

The cab driver had already grabbed his luggage and put it in the trunk.

"Marriot Hotel," he indicated as he got in the back.

"I know it well," the driver said as he got behind the wheel. "It's barely twenty minutes down the road."

Time went quickly, and it was barely fifteen minutes when the hotel finally came into view. Even in the short drive, he was sweating profusely since the temperature was well over ninety degrees, and he had already unbuttoned his shirt. As the driver maneuvered to the front door, he let out a sigh of relief. Soon, he could get a shower and try to relax.

"We are here," the driver said, jumping out.

Getting out he looked up at the building. It was supposed to be the best in the region and was over four stories tall. Beside the main entrance were two large fountains spraying water almost twenty feet into the air. Closing his eyes, he could feel the fine mist hit his hot face. It also said in the brochures that from the roof area, you could overlook miles of the Nile River shoreline. If he had a chance, he would check that out.

"Here you go," the driver told him.

His voice brought him out of his trance and, noticing his bags, handed him the fare plus a nice tip. As he thanked him and went back to the cab, a doorman had already come out and picked up his bags. He was standing patiently waiting for him to enter. There was a big grin on his face as he waited. Nodding, he entered the hotel entrance and headed for the front desk to check in.

Inside, he could see large red-and-gold trim curtains draped and tapered back on each archway above him. The long hallway leading to the concierge desk also had two large statues of lions. He passed by a set of double doors and could see a casino with poker tables and slot machines. Off from the desk was several elevators covered in gold and a beautiful white staircase that went up to the next floor.

"Good evening, sir," the front desk clerk said to him as he approached. "And how may I help you?"

"Yes, my name is Johnny Cortez, and I have a reservation," he told her.

"Thank you." She smiled. "Just a moment and let me check."

As she looked for his name in the computer, he leaned over on the counter and looked around the room. He then saw a woman come out of a crowd of patrons and appeared to turn her head and look over at him. She was the only one out of the entire group that looked in his direction, which he found puzzling. A man was walking beside her as they disappeared in the crowd and out the front door.

"Yes, here is your reservation, and we have you in room 126. It shows as a single," she said, looking at him. "Will anyone be joining you?"

"No, I'm all by myself."

"Okay," she commented with a cough. Moving a strand of hair over her ear, she looked back at the monitor. "I wanted to make sure you didn't need another key."

"No, one key is plenty, thanks."

"Your room is located right here on the main floor and just down the hallway to your right."

"Great," he said, twisting and looking to where she pointed.

"May I have your passport please so I can put it in the system?"

"Certainly," he said, pulling his documents from his jeans.

He handed her his passport and watched as she began to type the information into the system. Watching her slowly place his information into the registry, he finally focused and actually noticed how really striking she was. The black hair along with the deep green eyes highlighted her soft face. As she twisted on her heels behind the counter, he couldn't help but notice her petite figure. Her physic was obviously shaped by the type of work she did, and when she bent over to get something, he saw the curved bottom beneath the red-and-gold hotel outfit she wore. It was obviously tailored and fit her like a glove. The jacket tails ran over her bottom like a short skirt. When she turned back, he then saw the name tag on her jacket.

"Mica," he said, "that is a beautiful name…It fits you."

"Thank you," she said, blushing at his comment.

"Uh, do you happen to have an open deposit box?"

"Certainly…would you like to put something away?"

"Yeah, it's just something from work that I don't want to drag around with me."

Checking her computer, she assigned a key to his reservation before turning around to the wall of boxes behind her. Opening one of them, she then pulled out the inner container and placed it on the counter.

"Will this be large enough for your needs?" she asked.

"It's plenty big."

Taking out the package from his bag, he opened the lid and slid it inside. When he closed it, he watched as she picked it up and returned it to the opening. Locking the door, she handed him the key and smiled.

"And here is your room key, sir. Will there be anything else?"

"No," he said, putting the room key in his pocket.

When he turned to pick up his bags, another attendant had already grabbed them and was waiting for him to go to his room.

"Room 126," she told the man.

He nodded and quickly headed off to the room. Before he could follow, she spoke up, sliding her hand across the counter to him.

"If I can ask," she started, "we don't get that many Americans in here, and I was wondering if it's true that all Americans drink only Scotch and beer?"

"No," he laughed. "An occasional beer, but I'm strictly a bourbon man myself."

"Oh." She smiled, leaning back. "Thank you."

"I hope that satisfied your curiosity."

"Yes"—she grinned—"yes, it does."

Walking down the hall toward his room, he saw the man with his luggage standing by his door. He inserted the key and opened it. The man followed inside quickly and arranged his luggage on his bed. Thanking him, he then gave him a tip and stood, examining the room as he heard the door close the door after he left.

I really need a shower, he thought, feeling sticky.

Stripping his clothes off and tossing them on the bed, he entered the bathroom and turned on the water. Feeling the water, he stepped inside and let the water run over his body before finally sticking his head under the flow. It felt good, and the turmoil of the day began to disappear. Standing with his hands against the wall, he began to think of what he needed to do the next day. He hadn't thought about it much since he left, and everything was starting to get to him.

As he was just about finish rinsing off, he suddenly heard a knock at the door. Turning off the water, he listened again to make sure it was coming from his door and not next door. The knock sounded again, and he knew it was his door. Grumbling, he grabbed a towel from the rack and, wiping the water off his face, wrapped another towel around his waist. Rubbing his head, he moved over to his door, wondering who would be knocking. The knock sounded again.

"Yes, yes," Johnny yelled out. "Just hold on a second."

Looking through the peephole, all he could see was the top of a head looking down at the floor. Unhooking the chain, he opened the door. His feet were still wet and slipped slightly as he opened it and moved to the side. When he caught himself with the edge and looking saw that it was Mica standing in the hallway, smiling. Her eyes widened, seeing him all wet and only dressed in a towel.

"Uh…hi there." She beamed.

"And what can I do for you?" he said, rubbing his hair.

"I'm sorry but you left your passport at the counter," she said, holding it out to him.

"Oh, thank you," he said, reaching over and taking it from her. "I probably couldn't have gotten very far without it."

He realized that she was not in her hotel outfit. She had changed and was wearing a thin summer dress that barely covered her body, her long legs sticking out tantalizingly from the short hem. Her long hair was no longer tied up on her head and was down, draped over her shoulder. With a smile, her other hand came out from behind her back, and looking, he saw that it held a bottle of aged bourbon. After showing him, she took a small step toward him.

"I didn't know if anyone had properly welcomed you to our country."

"Properly?" he asked, confused.

"From that, it's obvious that didn't happen. If you're not too tired, I thought that I could be to one and…" she said, holding the bottle up, "first up, share some of this with me."

"I don't really—"

Before he could continue, she stepped past him into the room. As she did, her hand grabbed the edge of the towel and yanked it. When she turned, the towel slipped from his waist and hit the floor at his feet. Not bothering to move, he released the door and let it shut behind him.

"Oh my!" she gasped, seeing him naked.

"If you insist, come in." He laughed.

He followed as she turned and placed the bottle on the counter before turning back to him. Slowly, she pressed her body up against him. As he took her waist, she ran her hands along the length of his arms. As she examined him, the thought of her in his room right now was definitely appealing, but he didn't know if he had the strength to perform up to her expected standards.

"Mica, I have to warn you, I've had a very long day."

She looked into his eyes as her hand ran down to his butt, squeezing the flesh in her fingers.

"I've had a long day also."

Knowing what might happen next, he reached over and grabbed the bottle of bourbon. Taking the top off, he quickly tipped it up and took several deep swallows, gasping as it began to burn going down his throat. She laughed seeing is face.

"Just to give me the strength, you understand," he told her.

"Completely," she said, taking the bottle from him, "and we might as well start out equal."

After several gulps, she placed it back on the counter. Reaching behind her, she unzipped her dress and, with a shrug of her shoulder, let it fall down around her ankles. Stepping over to him, she took his face in her hands and, leaning forward, kissed him. As their lips met, he swept her up into his arms and carried her over to the bed.

"I guess in the end, we'll see who's equal," he commented.

"Really," she said, kissing his chin, "I like a challenge."

Johnny liked to be challenged, and she had obviously thrown down the gauntlet. With a smile, he slowly lowered her to the bed. As her legs wrapped around his waist, the time together slowly blended until, exhausted, he noticed it was early morning. With a deep breath, Mica rolled over onto her elbow and smiled at him.

"Welcome to Egypt, sir…"

"It was a great welcoming," Johnny said, pulling her against his chest.

With a deep kiss, she got up and, grabbing up her clothes, began to dress. Once she was fully dressed, she came back over and kissed him once more.

"From my point of view, it was a tie. Maybe we can break that tie another time."

"Maybe I'll be up for it," he laughed.

"Oh, you were up for it," she laughed. "You need anything just call me."

"I will."

Mica then turned around and left. Watching the door close, he leaned back into the pillows and gave a sigh of relief. Now he needed another shower, and noticing the time, he got up and went back into the bathroom.

After the shower, he didn't know what he felt like doing. After the long flight and now with Mica, he didn't know what he felt like. Knowing he had to get adjusted to the time and get his body on the same page, he felt he had to rest. It was only a little after midnight and, reaching over, turned on the TV. Scrolling through the channels, he saw an American broadcast of an NBA basketball game between the Philadelphia 76ers and the Los Angeles Lakers. From what he could see, it was a home game in the Coliseum. Watching for a moment, it appeared the score was tied and was only in the second quarter.

Good deal, he smirked.

Fixing a drink, he came back and settled onto the couch. While watching the game, he heard his stomach rumble and realized he hadn't eaten in hours. Checking the room service menu, he saw that he still had time where he could order. Looking through it, he found something he could eat that was not all that heavy.

The next thing he knew, he woke up stretched out on the couch and the game was over with. Looking at the clock, he had been asleep for about two hours. Now that he was half awake, he knew he was still tired and didn't feel like going out. There would be time for that later. Ordering a sandwich and fries, he slipped on his pants and waited for the food to arrive. He was surprised when only about ten minutes later, there was a knock at the door. As he opened it, there was an attendant with a platter in his hands.

"Your food, sir," he said, walking past him.

"Just put it on the coffee table," he said, digging in his pocket for a tip.

After he had set his food out and arranged it, he came back and, taking the tip, gave him a smile and a small nod.

"Thank you, sir," he said, heading for the corridor. "You have a good evening."

"You too."

Closing the door, he went over and sat down on the couch. Sitting on the edge, he began to eat his sandwich, almost inhaling it. Within minutes, he had inhaled almost the entire plate. Wiping his mouth, he grabbed his glass and sat back. With a belch, he started to laugh since he tried to remember what it tasted like. He realized that he was hungrier than he though. Taking a sip of his drink, he settled back to watch the game.

CHAPTER 6

THE SHARP RING of the phone made Johnny sit up quickly from the couch. He let out a gasp as the blood raced from his head. Reaching over, he picked it up and didn't bother waiting to hear the hotel wake-up message. Leaning over on his knees, he slowly rubbed his face, noticing his aching body. He then saw that his pants were on the floor and a towel he had probably grabbed to cover him was lying on the floor at his feet. Laughing, he slowly looked around the room. The television was still on and the plate of half-eaten food sat on the small table. Beside it was the bottle of bourbon Mica had brought and an empty glass. Seeing that the bottle was almost a third gone, he understood his head.

Really need to eat first and not after, he thought.

Checking the time, he knew he had to get up and get ready. Today he was going down to the main police station and see if they had any more information on the disappearance of his father. It had now been over a week, and he needed to know more details than what the officers had provided when he was in New York.

He slowly made his way into the bathroom and got into the shower. The hot water felt good, and as he finished, he turned it to cold. The change in temperature made him instantly shiver, but he also knew that the day would be very hot and wanted to enjoy some form of cold before that happened. Finished, he dried off and looked at himself in the mirror and wondered about his father.

Where the heck are you, Dad?

Staring further into the glass, Johnny saw the glistening diamond sapphire in his ear that his mother gave to him when he turned eighteen. As he shaved, he began to reminisce about the times she took him to school and encouraged him to just do his best. Then, he thought when his father would help him to learn Egyptian history and taught him to dig up artifacts with a brush and scalpel. Now they were both gone, and he was all alone. As he thought of that fact, he nicked himself with the razor, and blood began to drip down his cheek.

"Damn," he cursed loudly.

Sticking his finger on the cut, he turned and looked at the damage. It was just a small nick, and once the bleeding stopped, he finished carefully and washed his face. Checking once more the water, closed the cut and it wasn't bleeding any more. With his face dry, he could finish dressing into something cooler for the area. Pulling a white polo on and his faded jeans, he tied up his work boots, knowing he would probably be walking quite a bit. Going back in the bathroom, he straightened his hair and, pouring out some cologne, splashed it on his face. When he did, the small cut on his cheek began to burn and he cursed again. Checking, he saw that it still wasn't bleeding and, making sure he hadn't forgotten anything, grabbed his bag and headed down to the lobby.

When the doors of the elevator opened and he walked toward the front doors, he turned and looked over at the main counter. He saw Mica helping another guest, and as he passed, she looked up and saw him. Never missing a beat, she produced a large smile and gave him a wink before going back to the guest in front of her. He just grinned and, shaking his head, left. Before reaching the outside, a man came up to him.

"Do you need a taxi today, sir?" the doorman asked him.

"Sure," Johnny said, slipping on his sunglasses.

The doorman quickly stepped over to the edge of the curb and, blowing his whistle, lifted his arm to hail a taxi from the waiting line. Once it pulled up to them, the doorman stepped over and opened the back door for him.

"Thanks," Johnny said, stepping inside the back.

"Where to?" the driver asked, leaning over the seat.

"I need to go here," he said, handing him the card. "You know the place?"

"Uh, yeah," he said, slightly puzzled by his destination and, handing him the card, turned back around. "That's the first time I've had to take someone there."

"First time going there myself," Johnny commented, leaning back in the seat.

At least the cab was somewhat cool since it was early morning as they drove through the city. After a while, the cab came to a stop. Looking out the window, he saw they were near the entrance of the station. Paying the fare, he stepped out of the back and looked at the entrance as the cab left.

The station was nothing special and was an all-brick building that looked very old like all the surrounding buildings. An Egyptian flag on a long pole waved above the front doors. The doors at the top of the steps were wooden and propped open to allow the breeze of the day to swirl through the entryway into the lobby. The only windows of the four-story building started up on the second floor, and all of them were covered in steel bars. A large sign in both Egyptian and English indicated that this was the Agouza Police Department. He shook his head and headed up the steps to go inside.

Once inside, he saw that there were probably twenty or thirty people sitting around or talking to officers. Some were waiting to go inside to visit relatives or friends or wanting help for help for their problems. Beyond a group of people, he saw an officer behind the counter not helping anyone but going through paperwork. Slowly pushing through them, he stopped at the counter.

"Excuse me, can I get some help?"

"What can I do for you?" he said, barely giving him a glance."

"My name is Johnny Cortez," he said, digging out the card and handing it to him. "I'm here to see a detective, Deniko Kashef."

"Is he expecting you?" the officer asked, looking at the card.

"I think so. He's investigating my father's disappearance."

Handing the card back to him, he reached over and picked up the telephone, calling the detective's office. After several minutes of talking to someone on the other end, he hung up and looked over at Johnny.

"Sir, if you take a seat, someone will be down shortly to get you."

"Thank you," Johnny said.

When he turned, Johnny saw an open seat on the near wall and quickly walked over and sat down. He didn't know how long it would take and tried to get comfortable. As he waited, he was intrigued at the type of people that came in. There were all aspects of the local people. A couple of times people would come in with livestock expecting help. Each time an officer would come from behind the counter and usher them outside. Time passed quickly as he watched the people coming in to the station.

"Johnny...Johnny Cortez?"

Hearing his name, he stood up and stepped forward.

"Right here," he said, lifting his hand.

The person calling out his name was a young woman officer who waited for him near a hallway and lifted her hand to indicate where she was standing. Approaching her through the moving crowd, she smiled when he finally got up to her.

"Sir, I'm Officer Somali and will be escorting you up to the detective's office. If you'll follow me, I'll take you to him."

"Lead on," he said, following her as she turned.

Walking down the hallway, they went up the stairs to the third floor. As they walked, he noticed that there were no elevators he could see. Everything was accessed through multiple stairs. The building looked like it was a converted apartment building the government had taken over because of its location. Reaching the third floor, they went down another hallway that opened into a large bay filled with desks and police. Along the walls were offices that covered the windows. Near the back, she walked up to an office and knocked on the door.

"Come in," a voice called out.

Opening the door, she stepped in and off to the side.

"Johnny Cortez," the woman announced.

"Thanks," the man behind the desk said never looking up. He pointed over to a chair near the desk. "Have a seat, and, Officer...please close the door when you leave."

"Yes, sir."

Obeying the detective, she stood holding the door and let Johnny move past her before stepping back outside and closing the door. Taking a seat, he waited as the detective finished writing in a file he had opened on his desk. A small fan on the cabinet behind him whined and was the only noise in the room. The window was open behind him, and he could barely hear the noise of the street below.

Detective Deniko was exactly what he expected. His white dress shirt had several buttons undone at the top to help cool him in the hot office, and he could see his dark chest hair beneath. The strap of his holster over both shoulders held the material in place. His dark hair was solid and thick, and he figured it wouldn't move even in a high wind. A layer of two-day-old stubble covered his face, and traces of gray hair mixed with the darker hair. A set of small glasses was pushed low on his nose. Beside him, a cigarette burned in the ash tray, and smoke circled lazily in the air until the breeze from the fan pushed it away. Finally, he dropped the pen in his hand and, picking up the cigarette, leaned back in his chair.

"Mr. Cortez," he started, examining him. "I didn't expect you but figured, at some point, you would show you. I hope you had a good flight."

"Yes, it wasn't that bad."

"Let me first say I'm so sorry about your father, and believe me, I'm doing everything I can to figure out what happened to him."

"I really do appreciate your office sending the officers to see me while in New York to let me know about my father, Detective."

"According to your father's visa files," he said, leaning forward, "you are his only living relative and so we reached out to find you. It took several days before the authorities could locate you and send some officers."

"Again, I appreciate it," Johnny said, now staring at the board on the other wall.

On it were at least a dozen pictures with his father's picture at the very top. He didn't recognize any of the other pictures, but being up there, they obviously had something to do with the case. Black lines and notes were written everywhere, and a couple of the faces had red lines crossed through the faces.

"I see you've noticed the storyboard concerning your father," he said, standing up and walking over to it. "Most of the investigation is placed here…and my notes."

"Is there any progress or suspects in his disappearance?" Johnny asked, getting up.

"Unfortunately, we've run into a dead-end. We still have several leads we are checking out but nothing solid. Nothing is out of bounds, but I'm getting pressure from my superiors who want this case closed quickly."

"And closing it means…what?"

"Well, it will mean the file is closed in the eyes of the department but will remain on the open list. That is similar to what you in America call…a cold case."

Johnny didn't like hearing that answer and continued to stare at the photos. Deniko noticed that his attention remained on the board even while they spoke. Leaning forward, he looked at Johnny.

"Johnny, any of those face or names familiar to you?"

"Well, just one of them is even familiar to me… It's Jarif Widdal."

"Tell me, what do you know of Mr. Widdal and his involvement with your father from your perspective?"

"Well…my father told me that he was a respected businessman and could get him the dig permits he needed for his dig. Widdal was very interested in his possible discovery. He was also willing to finance the operation. He ran all the business operations, and my father would hire all the crew he needed but within reason."

"Do you know if he had any issues with him?"

"I guess he could be but never said anything about it to me."

Deniko didn't say anything further and scribble some notes in his file. Once again, Johnny could hear the noise of the traffic below. Finally, he leaned back and, glancing at the board, turned back to Johnny.

"Mr. Cortez, your father was invaluable to our people and our country to understand so many things about our civilization."

"It's the thing he loved to do," Johnny said.

Deniko continued to notice that he was focusing on the board. His curiosity with it intrigued him and, in the back of his mind, thought that he might know more than he was leading on.

"In my investigation, I've had not only Jarif Widdal under surveillance but everyone one else on that board. After we interviewed them, we watched and followed up some other leads but still maintained a watch over them. We wanted to see if after all our questions one of them would do something out of the ordinary."

"And did any of them?"

"Unfortunately, none of them did."

"And what about Widdal?" Johnny said, walking up to the board to get a better look.

"Even though he is very influential in the area, Widdal has been a subject of other investigations. So far there has been nothing we can find that would convict him. The only thing is minor infractions that in court they simply got a plea deal and paid the fine, thus dropping and conviction."

"Same sort of thing happens in America, Detective."

"My problem with it is that, in several of the cases, critical witnesses suddenly disappeared only to be found later dead. I really don't know if he had anything to do with your father's disappearance, but everything in my body says he does."

"And," he asked, sweeping his hand at the board, "what about all these other people?"

"Each one of them had very tight alibis for the night he vanished…even Widdal. In the case of a missing person's case, we simply can't arrest someone with no evidence. This missing person's case has no weight without a body or foul play motive that we can prove. The internal department will review it for closure next week if nothing else turns up."

"There has to be something out there," Johnny said, wondering if he would ever find out what happened to his father.

"Would you like to see the dig site?"

"Yes, I would."

"We have it all quarantined and have the help of the military thanks to your father's find. Maybe with your expertise, you might see something that we missed."

"If I can help," he said, still looking at the photos. "I'll do anything that might help me know what happened to my father."

"Thank you."

Hearing a buzzer, he saw Deniko stand up and also stood. When he turned hearing the door open, he saw the female officer that had brought him up earlier appeared.

"Would you escort Mr. Cortez down to my squad car?" Deniko said. "I'll be down there shortly as soon as I finish making some notes."

"Certainly, sir," she said, stepping to the side. "Mr. Cortex, please follow me."

Knowing he couldn't get any further information, Johnny figured there might be something at the dig site. He walked out the door and headed for the stairs, following behind the officer.

Sitting down, he watched Johnny walk away until he disappeared. Leaning back, he ran his fingers through his hair. As he stared blankly at the ceiling, another officer walked into the detective's office and shut the door behind him. Walking over to the desk, he leaned over and opened one of his drawers. Pulling a bottle of whiskey out, he poured himself a drink and sat down. It was his chief, Omar.

"Uh, just help yourself," Deniko said, watching him.

"Don't mind if I do," he commented, taking a long swallow. "It's been a hell of a day and this will help. So is there anything new from the son?"

"No," he said frustrated, "nothing that I didn't already know or expect to hear."

"You know that I can't keep the commissioners back for much longer."

"I just know there is a piece of evidence that we're missing, and with his son now here, that might just appear."

"Well, you better hope so for your sake."

Deniko just looked at him.

"How long do I have before they close it?"

"The best I can do right now is..." he began slowly sipping his drink before looking over at him, "two weeks tops."

"Shit," he said, tossing his pen across the room.

"Like I said, it doesn't look good that a renowned American archeologist disappeared and we can't find him. I've heard that our superiors are already formulating a satisfying response to close the book."

Getting up he walked from behind the desk, and as he passed the chief, he snagged the glass from his hand and finished his drink. Handing the empty glass back to him, the chief grinned as he took it and watched Deniko head out the door.

"You know where the bottle is," he said to him with a wave.

"Yes, I do," he said, getting up and pouring his glass full. "Yes, I do."

CHAPTER 7

ONCE DOWNSTAIRS, DENIKO went around to the back parking lot and, sliding between the parked cars, saw Johnny and the officer standing over by his car. They appeared to be talking as he came up to them. The officer turned and saw him, tapping Johnny on the arm before pointing in his direction.

"Thank you, Officer Somali," he said, "that'll be all."

"Yes, sir," she said, walking back to the building.

"You ready to go?" Deniko asked, opening the doors.

"I sure am," he said, getting in.

As Deniko drove out of the city to the dig site, Johnny didn't say much. He sat quietly and watched the scenery of the buildings go by. Finally, the buildings vanished, and there was the normal brown sand of the desert. It was only occasionally that he saw any sign of civilization or people. Even the horizon was empty and merged with the sky.

After about twenty minutes, the detective turned off the main road onto a dirt service road. It wasn't paved and had ruts everywhere from the traffic passing across it. Moving along, the tires hit bumps and holes, jostling them, causing Johnny to hold on. Soon, a small sign appeared next to another small road. The makeshift pole indicated they were heading to a site managed by the Widdal Company, and below it was a black arrow pointed to the right. As they turned, the sandy road began twisting between the hills. Finally, the hills parted, and they came to a small rise containing several tents along with parked vehicles. Johnny noticed that there was one truck containing several military personnel. Deniko drove to an open spot beside one of the larger tents and stopped.

"Well, we're here," Deniko said, turning off the car.

Turning, he watched the expression on Johnny's face and waited for him to get out of the car first. Once he was out and closed the door he got out. Johnny stood and looked around the area trying to take it all in. Deniko motioned for him to follow and led him over to the security officers guarding the area. Showing them his credentials and telling them that Johnny was with him, they allowed both of them to pass.

Both of them walked over to the top of the small ridge and up to the main tent. There was the yellow police tape hung across the entrance on two poles, and when they entered, Johnny knew that it was his father's tent. He bent over under the tape, and once he was on the other side, stepped inside. Just before they entered a tall worker from the dig site approached them. He wore overalls, army boots, and a plaid long sleeve shirt. He wore glasses and his skin was darkened from years in the sun.

"Hello, Detective," He smiled, "and how are you doing?"

"Jorge," he said, shaking his hand. "I'm well thanks."

While they shook hands, the man turned and looked at Johnny.

"I'm sorry," Deniko said. "Jorge this is Dr. Cortez's son, Johnny Cortez."

"Greetings, sir," he said, shaking his hand.

"Hello," he said. "You may not remember me but I know you. Your father and I have worked on many projects together. Every time he comes here, we worked together and that has been now for almost thirty years. The last time I saw you, you were only a small boy."

Johnny looked at him and tried to remember. Even though he said they had met, he couldn't place him in his memory. Grabbing his handkerchief from his back pocket, he wiped the sweat from his brow.

"Maybe, but that was a long time ago…sorry."

"That's all right," Jorge said. "It was a long time ago."

"I do remember something about being stuck in some quicksand and someone saving me and also about making a…fire that burned down a tent?"

"Yes," he laughed. "That was me and I didn't even remember the one about the tent and fire. Boy, was your father mad about that."

"I remember the glow in the darkness," Jorge said, rubbing his chin.

While they talked, Deniko reached over and moved the tape away and opened the flap of the tent entrance flap. Turning, they saw he was holding the flap, and both of them entered before he followed, releasing the flap. Johnny looked around and saw several things that his father always took along with him. He turned and looked at Jorge.

"Jorge, do you know what happened to my father?"

"No," he said softly. "If I did, I would have told the detective."

As Johnny surveyed the room and picked different items up, Deniko and Jorge stood to the side and watched. The tent looked like nothing had been touched or moved since his father was last there. On a table near one side were a set of walk-ie-talkies to direct the various dig activities. There was also a table with a large map of the area that had markings all over it along with a compass. In one corner was a bed, which was still made and straightened like one was in the military. The room was dominated by the large work table in the middle, and he saw a bottle of wine with a glass next to it. Picking up the glass, he saw that there was still a small portion of the wine in it.

"Is this the way you found it?" Johnny asked.

"We have gone over it, but yes, everything is where we found it."

Sitting down in the chair, he saw that it was turned a specific way. Ahead of him there was another flap in the tent. He asked Jorge to open the flaps so he could see what he would see while sitting at the table. When Jorge pressed the flaps to the side and held them, Johnny could see the dig site in the distance. Leaning forward, he could see that the map was aligned with what he saw.

He was always a stickler for the little details, he thought.

"It looks like the military captain is coming over to see us," Deniko said, looking out the other flap.

If he was to figure out if there was anything here, he had to have some time alone. He couldn't do that with people around him.

"Detective," Johnny said, "is it possible to give me a minute alone?"

"Sure," Deniko said, motioning for Jorge to go outside.

Jorge could see the pain in his face and felt sorry for Johnny. He nodded and, as he passed him, rubbed his hand over his shoulder. Johnny looked up at him and smiled to indicate he appreciated it. Deniko held the flap open until Jorge passed him before exiting. Now that he was alone, Johnny didn't know where to start. He didn't have much time since the captain would want to see him.

As he swallowed, he almost choked on the piece of gum he was chewing and knew he had to get rid of it. Taking it out of his mouth, he looked around, looking for something to put it in, and saw there was no trash can. There wasn't even a simple slip of paper he could wrap it up in. Tossing it in the sand was not an option. With little choice, he figured he would do just like the kids did in school and stick it under the table.

Trying to get it to stick underneath, his left hand hit another dried piece of gum. Feeling, there was something else attached to it. Leaning over, he saw that a small piece of paper was jammed into the crack between the top and the legs and the gum was holding it into place. With a quick glance over at the tent flap, he pushed the gum away and pulled it out. It was a small piece of paper folded in half and, when he unfolded it, saw that there were no words on it. There was nothing more than a strange single string of numbers.

What the hell is this?

Staring at it, he didn't know the significance of the note or why it would be stuck under the table. It was definitely in his father's handwriting though. Before he could think about what it might mean, he heard voices growing louder outside the tent. Sticking it in his pocket, he leaned back in the chair. Just then the military captain, Deniko, and Jorge entered. Seeing them, Johnny stood up and walked over to them.

Deniko introduced the captain to him and, after shaking hands, went over what was going on at the dig and why they were there. He didn't have a problem with them being there and thought it was probably better they were. Between the police and the military, nothing would get out of hand or disturbed.

While Johnny talked to the captain, Deniko and Jorge went outside and waited by the tent. They then noticed a rising cloud of dust above the hills on the entrance road. Between the hills, a black Cadillac rumbled down the road. They watched as it pulled up near the main tent besides the detective's car. A large man stepped out of the driver's seat and opened the back door. He stood holding the door. It allowed the passenger in the back to step out.

The man stepping out stood for a moment and looked around. Even in the heat of the day, he stood as if he was heading to a board meeting. His white hat that he adjusted matched the white and black suit and the black leather shoes shined in the sun. When he looked up, he smiled, and the bright sun glared from the gold caps on his teeth. Adjusting his suit, he began to walk toward them while the other man closed the door and followed him.

"Shit," Jorge grumbled. "What the hell does he want?"

"I don't know," Deniko said, studying them, "but I'm sure we'll find out shortly."

"There isn't much left for him to grab."

"Maybe he just wants to double check," Deniko chuckled.

"Good afternoon, gentlemen," Mr. Widdal said, walking up to them and holding out his hand. Jorge just looked at him and simply stood there.

"What can we do for you, sir?" Jorge said, folding his arms, somewhat irritated.

"There's no need for the attitude." He smiled, noticing his demeanor. "I simply heard that Dr. Cortez's son had come to Cairo, and when I found out he was out here, I wanted to come out and personally give him my condolences."

"He's over in the main tent," Deniko told him, pointing over to him. "He's talking to the captain right now, so maybe you shouldn't bother him until he's finished."

"I understand the delicate nature of this time, and when he's done, I promise I will only take a small moment of his time," he said with a grin.

"Does it really have to be right now?" Jorge asked, gritting his teeth. "There is the ugly part of his father that is missing."

Hearing the voices outside, Johnny peered through the tent flaps and saw the group of gentlemen talking. He quickly concluded the conversation with the captain and, excusing himself, stepped out of the tent. As Jonny flipped open the tent flap to go over to them, Jorge then turned and saw him. Seeing him approach, Jorge stepped to the side.

"Sir," Jorge began, "this is Mr. Widdal, your father's employer, and he would like to speak to you."

Surveying the man, he held his hand out.

"Glad to meet you," Johnny said.

"It is good to finally see you again, Johnny," he said.

"Again," Jonny said, surprised.

"Yes, you may not remember since you were only a small boy when I first saw you digging beside your father on that desolate dig site," he said, examining him. "I see you're all grown up."

"The years do that," Johnny told him.

"I actually came here to give you my personal condolences. Your father's loss not only hurt me but hurt the entire archeological community."

"Thank you, I appreciate it," Jonny said, looking at the man behind him. "And who is your friend?"

"This is my bodyguard." He turned and smiled. "In this day of unknown issues, it's always better to feel safe. I always want to feel safe."

"Hey," Johnny said, holding out his hand to him.

The man never moved and simply looked down at his hand.

"Don't be offended," Widdal laughed. "His hands are used for many things but not greetings."

"Is that all they are used for?" Johnny asked him.

"Yes, except…"

Mr. Widdal waved his hand to the man while taking a few steps toward Johnny. His bodyguard nodded and, turning, went back to wait at the car. Deniko and Jorge watched and grew somewhat nervous by his outward concern.

"Johnny, I know there are many questions going through your mind. We will have time later, and I'll answer any question you might have. Your father and I had a wonderful relationship, which I will tell you I sorely miss."

"I'll see if we can arrange for a meeting," Johnny told him.

"Now that you mention it," he said, looking at the others, "I'm having a small dinner party and would like you to come. There will be plenty of time and we can discuss anything that's on your mind."

Widdal looked over at Jorge and Deniko.

"And of course both of you are also invited."

All three of them looked at each other before agreeing.

"We'll be there," Johnny said.

"Excellent," Widdal said. "I'll let the good detective know the date and time."

Turning, he walked slowly back to the car. As he came closer, the man opened the back door and waited. Getting into the back, the man closed the door and quickly got in the driver side of the limousine. Starting the engine, it backed up and turned to head down the road back to town.

"Well," Deniko said to the others, "that was interesting."

"Yes, it was," Jorge said.

"I think it's time to get you back to your hotel."

"In a little bit," Johnny said, looking back at the dig site. "I want to look at what my father discovered."

"There isn't much left."

"That's all right… It won't take long."

"I'll take him down to the chamber," Jorge told the detective.

"Thanks," Deniko said. "While you're doing that, I'll check in with headquarters."

"Let me go and get a few things, then we can go."

CHAPTER 8

WIDDAL SAT IN the back of the limousine and wondered about Johnny. Opening the collar of his shirt, he leaned forward and, dropping a few cubes of ice into the glass, poured a drink from the bar in front of him. His mind raced as he sat back and sipped the drink. Was his son simply here in the country to see what happened to his father, or was there perhaps more to his arrival? When they get to the party, he would find time to see.

His cell phone began to ring, and pulling it out, he recognized the number. He gritted his teeth and, answering it, placed the call on the speaker so his hands were free.

"Yes," Widdal responded.

"I just wanted to make sure our payment will be made as promised and in full," the voice said. "Considering the large sum and what has happened with the dig site, we have concerns."

'The payment will be made at the appointed time," he said, trying to calm them, "as was promised."

"Since you have already missed one payment, we have to ask."

"You were gracious to slide the one payment, and I understand fully that this next one is doubled. I'm gathering the funds even now."

"We are glad to hear that."

"It just has been tough with the disappearance of the doctor."

"And what of the son who has arrived? Does he suspect or have any information?"

"I have not had a chance to actually question him yet."

"You have seven days," the voice indicated. "No more. Do not disappoint us."

The line went dead, and he slapped at the phone angrily to turn it off. Emptying the contents of the glass in his hand, he grabbed the bottle and filled it again. As he placed it back in the holder and leaned back, he pressed the button on the console, allowing the window between him and the driver to slide down.

"Where do you want to go, sir?" the driver asked.

"Back to the house," he said. "I feel…dirty."

"Yes, sir."

CHAPTER 9

S TANDING ON THE hill waiting for Jorge to return, Johnny watched the cloud of dust slowly disappear in the distance. Johnny wondered if Widdal had come to really give his condolences or had some other purpose in mind. Hearing footsteps behind him, he turned and saw Jorge coming toward him. There was a strange look on his face, and he sensed that he was hesitant to say something to him.

"Sure seems a bit full of himself," Johnny said with a grunt.

"Yes…yes, he is," Jorge commented.

"I almost expected it when he told me who he was," Johnny told him, glancing back at the hills. Seeing that the dust was now gone, he turned to Jorge and smiled. "Shall we go?"

"Yes, follow me."

He had a lantern in his hand, and Johnny followed him down into the dig site.

"So where are we going?" he finally asked.

"There was an area by the wall that he found."

"What exactly was my father digging for in the site?"

"I'm not exactly sure of the actual significance, but I can show you the chamber," he said, walking down the slope.

The two walked down into the dig site and through the workers still clearing the sand away in several areas. In his mind, he slowly counted them and realized there were approximately twenty men working that glanced at them while they came through. As they would pass, Johnny saw them staring at him and tried to see their facial expressions. Could one of them know more than they might have told the police? Jorge saw that he was examining each man as they passed and stopped him.

"I know what you're thinking, sir, and can tell you that these men were extremely loyal to your father. If needed, any one of them would give their life for him. He was very generous to them when they needed help. If one of them knew anything about your father, they would have freely provided it, believe me."

"I didn't know you could read minds," Johnny laughed.

"I can't, but your eyes betrayed you."

"I have to work on those tells."

"Your father knew all their names and family members. He always joked with them and cared about what was happening with them. That was the reason they were so loyal and would never let any harm come to them."

"Sounds like my father," he said, knowing that he was judging them unknowingly. "Do you have any idea what happened to my father?"

"I'm sorry but I do not. The last time that I saw him, he was watching them pull all the items from the chamber. He was quite excited while inspecting each item as it came out. There was a sense of pleasure as he looked at Mr. Widdal after he arrived."

"Something so extraordinary couldn't just be left for one person."

"But he thought so since he paid for all of it. Seeing all the objects being loaded into trucks made him extremely angry. I don't know why, but seeing his face contort appeared to please your father. I think he did it because he figured that many of the objects would simply have disappeared and not been shown to the world."

"He always believed discoveries were for everyone and not a few chosen few," he said with a smile.

They walked to the far side of the dig where several workers were clearing a long portion of an inner wall. Several feet of sand had been removed, and he noticed that walls on either side of the entrance had magnificent paintings along with delicate carvings. Several were on three entrances formed into the surface of the walls. Stepping over to one of them, he ran his hand over the lines of text. Studying them he found he could read some of it, but other pieces he couldn't make out and was unrecognizable. Shaking his head, Jorge then led him over to the main entrance.

"This is where your father found the main chamber."

"I wonder what it was originally built for," Johnny asked, looking around at the entrance.

"We may never know, but once they study it, they may find out."

As Jorge turned on the lantern and began to walk inside, one of the workers walked over to him. The worker's coveralls were covered completely in dirt from digging. Noticing him approach, he saw Jorge stop and look over at him.

"Yes, what is it?" he asked.

"Can you come over to the far wall? The men there need instructions about excavating the last portion of the far wall. They are confused and need some direction."

Hearing the man speak to him, the strange tone of the voice caused Johnny's eyebrows to rise. Standing beside him, he instantly knew that this was definitely not the voice of a man but a soft voice, that of a woman. Taking her cap off, she began to beat it against her leg, sending the layer of dust into the air before slowly dissipating. He couldn't take his eyes from her as she began to straighten her clothing. Jorge began to chuckle seeing him stare at her.

"Very well," he said and then looked at Johnny. "Since you're here, let me introduce Dr. Cortez's son, Johnny."

Jorge pointed to the worker and smiled, standing straight and proud.

"And this, sir, is my daughter…Ani."

"Nice to meet you," she said with a smile. "Sorry for butting in."

He couldn't help but notice the beautiful green eyes looking at him and the long black hair tied into a ponytail beneath the hat she wore.

"Uh, no problem," he said, reaching over to shake her hand. It was all that would come out of his mouth. When their hands touched, there was a large blue spark that jumped between them. His whole body began to tingle from the charge and, shaking his tingling hand, smiled over at her.

"Sorry about that," Ani said. "Happens all the time in this dry desert."

"Yeah, I forgot about it also."

"I'm sorry about your father," she commented, taking his hand again.

There were no more sparks, and now they were just staring at each other with only silence between them. After a few moments, it became quite noticeable. Neither would move nor speak as he delicately held onto her hand. From working, he noticed how smooth her skin was and wondered. She didn't bother pulling away from him or seem that it bothered her that he hadn't released it as they just stood. Finally, Jorge shook his head and jumped in.

"Ani, how about if you show Johnny the inside the chamber while I go and handle the excavation crew?"

"Sure, Dad."

Jorge held out the lantern to her, and once she slipped her hand from his grip, she took it from him as he walked to the men waiting over by the wall, leaving them alone. Ani took a breath and placed the lantern on the ground before slipping her arms from the top of the coveralls. She then tied the loose arms around her waist. Beneath the coveralls she wore what looked like a man's muscle shirt with open arms. He could see the dark outline of her bra beneath it. As she finished tying the sleeves, Johnny coughed roughly, clearing his throat. She glanced at him and laughed as he tried not to be obvious. He then looked at the entrance.

"This leads to the inner chamber?" Johnny asked, still trying to clear his throat.

"Yes," she said, still smiling as she turned on the lantern. "Ready?"

"Oh yes, lead on."

Ani held up the lantern and entered the opening while using the wall of the entrance to steady herself. Noticing how slippery the footing was beneath his feet, he tried to stay close so the light shined on where they were walking.

Moving farther inside, he couldn't help but watch her curvy hips and round buttocks move as she walked along. The shadows reflecting from the wall made them tantalizing for such a small frame. Every few steps, she would turn to see if he was right behind her. Even with a layer of dirt and sand, she was striking. As dirty as she was, it didn't seem to bother her like it would most women.

"Johnny," she said, pointing to an outcropping of rock. "Need to make sure that you don't hit your head coming in here."

"Thanks," he said, realizing he wasn't watching where he was going.

As they finally came into the inner chamber, Johnny began to gasp. The air was still thick and musty with little breeze to circulate the air. Standing near the entrance, he let Ani walk in farther so the light could shine on most of the area. He was totally amazed that they had found something this special after ten thousand years. There was a huge painting on a wall with what looked like early Egyptian writings. There were still a few pieces of wood furniture that hadn't been removed sitting off to one side. Off to the side near the furniture was an odd place that had been cleared that to him looked like a holding area for a burial tomb, but he couldn't see where the tomb could be located.

"Did the government take all the artifacts?" Johnny asked, walking around the room.

"After your father called them, they brought a whole army of people from Cairo and immediately began removing everything after cataloguing it."

"Was Mr. Widdal here when they took it all?"

"Oh yes," Ani almost whispered. "He arrived a few hours after they did."

"I can understand why he was so upset if this place held what they say. He probably felt he was cheated out of his profit."

"He's all about profit," she said.

Ani could see that as he talked, there was an anger growing inside him. Walking over to him, she placed her hand on his arm and looked into his face. He could see a small tear beginning to form in her eyes as she looked at him.

"I could tell when I met him."

"Your father was a good man and I'll miss him."

Hearing her voice, Johnny's heart started beating faster. He couldn't tell if it was because he was thinking about his father or because of her. Even in the dim light of the lantern, her face seemed to almost glow. Seeing her smile at him produced strange feelings within him. Feeling the calm, he took a deep breath.

"Thank you," he said, returning her smile. "I just need to know the reason for my father's disappearance. It's not something he would do. I owe it to him and myself to try and find the answers."

"I'm sure the answers will come…in time."

Ani continued to smile as she flipped her hair from her shoulder. Johnny found himself unconsciously staring at her when suddenly his stomach made strange gurgling sounds that echoed through the chamber. The odd sounds caused her to look at him strangely.

"Seems you might be a little hungry," she said, hearing the sounds.

"Well, maybe just a little," he laughed.

"If you like, we can come back later after you get some food."

"No, we're here and I want to examine this chamber first."

"As you wish," she said, shaking her head.

Johnny walked in between the stanchions of lights that were off staged around the room. The main generators to the chamber were turned off for the night and that's why they needed to use lanterns. He went over to the main wall in the back and began to survey the writing and reliefs. It was an amazing sight. Nearing down to the one section below the reliefs, he tried to read the inscriptions. Several of the strings he didn't recognize and turned to Ani.

"Ani, do you know what these symbols here mean?"

"It is ancient an Egyptian language they said. The symbols are the words, but the archeologists couldn't read them either. Several thought it was an amazing discovery of something older than what had been found before."

"They look older than any of the writing from even the early kingdom."

"One of them said maybe earlier than that."

Johnny smiled at the beautiful script and ran his hand over them. He thought of the men who had chiseled each item into the hard stone. Feeling the depth of the words, he tried to think of his next question but figured that Ani would not be able to answer them. Looking at one of the reliefs, he thought it odd. It was probably eight feet high and four feet wide and placed on either side of the center structure. Checking the edges, he wondered if they might have been placed to conceal something behind it. That was something for a later time. About twenty minutes later, after going over every inch of the chamber, they walked out into the pit. He could see Jorge walking down to them from the hillside.

"Thank you," Johnny said to Ani.

"It was my pleasure," she said, taking his lantern. "Maybe we can see some of the other sites around the city. I'm sure some of it has changed since the last time you were here."

"A lot has changed," he said, smiling at her.

"So have you seen enough and ready to go?" Jorge asked, reaching them.

"Yes," Johnny said. "I need to relax for a little while and let this all sink in."

Johnny thanked Jorge for everything and, while following him, glanced back at Ani. She stood watching them and then waved. Waving back, he followed him up to the detective who was leaning against his car, waiting. As he paused, he looked around the dig site. Deep within him, he knew that there was still something he was missing. He wondered if it just might be hiding in plain sight and he was overlooking it. Rubbing his chest, his handed felt the small slip of paper he had tucked inside. A smile rose on his face as he got inside the car.

It must be important if Dad hid it, he thought.

Shutting the door, he buckled up for the ride back into town.

CHAPTER 10

ENIKO DROPPED JOHNNY off at the hotel entrance and, after thanking him, walked into the lobby. Hitting the coolness in the room, he sighed and swallowed. It almost stuck as he tried to move it. Knowing that his throat was dried out parched and turning saw the sign of the hotel bar off to the side.

A couple of drinks would certainly help, he thought

He would have plenty of time for a shower and change of clothes later. Entering, his nose was hit with the smell of two-day-old cheap wine and the lingering odor of cigarettes. Hidden within the pungent air was another smell, a great smell of cooking food that was trying to mask the odor of the other. He knew this type of environment all too well, and as the odors swirled around his nostrils, the memories flooded back. As he stood at the entrance and took in the fragrance, he looked around the room.

He was surprised at how few men were actually in the bar. There were probably a dozen females at a couple of tables and the bar. They all turned as he walked in the room. There seemed to be at least a four to one ratio of women to men in the room. He always had a thing about blondes, and looking over the crop, there seemed to be plenty of them waiting for single a guy. Before he could reach the bar, a sultry blonde pressed through the others and walked over to him, grabbing his arm.

"Hey there." She grinned. "Want to buy a girl a drink?"

As she held his arm and began to stroke his chest, he noticed she was definitely better than the others that were waiting. Even in her heels, she was only tall enough to come up to his face where he could kiss her forehead. Looking up at him, she fluttered her eyes, obviously hoping he would take her invitation.

Not bad, he thought.

Surveying the woman, she had on a beautiful but simple black dress that covered her curves just right. The dress was cut low in the front to show off a long line of cleavage. Looking down, the dress was just short enough to expose her long legs. After his examination, he looked back up into her face.

"Sure, baby," he told her, trying to get the bartenders attention. "So what is your name?"

"It's Carmen." She smiled with a delicious twist of her mouth. Several of the other women at the bar tried to slowly move over to him, but she easily blocked them from coming closer. "So do come here by yourself all the time?"

"Well, I wouldn't say...always." He laughed, watching her play the dominate female in the room.

She was outgoing and very sexy, but Johnny was not in the mood for a possible hookup due to thinking about his father. But she was funny and interesting. The raggedy juke box had buttons that were faded and seemed to skip every now and them. But this was a bar, and Johnny was trying to drown his feelings for his father.

"Bartender," he said, trying to get his attention.

The bartender strolled over and, leaning on the bar, looked at him.

"I'll take a rum and Coke," he said before turning to her. "And what will it be for you?"

"Just make mine a glass of red wine."

Johnny looked back at the bartender and nodded.

"You got it," she said, beginning to make the drinks.

The place had changed since the last time he came here. It appeared to have many seedier individuals than he remembered. Trying to forget his father at least for a while, he was reverting into his normal behavior. He had already downed two drinks, and each one disappeared in only about two swallows. Carmen stood beside him and began to laugh.

"Seems that you've had a long day." She laughed, grabbing his hand. Moving closer to her bosom and centered in front of his chest and face. Johnny's heart began to pound in excitement.

"So...you know my name. What's yours?"

"My name is Johnny Cortez."

Her long body pressed close against his, and she said those words that Johnny wanted to hear.

"Let's dance?"

She reached toward Johnny's face and touched his ear. She moved her fingertips around his small diamond earring in his ear. Johnny's mind flashed back to his mother as this was her diamond in his ear. He remembered his mother grabbing his hand and teaching him to dance. She was a dancer and taught him all his moves as a young teenager. Johnny stood quiet for a second and then paused. Carmen was looking at him and knew that his mind was on more than just her.

"Johnny, are you okay?"

"No, I'm really not."

She drew closer to his face. Johnny pierced into her blue eyes and saw a sea of waves. His boat was there on the waves of her deep blue eyes, and he felt the wind rush by his sails as she began to speak softly. She lifted her arm and rubbed his neck and slightly pulled his neck to move his ear by her lips.

"I can't stand that you feel bad. Tell me what I can do to make you feel better?" she whispered in a sultry voice.

Johnny straightened up and looked Carmen in her eyes.

"Carmen," he said. He had come down here to play, but he was finding that didn't appeal to him any longer. She had to know why he was acting the way he was. "I'm only here because I wanted to forget things. I was told my father is dead."

"My god, I'm so sorry. And if I came on a little strong, please forgive me." Carmen's demeanor changed, and she immediately became the church girl all men want to marry—a great confidant and very respectful.

"It's okay... I'm trying to deal with it."

"Do you want to perhaps sit down and talk about it?" Her eyes danced with excitement.

"Carmen, you are very nice and I…I really can't."

Just as he finished, the figure of another woman moved behind her. She was heading out of the bar but looked at him as she passed. The look caused him to focus on her like the piercing focus of a cheetah hunting its quarry. She was dressed simply in designer jeans and a light shirt, but there was a long flow of blonde hair. When she had looked at him, he could see the most gorgeous blue eyes. Never stopping, she moved away, and he tried to refocus back on Carmen, but his gaze remained on the woman until she disappeared. In the back of his mind, there was something about her that he couldn't put his finger on.

Where the hell do I know her from? he thought.

He returned his focus back on Carmen, playing as though he was still listening.

"Ah…I'm sorry, my mind drifted. What did you say?"

"I said, silly, you should come over to my place tomorrow. I'm having a little get-together with some of my close friends. There will be food, drinks, and music. You'll have a good time I promise."

As she talked, he was nodding his head side to side, indicating what his answer would be.

"Oh, please, please say that you'll come," Carmen said, seeing his hesitation.

"I'll have to think about it."

She moved in closer to his face and he was not distracted, but his mind was still thinking about those green eyes that left the bar. Carmen was all her sexiness and gave him a quick kiss on the cheek and wrote her number on a napkin.

"Carmen, you really didn't have to do this."

"I wanted to. Not very often you meet a nice man around these dig sites. You can call me later to tell me you're coming. I'll give you the directions." Carmen suddenly moved her eyes down, looking at the floor. Moving over closer to him, she twisted her body, and he could tell that she was trying to use him to block her from being seen. Turning around, he saw a man along with several others had walked through the dining room entrance. When he looked at her, she was now cowering next to his arm in an attempt to blend into the bar and disappear.

"So who's that?" he asked her.

"Crap…that is my asshole boss," she said in surprise.

"Really, you're not supposed to be able to have a good time?"

"He's a control freak," she began, glancing up at him.

"You don't have to say anything, Carmen."

"Thanks," she said with a low voice, moving closer. "Damn, he's coming over here."

"Carmen, I see that you've met Mr. Cortez," Mr. Widdal stated to her.

When he heard him speaking his name, his eyes widened in amazement. Did his father talk to him about him? Mr. Widdal looked taller than he would have thought and was about the same height as he was even in his boots. Taking off his black gloves, he handed them to the man standing behind him. He wore a black hat and white collar shirt and believed him to be a businessman. Raising his arm, the Gucci watch he wore appeared to be pure gold. When he smiled, a gold tooth in the front glistened.

"Well, I can see the resemblance between you and your father," Widdal said with a smirk, looking him over.

"I am my father's son," Johnny replied and stood his ground.

"That is a good thing. You know, Johnny…your father was in search of something very important. He tried everyone he knew, and they all turned him down. I guess that was why I decided to sponsor his dig in the first place. After listening to his research, I began to believe deeply in his quest," he began, pausing to light his cigarette. As the smoke rose around them, he exhaled and stepped closer to Johnny. "I was hoping he would accomplish that goal."

"He believed in many things," Johnny stated bluntly.

"And what of you? What do you believe in?"

Johnny wasn't sure he wanted to answer him. It was really none of his business what he believed in. He was only here to find out what happened to his father, not continue his father's work. Noticing how Johnny's face was beginning to tighten, Carmen reached over and put her hand on his arm as if to calm him.

In the silence, Widdal and Johnny were now squared up in front of each other as if the boxing match was about to begin. Glancing around, Carmen noticed that most the people at the bar had backed away to give them some space. The tension in the air was becoming uncomfortable, and she tried to lighten the moment a little.

"Mr. Widdal," she quickly interjected. He never responded or even bothered to look over at her. She then tried to break their stare at each other once again. "Mr. Widdal…sir, please!"

"What is it, Carmen?" he finally said with a smile.

"How would you like to dance with this little lady?" Carmen placed her hand on her hip and pointed to herself as she removed her hand from Johnny's arm. Moving over, she took Widdal's arm, leaning up against him. As he looked over at her, he could see a sad, puppy-dog look on her face. "My favorite song is playing on the jukebox."

"I don't think so. I have some business to take care of," Widdal said, nudging Carmen away. His gaze went back to Johnny again and knew that her comments were done in an effort to break his concentration.

"Johnny," he began, "let's not become enemies with our first meeting. I only want what belongs to me and that dig site holds the answers. My benefactors are very demanding, and we receive top dollar for artifacts from this era. Your father gave them a small taste of that, and they want to receive more. In the Cairo history museum, many of your father's recent discoveries are displayed there."

"Mr. Widdal, my father can't give them any more. Now that he's disappeared, he can't give them what they want…can he? Have you even bothered to look for him if he was all that important to you?"

"Believe me, I've used every asset I have at my disposal to try and locate him with no results. If you ask, the police can tell you that fact."

"I'll definitely check that out," he told him.

The room became silent once again before Widdal finally began to laugh.

"You have the same fire that your father had, that's good," he commented, slapping his arm. "I'm sure that our paths will cross again, Johnny, as we both try and find answers in our own specific ways. With that, I'll leave you then for the evening. May you all have a good night."

With that statement, he turned around and left the bar followed by his bodyguard.

"Well, that was really interesting," Carmen commented, gasping, watching him leave.

"Yes, it was," he said, letting out a sigh.

Turning, he placed his elbows on the bar and, getting the bartenders attention, motioned with his hand for more drinks. As he thought about what had happened and what Widdal had said, Carmen pulled up a stool very close beside him and sat down. Leaning over near his elbow, she began to slowly press the tip of her toe and then the rest of her leg in between his tight legs. Now between them, she moved it delicately up and down, trying to caress his inner thigh. After a moment, he turned and looked over at her, watching her tongue lick her glistening lips.

"So do you want to get out of here?" she then asked him.

"Sure," he then told her watching her tongue, "what the heck."

"My place is really close, so let's just go there," she said as a big grin appeared across her face. "You'll then know where to come tomorrow."

"Still trying, aren't you?" He grinned.

"Just about every minute of the day," she said, "especially when there is something I want."

"I'm sure."

Sliding off the stool, she stood beside him, waiting patiently for him to finish his drink so they could leave. Paying the bill, he took her arm and they headed outside for her place. There was a certain strut in her walk as they moved down the street. Holding his arm tightly, every so often, her swaying hip would bump against him. There was a wicked look in her eyes, and he didn't know who was being led to the slaughter, her or him.

I sure hope this is worth the effort, he thought, staring at her.

CHAPTER 11

A
FTER THE LONG night with Carmen, all he could think about the whole time was that strange girl. It was eating him up inside, and he had to satisfy his growing curiosity about her. He noticed that it was already late in the morning as he left Carmen's place. Going back to his hotel room, he still hadn't gotten to his room and definitely had to freshen up and change his clothes. Walking back to the hotel, he glanced into the bar. He hoped the woman would perhaps be there.

Just a quick look to see, he thought.

Stepping into the bar, he scanned the sea of faces, looking for her. His eyes widened as he thought he recognized her sitting by herself near the end of the bar. She was leaned over on the edge and sipping a drink. Approaching her, he definitely thought it was her even though she was wearing a baseball cap. He just knew it had to be her. Walking over to her, she never moved as he stopped and produced a small cough to get her attention.

"Hi there," he said, causing her to slowly turn and look.

"Hi," she said simply.

"Uh, I'm Johnny Cortez."

"I know who you are," she said with a large smile.

"Really?" he said, surprised, "How do you know that?"

"We met each other yesterday at the dig site, silly."

"I really don't remember…" he said, trying to think.

"I'm Ani," she said, holding her hand out. "My father is Jorge, the dig supervisor."

"Interesting," he said, staring at her. "You certainly don't look like the same girl I met the other day."

"Yap…that was me."

She definitely appeared different than when he met her. It was amazing how a change of clothes would make someone entirely different. Her long black hair was pulled back and tied up in a ponytail, sticking out the hole in her cap like a tail. Wearing a shirt with rolled-up sleeves, it matched the jeans with holes that everyone seemed to be wearing. The leather sandals she wore on her feet showed off a bright nail color that was quite bold. It didn't look like she would be a person that would go around digging around in the desert.

What is it about this woman? he thought, looking at her.

There was none of the usual lines he would normally use coming from his mouth. He found it strange that he was simply sitting here, talking to her as if they had known each other for years. She made him feel comfortable where he could just be himself. Maybe it was that he really had no expectations about what was going to happen.

"So what are you doing here?"

"The military has the dig tied up as they secure the site, so I have a day off."

"Do you work all the time?" he asked as the bartender came up. Ordering a drink, he waited for her to respond.

"I like working."

"What do you do when you're not working?"

"Normally, I like to check out the sites of the city," she said, sipping her drink. "So have you had a chance to get out and look around?"

"No, I haven't seen anything for some time. I'm sure it's changed since I last came here with my father years ago."

"Would you like to see them? I can be your tour guide."

"Sure, that would be nice."

"Then let's go."

Finishing their drinks, they went out to the front and grabbed a taxi. They cruised around the city, stopping at several locations. As they walked around the area, she would tell him about almost every stone. He was surprised that she knew so much about where they were and the history behind each item. After a few hours, they stopped at a little café to have a late lunch near the river. While they ate, she looked at him.

"Do you want to see some of the stuff your father found?"

"Can we do that?" he asked.

"I can get us in if you want."

"Absolutely, I'd love to see them."

Grapping a taxi, they went to the museum located back in town. When they walked inside, she waved her hand and yelled out one of the guard's name. One of them looked up from the main guard station and greeted them when they came closer.

"Caleb, this is Johnny Cortez," she said, pointing to Johnny. "His father is the one that brought all the stuff you have stored down in the warehouse. Is it possible to let us in just for a little while so he could look at them? I promise we won't be long."

"I don't know, Ani, you know the rules," he told her.

"Oh, please, Caleb," she begged. "It's important."

"I guess so," he said, giving into her request. "You can go down there, but you only have thirty minutes and then I'll come and get you."

"Thank you, Caleb," she said, going around and kissing his cheek. As they moved off toward the warehouse, she turned back to the guard. "I promise I won't tell anyone about you doing this."

"You better not," he yelled after them, smiling.

Moving into the warehouse, Johnny was surprised at how big it was. He was also surprised that Ani knew where almost everything was located in the room. It was almost as if she had placed them there herself. After showing him several objects, she walked over and stood beside a small stone obelisk. She smiled as he came over to her.

"Your father was very fond of this one in particular," Ani said.

"This writing is something I've seen before."

Kneeling down, he took the light to get a better view of the inscription. Running his finger across the surface as he always did, his mind began to try and decipher the ancient words. Ani knelt beside him and placed her hand on his back. While they stared, he would glance back at her and then look back to the writing. Focusing, he found he could read only bits and pieces of the inscriptions near the bottom. Rubbing his chin as he studied it, he finally stood up.

"If I didn't know any better, I'd swear that these were a set of coordinates," he said, "but they are modern numbers, and they wouldn't know about them back in those days. I just can't be reading that right."

"That is strange," Ani commented.

"True, but even if they are not, they still have to mean something," Johnny said.

"I'm sure it does, but I think we need to go," she told him.

"Yeah, probably," Johnny said, agreeing. "Do you have any paper?"

"I have this," she said, handing him a napkin.

"That'll have to do."

Taking it from her, he laid it across the inscription and, using the pencil from his pocket, etched it on the surface. After a moment, he held it up to make sure that he had gotten it all. With a grin, he folded it up and put it in his pocket.

"All done," he said, standing up.

Still staring at the small obelisk wondering what the writing meant, he slowly turned to her. She took a step forward and caught her foot on something on the floor, stumbling. He caught her and held her. Pressed against him, she looked at him. After a moment, she coughed and stepped back away and looked around the room.

"I'm sorry," she said, almost blushing.

"Glad I could help." He smiled. "It was actually nice."

"We really need to go. My father will worry since it's late," Ani told him.

"Yeah, I probably need to get back too. It's been a long day."

Thanking the guard, they grabbed a taxi and took her back to her house. When it stopped, they both got out. As they said their goodbyes, she started to turn before stopping and looking over at him. The talk had ended and they now stood in silence. Ani shook her head and, jumping back over, kissed quickly. After kissing him, she turned around and headed for the house. At the front door, she turned. He could see a smile across her face.

"See you tomorrow," she yelled out.

"Oh, absolutely," he said with a wave.

"Bye," she responded, bouncing into the house.

CHAPTER 12

AFTER SHOWERING AND dressing, Carmen wanted to simply get out of the apartment and get some food. Locking her apartment, she walked down the stairs and out the front door. The day was already becoming hot as the sun rose higher in the distance. Standing on the sidewalk near the doorway where there was a bit of shade, she pulled a cigarette from her purse and lit it, taking a long drag. Trying to decide where to eat, she exhaled and blew smoke up into the air. Before she could move, a hand came over and grabbed her arm. Looking at the figure, her eyes widened and knew her choice was now limited.

"He wants to see you," the man said, turning her. "Now."

"Uh…sure," she said, dropping her cigarette.

As her foot crushed the cigarette on the sidewalk, he led her over to the black limousine parked near them. Reaching the side, he opened the back door and forcefully shoved her into the back. Settling in the seat, she turned and knew exactly who was waiting and looked over at the man sitting comfortably beside her. Leaning against the side armrest, he held a glass in his hand, sipping it slowly. Watching him, the slamming door startled her.

"And so," he said never looking at her, "how did it go?"

"It went as you expected," she said, leaning back and straightening out her dress.

"Did he indicate anything that could be useful?"

"Not this time," she indicated with a grin. "Since it was only the first time, he needs to get used to me and feel comfortable around me."

"How comfortable does he have to get?" he asked, looking at her.

"Enough to answer questions, but I'm certain he will with another chance."

"Are you sure?"

"He's a man, isn't he?" She smiled.

His eyes began to narrow as he looked at her. There was a look on his face as it contorted and began to grimace. It was a look she had not seen before, and it worried her. She began to slowly squirm in the seat.

"I remember not that long ago that I was visiting a dear acquaintance concerning a small job I needed done, and he was in the midst of surveying his crop of girls. It was early morning, and they had just returned from working the streets, and I was watching him collect the daily receipts," he began. "As I was having a drink, he happened to ask me to judge his women. A male lion always keeps the most faithful close to them and gets rid of those that aren't. When we walked into the room, I looked around and gauged each of them. There was only one that caught my eye. You were the only one I noticed. You were sitting on the couch smoking a cigarette. Do you remember that day?"

"I remember," she said, looking at him.

"Do you remember the girl that held back part of the daily funds on him?"

"Yes," she said, glancing at him.

"Without any hesitation, he pulled his gun out and put a bullet in her brain."

"Her name was Felicia," she said, remembering.

"The key to that statement was the word...*was*."

"I just remember the long trail of blood on the floor from them dragging her body out, and then we were ordered to clean it up."

"So did it leave an impression on you?"

"I'll never forget it as long as I live."

"That happened because he was a businessman, the same as I am. Because he was my friend, he knew I wanted a companion, and he allowed me to pick from the group and I decided to purchase you."

"And I will always be grateful for that day."

Widdal grinned at her comment and, reaching into his jacket, pulled his pistol out. Holding the silver pistol, she watched him lean forward and place it on the ledge. As he leaned back, the pistol was within her view. Settling back, he looked at her.

"Good," he said, looking at her. "Now, I only want to hear two words ever coming from your mouth when I ask you something."

"Certainly...anything you want."

"The two words I want to hear are very simple...'yes, sir' or 'no, sir.'"

"Yes, sir," she then responded.

"Good, and so, tell me. How would you judge his lovemaking? Did you enjoy him?"

"Not really...he was nothing special," she told him, not knowing what else to say. "He was a job as you told me to do."

His hand moved over and came to rest on top of her knee. Slowly, it moved down her leg and moved to her inner thigh, groping her skin with his fingers as he went. She knew resisting would not go well and sat quietly, allowing him his pleasure. Feeling his fingers slip beneath her underwear, her back arched when he entered her.

"And what was the taste like," he asked, watching her eyes slowly close.

"He was," she began before letting out a soft sigh, "I guess like any other man."

Hearing her words, he instantly slipped his hand from beneath her skirt and, reaching around, grabbed the back of her head. His fingers twisted in her hair harshly and snapped her head back. She screamed out in pain while looking at him.

"Am I like any other man?"

"No, not even close."

"Sir," he stressed, hearing her voice tremble.

"No, sir," she said softly.

"I own you and pay for you to live the way you do. If I want to change that arrangement, I will do at my pleasure. That arrangement is complete until I say otherwise. If you think in that pretty little head otherwise, then I absolutely guarantee you will end up right back where I found you," he stressed, "and in a worse position than you were then. Do you understand?"

"Yes, sir, I understand," she said, knowing he was in control and didn't want to go back to that life.

"That's a good little girl." He smiled. "Now, since I've not seen you in some time, we need to get back to the way it was…the reason that I paid for you in the first place, right?"

"Yes, sir," she said with an obliging smile.

"Don't make me regret my decision."

Slipping his hand from her hair to the back of her neck, he began to guide her head down to his lap indicating his wishes. Knowing what he wanted, she didn't struggle against him as her hands came over and began to unbuckle his pants. Sipping his drink, he slowly settled back into the seat to allow her to please him. Looking up, he saw the driver in the mirror glancing back at them.

"Just drive around until we finish," he told him, raising the glass privacy window.

CHAPTER 13

A FTER PAYING FOR the taxi, Johnny walked slowly into the hotel. He hadn't had a shower in what seemed like days and could almost feel the hot shower flowing over his skin. Entering the front doors, he went over to the counter where one of the attendants was working and leaned heavily on the edge.

"Do I have any messages?" Johnny asked. "Cortez in room 312."

"Mr. Cortez," the hotel attendant said, looking. "So did you have a good day?"

"Yes, it's been a really good day," Johnny replied.

"Uh," she began still looking through the notes, "it doesn't appear so, sir."

"That sounds perfect, thank you."

All the way to his room, he found himself oddly thinking about the day with Ani. He wondered why out of all the women, she would have been so available and she would flood his thoughts. Leaving the elevator, he walked down the corridor to his room. Taking his card key out, he swiped the reader on the door and opened it.

When he entered, he noticed that the curtains were closed and the lights were off. He knew that he left one on and wondered if the cleaning people had turned it off. Going over to the counter, there was a strange scent filling the air.

As the door slowly closed, he could just see into the room, and with the odd scent, he peered cautiously around. He slowly moved from the kitchen area before the light from the corridor was cut off by the closing door. There was a nagging feeling that he was not alone, but in the dark, he might have an even chance if there were someone. Taking a kitchen knife from the drawer near the sink, he slowly moved through the living room, listening for any noise. It was again odd that the door to the bedroom was closed.

Someone has to be in here.

Placing his ear against the door, Johnny could hear a soft moan, and there was whispering coming from the other side. There was definitely someone in the room. Grasping tightly to the handle of the knife, he took a deep breath and quickly swung the door open. Rushing into the room, the voice of a female screamed out, startled by his sudden appearance.

"Please don't hurt me," the figure begged, covered up in the sheets.

With only the bathroom light on, he could only see a large bump in the middle of the bed. Hearing the plea, he reached over and turned the room light on. He then saw the sheets of the bed begin to move and shake. Holding the knife, he wondered who was there.

"Show yourself…now," he commanded.

Slowly, the bed sheets slipped away, and he saw who was in the bed.

"Mica," he said, surprised.

"Hi." She smiled crazily. "It's me."

"What the hell are you doing in my room?" he asked, tossing the knife on the dresser.

"You weren't planning on hurting me with that, were you?" she said, watching the knife come to a rest beside the lamp.

Johnny could only stand and look at her, wondering what was going on.

"Why are you here?" he asked her, stripping his shirt off. "Sneaking in here like that could have gotten yourself hurt."

"I just thought I would wait and surprise you," she said, noticing him wipe the sweat from under his arms before tossing it onto the floor. "You are surprised, aren't you?"

"I'm surprised, but I also have a meeting that I have to attend in an hour or so."

Somewhat disappointed by his reaction, she wadded the sheets in her lap and around her waist. By her being here, Johnny knew that Mica was probably infatuated with him, and their first encounter probably reinforced that feeling. Johnny stood near the sink and, glancing at her, saw that she just stared at him.

"Not even a little time for me since I went to all this trouble."

She couldn't keep her eyes off him. His body was perfect to her, and she watched as he moved, noticing each muscle flex. When he was done wiping his face, he walked back over to her. Looking down at her, he watched her breasts rise as she breathed. They were like mountains of inviting flesh, waiting to be devoured. Feeling his eyes, she tossed the sheets away to show that all she wore was a very skimpy G-string.

"How did you get in my room?"

"Silly, I work here."

She moved toward him on all fours to show her anticipation.

"And you being in my bed is supposed to be a clue?"

She was now close enough to lift up on her knees and kiss him. Holding his waist, she looked at him with desire in her eyes. Lifting higher, she kissed him softly and nibbled on his ear before her hands slowly slipped down to his crotch. Standing still, he waited and didn't resist before she then whispered in his ear.

"It's a clue to have anything you might want."

"Mica, it's just that…"

She grasped him and he instantly reacted to her. He reacted solely on reflex and wasn't thinking. He picked up Mica by her waist until her legs slowly curved around his waist. He felt her muscles flex in anticipation. He lowered her torso softly to the surface of the bed and kissed her. His tongue moved down and, circling her breasts, felt Mica tighten while kissing the top of his head. As he pressed against her, he could tell that she was getting excited and already becoming lost in the utopia of passion.

"I have no time to do this you know," Johnny told her as he moved down to licking her stomach.

"Johnny, please…just take me."

Johnny could feel her pelvis contracting around his lower intestines. The sand on his skin had transferred to hers, and the rubbing of their bodies against each other felt erotic and like sandpaper. He hesitated and began holding back. In his mind, he tried to think when he ever held back. Out of all the reasons, there could only be one, and the word escaped his lips.

"Ani."

Johnny couldn't believe that he said her name with another woman. But out of all the thoughts running through his head, it had to be the only reason. With Mica in his arms, he was thinking of her.

"What did you say?" Mica said, sitting up.

Johnny was shocked he had said it and tried to think of a way to explain it. He knew that he was guilty of leading her on then breaking it off. She would be mad. Johnny straightened up and thought about using his father's death as a way out. But decided against that as that was purely shameful. He had to think of something quick. Mica stopped moving and opened her eyes.

"I'm sorry, Mica," he said. sitting beside her. "My head just isn't in it."

Hearing him she rose up beside him and put her arms around his neck. She flipped one leg over his and was now wide open for him, waiting and inviting. Flipping her hair, she looked into his eyes. Johnny reached over and taking her leg, moved it over beside him. Mica watched and couldn't understand his action. He stood up and went to the bathroom to bring back a towel for her. Placing it around her shoulders to cover her, he looked at her.

"Sorry, Mica, I can't do this."

"I don't want you to have any regrets or reservations about what has happened between us," Mica told him. The tone was very confident and with conviction before noticing his face.

"I heard you say *Ani*," she said. "Is she a local girl?"

"Yes," he said, not wanting to lie to her.

"It appears you've been a busy boy since we last met."

Mica knew the answer, and a flash of anger grew within her, but deep down she knew he wasn't hers or would be exclusive. He had some feeling for this other woman but also knew that given the chance, he might come around and back to her.

Mica got up from the bed and began dressing. Johnny watched her and didn't know what to say.

"All I can say is, 'I'm sorry.'"

"I was only trying to make out with you in a romantic way."

"Through all this, you never asked me if I had a girlfriend or wife."

"It didn't seem to matter to you when we hooked up and you were all over me. When did you realize your feelings for this other woman?"

Johnny paused, looked out the window, and then back at Mica.

"Just recently," he said still watching her dress.

She finished and, grabbing her shoes, slowly walked out the room. She stopped at the opening and turned to look at him once more.

"Just remember that I'm always here." She grinned. "Just call me if you need company."

"Thanks." He smiled. "I'm glad you understand."

Tossing her shoes over her shoulder, she left, and after a moment, Johnny went into the bathroom. He cut on the water and looked into the bathroom mirror as his thoughts were elsewhere. Looking over at the clock, he knew there wasn't any time left. Stripping his pants off, he jumped into the shower. Deniko would be there soon to pick him up.

CHAPTER 14

AFTER HIS SHOWER, he dried off and tried to decide what to wear to this party. He stood in front of the little hotel room closet and looked at his clothes. It wasn't supposed to be a formal occasion but expected it to be upscale. There wasn't much to choose from considering he packed lightly for the trip. All he could come up with was his good black jeans and white dress shirt for the occasion.

I guess it will have to do, he thought, holding up his shirt.

Dressing, he looked at himself in the bathroom mirror. Between the shirt and the jeans, he thought he didn't look all that bad. Splashing on some cologne he went out to the other room to wait for him to arrive. Glancing at the clock, he had close to ten minutes before Deniko got there and really didn't want to wait in the room. Grabbing his key, he figured he would go down to the lobby and get a drink and wait there.

Walking into the hallway, he locked the door and, as he turned, saw another guest heading for the elevator. As he came up to the elevator the man turned, and he saw that his face was covered in a black mask. His eyes widened and, turning to get away, saw another man standing behind him. This man also wore a mask covering his face and, before he could move, felt the heavy blow to his head from behind.

The blow made his legs crumple beneath him, and he folded weakly into a heap on the floor. As he dropped, the men on either side of him began to violently kick him over and over in the stomach and back. It became clear that they wanted to be quick and make sure that he couldn't fight back. With one final kick, he gasped and rolled over.

Gasping and trying catch his breath, he produced a low moan of pain. The men knew they had accomplished their task and hurriedly began digging through his pockets. Grabbing his watch and wallet, they stood up and kicked him once more. One of the men leaned over and grabbed him by the collar and yanked him up.

"You better give it up," he growled in his ear. "If not, we'll be back to finish this."

As he stood, one of the room doors opened and a lady walked out. Seeing them, she began to scream, causing them to run and disappear into the stairwell. Rushing over to him, the lady checked to see if he was alive.

"Is he alive?" her husband asked her, coming out of the room.

"Yes," she said. "Call the police."

Checking his watch, Deniko noticed that he had made good time through rush-hour traffic and saw the hotel just ahead. Slowing down, he turned to park but immediately saw that there was an ambulance with flashing lights parked next to the front door along with several police cars. Pulling up and parking in the closest space, he got out and looked around for an officer. Walking toward the front doors, an officer came up and stopped him. Opening his jacket, he flashed his badge and started to walk past him before stopping.

"What's going on?" he asked him.

"Ah, there was a mugging to one of the guests up one of the floors."

"Do we know who it was?"

"All I know is one of the guests," he told him. "I'm here just to make sure the crowds are held back and don't interfere."

Pushing through the people mulling around in the lobby, he saw that there were at least a dozen people at the counter and figured he would just go to his room. Even the elevators were packed with people waiting to get on. He thought that taking the main stairs would be a lot easier than cramming into the elevators. After reaching the first floor and turning, he began to pant.

Great, that's all I need is to have a stroke, he thought, looking at the new set of stairs.

Holding his chest, he took a deep breath and kept going. The floor and Johnny was now in view, and he smiled, knowing he was nearing the end. Reaching the top, he leaned against the wall and tried to let his heart settle down. As he rested, he heard the sounds of multiple people down the hallway. Looking he saw Johnny sitting on the floor.

"What the hell," he said, wondering what happened.

Walking down the hallway, he pushed through the crowd until he had reached him. There were two medical attendants on either side of him as he sat on the floor with an officer standing nearby. He looked up and saw Deniko coming over.

"Detective," he said.

"What's going on here?" he asked, trying to access Johnny's condition.

"Appears to be a simple mugging," he said, checking his notes. "Seems to be a random act but still pretty brazen especially for a large hotel and in the daytime."

The whole time he watched the medical staff working on Johnny.

"Johnny, are you all right?"

"Yeah, I'll be fine," Johnny said, trying to push the medical assistant away that was checking his eyes.

"What the hell happened?" he asked, motioning them to leave him alone.

"Ah, got jumped by a couple of stupid muggers."

"Any way you can identify them?"

"No, their faces were covered, and it all happened so quick."

The door leading to the fire escape stairwell opened, and an officer came out and over to them. He held out his hand to them.

"Sir, we found this in the stairwell."

Taking the stuff from him, he saw that it was Johnny's keys, wallet, watch, and some cash.

"I wonder why they would just drop them if they went to all the trouble to come up here and mug someone."

"Maybe someone came into the stairwell and scared them," the officer said.

"Yeah…maybe."

"Listen," Johnny said, standing up, "we have a party to go to that I really don't want to miss. I really need to get cleaned up?"

"Are you sure about this," Deniko asked, helping him to his feet.

"Absolutely," he commented, taking a step toward his room.

As he took his step, he became wobbly, and Deniko caught him by the arm. Johnny looked at him and shook his head. With a smile he helped him to his room. Waiting, he let the officers in the hallway leave before going inside and watched him clean up and change clothes. Once he was done, they went downstairs and headed for his car.

Driving down the highway, Deniko would casually turn and glance over at Johnny. He was slowly rubbing his forehead and blinking his eyes while making funny sounds as he looked around. Each time he looked over at him, he wouldn't say anything but just slowly shake his head. Johnny happened to turn and noticed he was checking him.

"You look like shit," Deniko then commented.

"Great," he smirked, "seems to match how I feel."

"You should have really gone to the hospital to get checked out."

"It's only my hard head," he said, reaching up and feeling the bump on the back of his head. "Right now, it feels like nothing more than a really good hangover."

"I'll tell the coroner that you said that during the autopsy."

His comment struck a chord in him, and he burst out laughing. Deniko couldn't stop himself, hearing him cackle and joined him. They drove along, laughing for no real reason until he then stopped and pointed as they slowed down. Looking, they could see the entrance to Widdal's home.

"We're here," Deniko said, turning slowly.

Pulling up to the gates, a guard stopped them and asked for their names. Once he told them, the man checked his guest sheet before letting them proceed. Standing on the other side of the iron gates, they could see a man holding an automatic weapon and guessed it was part of his security force. Stepping away for the car, he waved them through into the courtyard.

"He's gone a touch more upscale from the last time I met him," Deniko said, "and found a few new friends."

"I'd say," Johnny said.

Sitting in the line of cars pulling up to the entrance, Johnny looked around the courtyard and saw rows of gorgeous cars off to the side. There were a couple of stretched limousines, BMWs, Lexuses, and even a Rolls Royce. As they slowly pulled up, there were several valets helping the guests out and taking their keys to park them. Finally pulling up, Deniko stopped, and one of the valets came over to his door, opening it. They both grinned, knowing that the police squad car was definitely out of place.

"At least I'll be able to find it." He laughed, stepping out.

"Good evening, sir," the man said, holding the door.

"Good evening," Deniko said, taking his ticket.

Johnny waited for him to come around and join him, staring at the front of the building. It was almost like looking at the front of the White House with the dome on top and columns around the front doors. There was definitely a hint of Egyptian flair in the overall design, but he could swear he was back in America. As Deniko came up to him, he turned and looked.

"I think we might be a little out of place," Johnny commented, seeing the state of dress by everyone.

"Don't worry, I usually am." He laughed.

Nearing the main doors, a large man dressed in a black suit and white gloves stood by the opening, checking off guests from his ledger. They paused as they got to him.

"Your name, sirs," he asked.

"Detective Deniko," he stumbled, clearing his throat, "and Johnny Cortez."

"Ah yes," he said, finding their names. "Please go in and have a good evening."

The man then turned his attention to the couple stepping up behind them. Entering, they saw that people were huddled in small groups everywhere. Before they could go into the main area, two men came up and stopped them.

"I'm sorry, sir," one of them said, "no weapons are allowed."

"I'm Detective Deniko, Cairo police," he said, showing his badge.

"Still, sir," he insisted, "there are no—"

"It's quite all right," a loud voice behind him bellowed.

Turning, Widdal was casually stepping toward them through the crowd with a glass of champagne in his hand. Hearing him, the man nodded and turned his attention back to the other guests entering. Taking Johnny by the arm, he led them into the main area before turning back to Deniko.

"I do know how you detectives love your weapons." He laughed. "I wouldn't think of stripping you of your personal companion. If you feel more secure, I'm sure none of the other guests will object since you are an agent of the law. Come…let me introduce you to a few people while I have the chance."

As they walked inside, Deniko casually leaned over to him.

"So what's this party for again?"

"This is just a small fund-raising event for one of my favorite charities, the Cairo hospital. They indicated to me that they needed help with a new wing they are building, so I'm throwing this to solicit donations"—he grinned—"big donations."

"Really," Deniko commented as he followed.

Widdal instantly noticed his expression and laughed.

"Please, Detective, I don't expect you to actually donate considering your meager salary and all"—he smiled—"but if you do decide, I certainly won't turn it down. It's for a very good cause."

"I'll think about it," he said almost sarcastically.

While he led them across the room, Johnny surveyed the guests. There were obviously a lot of very important people at the gathering, and they were all dressed as if going to a prestigious gala. Most of the men were in black tux, and the women were in long, delicate evening gowns glowing with jewelry. He also noticed that there were several dignitaries and even a few military people attending. Looking at their faces as he passed them, he realized that there was not one person he recognized. Walking through them and nodding politely, he began to feel really out of place wearing just his white shirt and black denim pants.

Too late to change that impression, he thought.

The place looked like the inside of one of those mansions you see in the magazines with all the decorations. There were tall columns circling the large open area that looked like marble where everyone was gathered. A small band played music in the corner.

Off to either side of the room were several tables covered in white linen with dishes of all variety of food. Near them were a large liquor bar staffed by several attendants. Staff walked in and out of the service doors to the back kitchens, keeping the trays full. Circling through the crowd slowly were a half-dozen women holding trays of champagne and offering them to the guests. Each one looked to be out of a Caesars Palace casino. They wore a long white gown that had a golden cord wrapped around their waists like a belt. Their hair was tied behind their head in a ponytail wrapped with golden ribbons to hold it in place. The gown only covered part of their figure and hung low off their shoulders.

Passing one of the women, Widdal grabbed a full glass and handed her the empty one. Still moving through the guests, Johnny saw near the back there were several open doors that led out to a large veranda. Most of the couches were taken out of the main room and placed outside where guests could sit. Beyond them he could see the lights of boats traveling on the river in the distance.

Not too shabby, Johnny thought.

Before long, Widdal had brought them over to a small group of three couples near one food table and interrupted their conversation. Seeing him approach, them they gladly stopped and greeted them.

"My friends, this is Johnny Cortez," he said, introducing him. "And this, Johnny, is Abdul Matriffi who is owner of the largest import-export company in Egypt. And of course, clinging to his arm is his extremely lovely wife, Sirena."

"Glad to meet you," Johnny said, shaking their hands.

"And may I also introduce Detective Deniko, of the Cairo police department."

"Nice to meet you all," he said politely.

After introducing the remainder of the group to them, they began to ask questions and talk casually about his father and the work he did. They all produced apologies about his disappearance. As they inquired about his work and that of the detective, Widdal glanced over Johnny's shoulder toward the door.

"If you'll please excuse me, I have some other guests to attend to," he said, slapping Johnny's shoulder. "Please, enjoy all that we have to offer you tonight."

Walking away, Johnny didn't know how long he could keep up the simple conversation and finally excused himself to get a drink. As he left and reached the bar by the wall, Deniko quickly followed him.

"You weren't going to leave me there all by myself," he asked, stepping up beside him.

"I figured you could handle yourself." He laughed. "You are a detective, right?"

"In crimes, but this is a totally different situation."

"Two fingers of Bourbon…neat," Johnny told the server.

"Make mine the same," Deniko said. "On second thought, make it a double."

"I thought police officers weren't supposed to drink on duty?"

"And who said I was on duty?" He grinned.

Deniko grabbed his drink and took a long swallow, finishing almost half of it. He let out a long sigh as the fluid burned down his throat. When the server finished making Johnny's drink, he picked it up and turned slowly to survey the people in the room. When a couple of people came up to the bar, he pushed Deniko over to the side to give them room.

What the hell?

He spotted a beautiful blonde enjoying a drink. She was standing near one of the back doors out of the crowd. The area was a small niche out of the way. Even though her hair was up in a bun and she wore an elegant purple gown that fit her perfectly, he couldn't help but instantly recognize her. He wondered why Carmen would be at the event and also who her escort might be. Before he could think further, he heard Deniko.

"Is that Carmen?"

"Do you know her?" Johnny turned and asked surprised.

"Oh yes," he said, keeping his eyes on her. "Yes, I do."

From his comment, there had to be some history between them. He wasn't about to bring up that he also knew her and quite intimately. If it did come out for whatever reason, he would just try to explain. As he finished his drink, he excused himself and walked over to her. Even from where he stood, he could see her eyes light up as Deniko approached her. Watching him the music faded away and stopped.

"Ladies and gentlemen, before we proceed, I want to introduce a very special guest tonight," Widdal began and pointed over in Johnny's direction. "Please help me welcome Mr. Johnny Cortez, son of the late Dr. Manny Cortez."

The crowd immediately looked over at him and began to clap. He smiled weakly to them and lifted his glass in acknowledgment. They continued for a brief time before finally focusing back over on Widdal.

"Thank you," he said. "And now, just one of the reasons you're all here."

"Yes," one man yelled out. "What do you want us to purchase this time, Widdal?"

"You'll like it I promise, and it's something very special." He grinned.

Stepping over to a table covered in a cloth, the two men on either side stepped back. He grabbed the edge and pulled it away. Everyone in the room produced a collective sigh seeing the object underneath. It was a golden statue about two feet tall and glistened in the light of the room. People started to move closer to look at it.

"I was able to purchase this fantastic object, and I'm placing it up for auction. All the proceeds will be my gift to the hospital. I will not bore you on the history, but I can tell you it is solid gold."

"Fantastic piece," a man said, leaning up closer. "Old Egypt it appears."

"I will give you a chance and let you all come around and examine it before the bidding begins. Just remember, have those checkbooks ready once we start."

The crowd around the table began to laugh at his comment. Several people approached Widdal, and as they surrounded him, Deniko figured it was his chance. He stepped over closer to Carmen, and before he could say anything, she motioned for him to follow her into the kitchen. Waiting for a moment, he paused, letting her go first. Checking the crowd, he finally walked slowly past the doors before sliding inside as a server came out. Once inside, he avoided several of the attendants exiting and moved to the side. He then saw her standing over by a table.

"Well, Detective Deniko," she said as he came up to her, "tell me what your opinion is of this cake they have for the guests?"

"It seems," he stuttered, "frosted well."

"And that is the whole problem," she said, seeing his confusion.

"If you say so," he said, watching people pass them.

When the staff wasn't looking, she took his arm and led him out the access door to the side of the back. As the door shut, she stood looking at him. His eyes were on her and the sultry dress she had on. Even when they went through the door, he couldn't help but watch as she moved in front of him, his eyes tracing every line. Carmen peeked back through the door and quickly shut it. Deniko touched Carmen's shoulder and she turned and looked at him.

"I don't know about the cake, but it pales in comparison to your radiance."

"That's sweet, but we don't have much time," she said.

Carmen began to blush and placed her hand on her breasts while he came closer. Deniko stepped back in his place as he realized that was out of character for him to do in his uniform. How could he do this, and he is supposed to find a killer. This is not what a police officer does and in the midst of people who could be suspects. Yet, he did it anyway. His heart was jumping seeing her. And she didn't reject the advance. She simply stepped forward to Deniko and faced him full frontal. Deniko saw her coming and was hoping she would not yell at him and tell him go to hell. Or worse, tell his boss that he made an advance in an inappropriate event while on duty.

"Mr. Deniko, thank you." She waited for his reply and she was intrigued by him.

Deniko noticed that she wasn't a whistle-blower and wanted him to flirt. He moved in further to her.

"Carmen, you're very beautiful and your dress is stunning."

Deniko reached for her hand and she gave it to him. He bent down and kissed it. He paused about a foot away from her face on purpose. Carmen was excited as his gesture and felt a rush of emotion. Her face turned flush red. She placed her right hand on Deniko's strong shoulders and lifted up on her tippy toes in her Armani heels. She rubbed her lips together to make the red consistent for her kiss. She wanted to leave her mark on him and a statement that she liked him. Carmen reached and kissed Sergeant Deniko on the cheek.

She whispered in his ear, "You sure have a direct way with a lady. I accept your compliments. Thank you."

Deniko tipped his head to her and she moved back to the floor.

"Excuse me." The cook coughed. "Is there something wrong?"

She didn't turn around immediately, even though she heard his question. She kept at looking him and, producing a smile, turned back around.

"No, we were just checking the cake. Someone had indicated there was something wrong and the sweet detective was escorting me."

"What's wrong with the cake?" he asked them, stepping over to the cake.

Carmen gritted her teeth because he had interrupted their only moment. Standing in front of Deniko she crossed her hands behind her back, hoping he would step forward and take them. He looked and noticed her hands and understood what she wanted. As the cook checked the cake, they slid to the side.

"We didn't find anything wrong either. Sorry to disturb you."

Carmen grabbed his right hand and escorted him over to the back door and out to a small area beside the kitchen. Once outside, she closed the door and jumped into his arms. Her quick movement caught him by surprise. Wrapping her arms around his neck, she kissed him deeply as she held onto him tightly. After a moment, she released her lips from his and looked at him.

"I missed that so much," she said.

"As I did," he said, squeezing her waist.

"We've been away from the party far too long and we'll be missed," she said softly, kissing him gently. "We need to get inside before then."

"If we must," he said, reluctant to let her go.

"We'll have another chance but not now," she said, stroking his cheek. "I just needed to see you, touch you after you came into the room."

"You don't see me complaining, do you?"

"Never." She laughed. "Let's get back."

Kissing him she went through the door first, and taking a deep breath, he followed a few moments later. Entering the main room, he walked over and ordered another drink. Turning, he watched as she walked away, wiggling her butt but never turning. Sipping his drink, he couldn't help but watch her as she began to mingle with the other guests.

"What was the verdict?" a voice beside him asked.

Turning, he saw Johnny standing beside him with a smile on his face.

"I was checking the food," he told him, sipping his drink.

"Well, it looks like there was also a little tasting going on."

"What do you mean?" Deniko asked confused by the question.

Johnny laughed and told him about the lipstick smeared on the side of his lips. Trying to wipe it away, Johnny shook his head, indicating it was still there. When he began to curse under his breath, Johnny couldn't help but laugh. Excusing himself, he headed off to the bathroom to clean it properly. Several people passing him greeted him and gave their condolences on the loss of his father. Thanking them, they would then proceed to another group. Watching the activities, a man walked up to him.

"Mr. Cortez," he said, "It's nice to see you."

"Jorge," Johnny said, not recognizing him. "It's nice to see you."

"Nice party, isn't it?"

"A little too formal and busy for me," he told him.

"I like it," Jorge said, snagging a glass of champagne from one of the passing servers. "I don't get a chance to go to these and like to take full advantage of my invitation."

"As I would also," he laughed.

"Listen, Jorge," he said, leaning over to him. "Can you get me a vehicle that's good for traveling in the desert?"

"The dig site has two Land Rovers. I can get you one if you want."

"That's great, but can you have it at the hotel in the morning?"

"I can have it there as early as you wish."

"How about 6:30 a.m."

"I'll have it all gassed up and ready for you."

"Here," Johnny said, digging in his pocket. "This is a few hundred pounds to pay for supplies I might need for three or four days."

"I don't think that it'll take that much," he said, watching him wad the bills in his hand.

"If you need more just—"

The band suddenly began to play music and, when he turned, saw that some of the couples were beginning to dance. Suddenly, several couples parted and he noticed that a sexy, beautiful woman was walking toward him. Stopping in front of him, she leaned close and kissed his cheek.

"And how are you doing tonight?"

"No way," he said amazed. "It just can't be."

Ani looked like a sculptured diamond. She was vibrant and smelled like roses. Her dress was long and wrapped around her. Her shape was athletic and noticeable. Johnny was happy she came to the party.

"I am glad you came." She grinned. "If you hadn't, I would have been very disappointed and wasted all this time getting dressed up to impress you."

"Ani, you look absolutely fantastic!"

"Then it wasn't wasted and you approve?"

"Oh yes," he told her.

"Do you dance?" she asked.

"I don't know if you want to call it that."

"Let's try, shall we?"

Ani grabbed his hand and led him out onto the dance area as the band began playing a new song. Johnny put one hand on the small of her back and the other on her hip. Ani wrapped both her hands around his neck and looked into his eyes while waiting for him to speak.

"I really meant what I said about you looking fantastic," he told her.

"Thank you." She giggled. "I like dressing up and don't get to do it since no one takes me out."

"Looking at you, that just isn't right."

"Quiet and dance," she told him, snuggling against his shoulder.

"Yes, ma'am," he said, obeying her command.

He smiled as his arms wrapped around her, and small moans echoed in his ear.

CHAPTER 15

T HE NEXT MORNING, Johnny stood over the open backpack sitting on the bed and tried to figure out what he might be forgetting. Excited, he had started before sunrise gathering the things he wanted to take. He knew that it would be a hot and dusty trip but would only last a few days. Beside the pack was the folded map that he had placed the coordinates on with a big red *X* to mark it. The location was out in the middle of nowhere and couldn't figure out why his father would have thought it was important enough to note.

I guess we'll see when we get there, he thought.

Checking the time, he saw that Jorge would be at the hotel shortly with the vehicle and stuffed the remaining items inside. Taking it into the other room, he checked the GPS that he had purchased to make sure it was fully charged. Making sure the coordinates were in the memory, he turned it off. Placing it and the charger in the side pocket, he then heard a knock at the door.

"Yeah, it's open," he yelled out. "Come on in."

Hearing the door open, he turned and saw Jorge standing in the entrance.

"You ready to go?" he asked.

"I think I got everything," he said, zipping the top and tossing the pack over his shoulder. Looking around the room, he stepped over to the door. "Guess it's time to get going. Is the vehicle downstairs?"

"It's parked near the front entrance. The doorman had me park it just down the way so it didn't interfere with other cars pulling up."

"Great."

Walking beside Jorge, he locked the door and they headed for the elevator. Just before they got to the doors, they opened and Mica came strutting out, almost bumping into them. She just smiled at them and, as she passed, lifted her hand and ran her finger across his chin before continuing down the hallway.

"Well, good morning, Mr. Cortez," she said, never turning.

"Uh…good morning to you."

"I hope you're enjoying your stay with us?"

"I am," he yelled as she continued.

Johnny barely got the words out as she simply walked away. Earlier, he had only seen her from the front when they were at the counter, but the uniform looked just as good going away as it did then. The sway from her hips was quite pronounced and suggestive. They both stood for a moment before turning to look at each other. Before they could comment, a bell sounded and the doors started to close. Jorge reached over with his hand, stopping them.

"Young people these days," Jorge commented before stepping inside.

"Really," Johnny said with a grin following him.

Pressing the button for the lobby, he turned and looked over at him. His face was stone-cold, almost empty of expression, and it was obvious that their comments didn't mean the same thing. He snickered to himself as he watched the doors close.

Once the doors opened, he followed Jorge through the lobby and outside. He pointed to their right, and he could see the Land Rover parked a couple of hundred yards down the street. As they neared, he saw a head sitting in the passenger seat. When they came up, Jorge stepped behind it and opened the back window. He continued down the side and stopped near the passenger door to see who was inside.

"Hi there," Ani said, looking at him.

"What are you doing here?"

"Haven't you probably guessed?" She smiled. "I'm coming with you."

Looking on the backseat, he could see several bags and assumed they were hers. Jorge had come around and tried taking the bag from his shoulder to put in the back. When Johnny looked at him, all he could do was shrug his shoulders.

"Jorge," he asked, "are you good with her going?"

"She has a strong will," he said, leaning back around the corner. "I've learned that if she wants to do something, there is nothing I can say to change it. Besides, she knows the desert probably better than most and could probably help you."

"Oh, really," he said, looking at her.

"Yes, really," she said, leaning on the windowsill.

Johnny walked to the back to inspect what was there.

"Did you get everything I asked for?" he said, rummaging through the back.

"Everything," he commented before leaning over to him and whispered, "You will take care of her while you're gone…right?"

"With my life, sir," he assured him. "I won't let anything happen to her."

"Good." He smiled.

"Johnny, do you need help with anything," Ani yelled from the front.

"No, we're good."

With the contents in the back secured, Jorge shut the window and walked around to where Ani was sitting. Johnny opened the door and slid in behind the steering wheel beginning to buckle his seatbelt. He glanced over at Ani and Jorge lean in the window to her.

"Please have a safe trip," he told her.

"I will, Father," she said, kissing his cheek.

Returning her kiss, he leaned away from the window and took a step back onto the sidewalk. He then looked over at Johnny. Knowing what the look meant, he gave him a quick wink and nod as he started the engine. Making sure he was set, he gave Jorge a wave and, putting it into gear, slowly pulled away and out into the street. After a few moments, she looked at him with dismay.

"Where are you going?"

"Well, I'm trying to get to the main highway leading west out of town."

"We'll never get there this way," she sighed.

"It's been a few years, but I'll get my bearings in a minute."

"Sure, you will," she said, straightening up in the seat and then pointing. "Take a left at the next corner and head straight. It'll run right into the highway."

"Thanks."

Taking her direction, he turned and moved into the flow of traffic. There were a ton of cars, and he tried to maneuver through them without hitting anything. As the road opened up, he glanced over at her. He saw that she was staring at him as if checking him out.

"What?" he asked.

"Oh, nothing," she said, turning to look back out the window.

"Come on, tell me… Is something wrong?"

"It's," she began slowly, "it's just that you look very…well, hot."

"In what way?" he said, looking down at himself.

"You do know we are heading into the deep desert, right?"

"Yeah, why?"

"You just seem to be dressed for a casual stroll around the square instead of the blazing heat. I was just wondering."

"Hey, I'm comfortable dressed this way," he smirked. "Have a problem with that?"

"Nope, not at all," she said, leaning back.

"Besides," he laughed, "it's nothing a little two sixty air conditioning won't fix."

"Two sixty air?" she asked, not knowing what that meant.

"Yeah…two windows down and sixty miles an hour." He grinned.

Shaking her head, she began to laugh at his thinking.

"Only an American would even think of something like that."

"Hey…it works."

As they drove along in almost silence, he would glance over at Ani and, seeing her, knew it was actually nice that she was coming along. It was obvious that he hadn't thought this trip all the way through. The more he thought about going out in the desert all by himself, the more he thought it was probably not a very smart idea. At least now he had someone to talk to on the trip and one never knows. She might come in handy with the locals he might encounter.

"I just want to say that I'm really glad you came along," he finally said to her.

Turning her head slightly, she just smiled.

"I wouldn't miss this adventure for anything. Besides, if you were to get hurt, who would be there to help you? You'd just die in the desert, all alone."

"Thanks for the visual," he said, shaking his head.

"You're welcome."

Staring at her, he didn't notice a car that came out of the side road and pull into the small space in front of them. He quickly slammed on the brakes and swerved to the side, almost hitting the car next to him. As he yelled and cursed, he then let the space between them increase to a safe distance. Moving back into his lane, he merged along with the other moving cars. When he looked over at her, Ani was staring at him. Without saying a word, she slid down in the seat and put her feet up on the dash, bracing herself and holding onto her seatbelt. He started to laugh, but he could tell she was not amused.

Oh, this should be really interesting, he thought.

CHAPTER 16

JORGE HAD WATCHED the Rover disappear down the street and, once it disappeared, walked back under the awning to wait by the side of the building for his driver to come get him. While he waited, a car pulled up, and a man stepped out. He instantly recognized him as Detective Deniko, and as the man turned and saw him standing by the building, he waved. Walking over to him, he then smiled and, reaching out, shook his hand.

"Jorge, what are you doing here?" he asked.

"Waiting for one of my drivers to come and pick me up. What are you doing here?"

"I came to talk to Mr. Cortez and then afterward have a little lunch."

"I'm sorry, but he's not here," Jorge said.

"Where did he go?"

"He said he wanted a vehicle to go check something out in the desert."

"Really?"

"My daughter went with him and said they would be gone for several days."

Deniko didn't know what to think of him going out into the desert but would have to worry about that after he returned. He wondered if he had held something back or found anything that they might have missed. The one thing he knew was he definitely was not going to go chasing after him. It wasn't that important.

"I guess I'll see him when they get back," he said, slapping his shoulder. "You have a good day."

"You also," Jorge said as he walked away.

Time for some food, he thought walking inside.

Detective Deniko walked through the hotel and out onto the back seating area. He came there often and found it peaceful. Many times, he would come simply to clear his head about tough cases. He was always recognized by his hat, a Dick Tracy-style hat that he would toss on the hat rack hook as he went by. Most of the time, he would never miss, but this time, it bounced off the wall and hit the ground. One of the waiters by the serving area picked it up and placed it on a hook. Seeing that he had missed the hook, he cursed and walked over to a table.

"Ah, Detective Deniko," a man said, walking up to him as he settled in his seat. "How are you, my dear friend?"

His voice the detective recognized immediately and, turning, saw that it was the restaurant chef dressed in his normal white outfit, limp hat, and with an apron tied around his waist. Standing beside him, he had a smile as always.

"I'm starving, Hector," he said, grunting. "What is the special today?"

"It's your favorite today—squid with crab meat."

"Yes," he said, closing his eyes and leaning his head back. "I can already taste it now. I'll take a generous portion."

Raising his hand, one of the waiters came over from the serving area. Hector gave him the order and, nodding, scurried past the counter and into the back to place it. Turning around he looked at the detective.

"I see that you are not at your normal table over by the edge," he asked curiously. "Is there a problem?"

He knew that Deniko always went to the farthest table on the north side of the seating area and pulled out one of the wooden chairs to use it to put up his feet. For more years than he could count, he had always gone to the same spot. It was almost out of character for him to do otherwise.

"No, just wanted to have a change." He grinned. "It might change my thinking."

Sitting trying to gather his thoughts as he waited for his food, he felt a presence move beside him. Looking up, he saw a woman standing beside him. Shaking his head, he wondered why she had come to him.

"Mica," he said. "What are you doing here?"

"Can't I just sit down and talk to an old friend?"

"Sure, you can…if we are still friends."

"That has never changed," she said, sitting down beside him.

"It's just that since that day, you've never really talked to me."

"I was hurt," she said, leaning over on the table. "I'm a woman, and my feelings get hurt more often than you know."

"I can only say that I'm sorry, but you were going in a different direction."

"True, but now I've got a good job and making money, so I'm getting my life turned around for the better."

"Every day I check to see if your name comes up on the arrest report."

"Haven't seen it on there, have you?"

"No, I haven't and that's a good thing."

"See, there." She laughed.

The waiter came out of the back with his food and placed it in front of him. He then looked over at Mica.

"Would you care for something to eat?" he asked.

"No," she said, standing up. "I just dropped by to say hello to my friend. I'll maybe see you later?"

"I don't know," he said, wondering what she really wanted.

Shrugging her shoulders, she leaned over and kissed his cheek before walking away. He watched her until she disappeared into the hotel.

I wonder what that was all about, he wondered.

Sitting in the back of the limousine, Widdal knew that nothing was going as he planned. He needed to find out more. Dialing a number and holding the phone up to his ear, he waited as it began to ring. Finally, a female voice came on.

"Hello."

"Where is he?" he asked abruptly.

"They just left the hotel a short time ago, sir."

"They?" he said, surprised. "What do you mean by…they?"

"He was with a man, and when they got downstairs, there was a woman already in the vehicle. I don't know where they were going, but from what I could see, they had a bunch of supplies packed inside. The man stayed here at the hotel."

"Do you know how long they might be gone?"

"I don't know that either, but I did overhear the doorman say something about it being several days."

"Thank you," he said, looking out the window. "Your services will no longer be required. Do not call this number again."

Before another word could be said, he hung up the phone and quickly dialed another number. When it answered, a man's voice came on but did not say anything.

"I have a job for you."

"Yes, sir."

"I want you to tear Cortez's hotel room apart inch by inch and search for anything that might be important. He's holding something back from me, and I want to know what it is. You have three days, so let me know if you find anything!"

"Yes, sir."

Widdal hung the phone up and, leaning back against the seat, began to curse loudly.

CHAPTER 17

"So...you going to be my navigator?" Johnny asked Ani. "Or just ride along, so I'll have to do everything?"

"I thought about just sitting here, but since you asked, I'm really good at navigating." She smiled, picking up the map between them. Just then the vehicle hit a deep hole in the road, bouncing them up and against the seatbelts, causing her to laugh. "And probably better than you are at driving."

"We'll see about that." He smiled.

The tightly packed buildings of the city, along with the concrete, soon disappeared, and the landscape started to become stark and empty as they headed into the desert. The concrete road quickly turned into a large one-lane road that stretched into the horizon. Several times along the way, they had to pause as men herded their animals across the road to another area. Waiting for them to pass, he would lean over the steering wheel and shake his head. Once they passed, he would go on increasing his speed to make up for lost time.

The suspension on the old Land Rover made for a rough ride, considering the road hadn't been fixed in probably twenty years. His butt could feel every hole in the road. With only the drone of the engine, they sat in silence, and he knew that if it continued, it would be a very long trip since the oasis of Amar was over seven hours from the city. That was where he planned to get gas for the vehicle.

"I wonder if there is any music on the radio," he said, reaching for the knob.

"If there is, it isn't anything either of us would like to hear."

"Well, you never know."

For several minutes, he went through the whole range of the dial, and at the end, he knew she was right before turning it off. When he did, she just produced a sly grin and stuck her head back out the window.

"Told you so," she said smugly.

"Okay...rub it in."

Driving along, he would occasionally turn his head slightly and glance over at her. She looked to be very comfortable with her feet up on the dash with the top of her body leaning out the open window to cool herself. The breeze made her tied-up hair flutter behind her and against the top of the seat. Every so often, she would reach up and wrap it up to try and tuck it into her shirt. After she did, the wind would catch it and bring it back out.

The tan shorts she wore rode up high on her thighs. It was especially noticeable by the way she sat in the seat with her feet up. He found he couldn't help but stare over at her. With her toes tapping her sandals against the dash to some music playing in her head, he could see that her eyes were closed.

You have to stop this.

Chastising himself, he tried to concentrate on driving. Still, it provided him a chance to stare and examine her closely without the chance of her knowing. Every so often, a big smile would appear on her face but her eyes never opened.

I'm sure she knows I'm staring, he then thought, noticing the smile.

Oddly, he found he couldn't stop from staring at her. There was just something about her that he couldn't put his finger on. With her white shirt open in the front, she had tied up the bottom of it just below her breasts. He then noticed the smooth surface of her stomach rise and fall as she breathed. The small halter top she wore beneath it held tightly to each mound as they rhythmically rose in sync with her stomach. Several times he would stare at her longer than he should have and almost run off the road into the desert. When he did and quickly corrected the vehicle, she would slowly turn and look at him.

"Eyes on the road, mister." She grinned. "If you run us off the road, I'm sure as hell not going to dig us out of some hot sand dune."

"Hell, what road," Johnny said, pointing ahead of them.

"Excuses…excuses."

For the next few hours, they tried following the twisting road through sandy ravines and over small hills. Many times, the road would just vanish and they had to check not only the map but the GPS on the dash. A couple of times, he had to put the vehicle in four-wheel drive to keep from keeping stuck. It appeared that Ani was having a great time as she held on with a big smile. From her attitude, this was the first time she had done anything like this. Still, everything from the map and GPS said they were going in the right direction.

"Having fun?" he would ask her.

"More than you'll ever know," she beamed.

"Want to try your hand at driving?"

"Oh…not a chance." She would grin, watching the road ahead of them. "I think you're doing just fine."

"You coward."

"On most things…including this."

By her statement, it then suddenly hit him.

"You've never driven a car, have you?"

"Nope…never have."

"And if something happened to me out here, what would you do then?"

"Oh," she said, slowly looking over at him, "probably just look at you and try to figure out when I was going to die."

The comment made them both laugh. In the back of his mind, he figured she would at least give it a try if something did actually happen. Picking up the road again, the pressing heat of the desert made his back to sweat and his shirt stick to him. With his hands occupied on driving, it caused him to lean forward to get some air on his back. When he did, she noticed and would reach over, pulling his sticky shirt from his skin. Instantly, the mixture of sweat and air felt good, and he would let out a small moan.

"Ah…thank you."

"No problem," she said, fluffing his shirt, forcing air beneath it.

Trying to drive yet not lean back against the seat, he liked what she was doing and didn't want it to stop. It was almost as good as an air conditioner. When she did finally stop, he leaned back and looked around. Glancing at the GPS, he figured that they were getting really close to the oasis where they could stop and cool off. As he got to a small dune, he stopped the vehicle and looked over at her.

"We have to be really close now," he said, scanning around the area. "What do those navigating skills say about it?"

Looking at the map, she then looked up and pointed.

"It should be right over that hill," she said as her hand indicated it was over the hill in front of them.

"Well, here goes nothing."

Placing the vehicle in four-wheel drive, he gunned the engine and headed for the top. All the wheels struggled against the dirt and sand, but slowly, they made it to the top when he stopped. Beyond the hill, they could see a small valley and tucked next to the far hillside was a lush green area. He could barely make out several buildings, and below them on the valley floor, he could see the road going toward it.

"Finally, the oasis of Amar," he said with a sigh. "We made it."

"Thank God! I'm dying here."

"It should only be another hour—tops." He laughed, reaching over and placing the GPS in the glovebox.

"What are you waiting for?" she said, slapping his shoulder. "Get this thing moving!"

"Yes, ma'am," he smiled, placing the vehicle in gear.

It only took them about forty minutes to cover the valley floor and reach the edge of the oasis. The sun was still high above the horizon but low enough that he knew in several short hours it would be down and get dark. They had to get gas and back on the road as quickly as they could since he was hoping to get much farther towards their destination.

Entering the edge of the oasis, it was pretty much like he expected. There was only one main road down the center of the town with worn sand block buildings lining each side. Trying to guess, there was only about thirty buildings in the whole place. Toward the end of town was the station that had a small garage that provided fuel to those that passed through. Pulling up to the only pump, he stopped and turned off the engine. With a sigh of relief at making it, he looked over at Ani. To his surprise, she was already out of her seat and gone.

"Ani!" he yelled out, trying to locate her.

When he got out, an older gentlemen came up to him and, noticing he was an American, asked what he needed in broken English. Johnny said that he needed fuel for the vehicle and to fill it up. With a nod, he turned and yelled out, causing a small boy to come out of the nearby building. The man began to issue commands and guided the boy to his post. It was a stationary bicycle with a generator attached to the chain. As he began to pedal, Johnny could begin to hear the motors in the gas pump begin to spin up. Waiting for a moment, he unscrewed the gas cap and pulled the nozzle out. Smiling to him, he began to fill the tank. Now he had to find where Ani had gone off too.

As the man continued to fuel the Rover, he placed his map on the hood and checked where they needed to go next. After a few minutes, Ani still hadn't come back, and he thought it might be better to go find her. Folding the map and tossing it into the front seat, he walked over to the edge of the building.

When he turned the corner, he saw her kneeling over by some palm trees. Surrounding her were several baby goats being attended by several young children. The goats jumped and ran around them but always came back as they tried to feed them. She began to laugh as one of the goats playfully bounced against her, almost knocking her down. The children joined in laughing as she finally fell over onto her rear-end.

Watching her was almost like watching just another child in the mix. When she hit the ground, she had one of them by the arm and pulled her over on top of her. As they laughed and rolled, the goats came over and nudged them before bouncing away. He then heard the man by the Rover tell him that he was full and ready. Waving to him, he turned to Ani.

"Ani, we have to go," he yelled out.

"All right," she said, beginning to get up.

Saying her goodbyes, she walked over to him.

"Having fun with your new friends?" he asked as she passed.

"I love children," she told him, never stopping.

"I can see." He laughed.

Handing the man a thousand-pound note, he argued that it was too much and he would get him change. Johnny shook his head and just thanked him as Ani got in. Shaking his hand, he got in and started up the Rover. Taking a water bottle out, she took several long gulps as he started to head out of the city. When the buildings began to get smaller behind them, she turned to him but never spoke.

"Good people," Johnny said.

"More than you could ever know." She grinned.

Driving along following the directions, there wasn't much to look at except sand. When he went down a small canyon between two large sand dunes, he heard a loud pop. Checking the dashboard, it didn't seem to be in the engine, and then the rover began to wobble and he knew what had happened. Pulling onto a flat spot, he stopped and turned off the engine. Ani looked over at him.

"What's wrong?"

"I think we have a flat tire," he said, getting out.

Checking his side, he walked around to the other side. He saw that the rear tire had dug into the dirt and sand and was definitely flat. Stripping off his shirt, he broke out the jack and began clearing out a spot to lift the rover. Ani got out and, walking over behind him, just stood and watched. Glancing over his shoulder, he began to laugh.

"You want to break out the spare from the roof?" he asked.

"Uh, not really," she said, looking up at the top.

"I take it that I'll have to do this all by myself?"

"You are the man." She grinned.

"And what will be your purpose in all this?"

"Moral support," she said, looking at him and then wiping the sweat from his forehead, "and water when you need it."

"Hope you won't strain yourself doing that."

"Me either," she told him.

While they laughed, he got the jack positioned and then began after a couple of pumps, lifting the Rover slightly. Before he jacked it off, the ground went around and climbed up the back and on top took of the roof. She at least handed him the tire iron, and he took the bolts off from one of the spares. Once it was loose, he lifted the edge and pushed it off the side. It bounced several times, but Ani ran after it and stopped it from rolling very far.

"Thanks," he said, watching her chase the rolling tire.

"Don't want you using all your strength running through the desert," she said, snagging the tire. "I do want to get out of the sun."

He didn't know how to respond and just sighed as he jumped down. Taking the lugs off the tire, he began to lift the rover as she rolled the tire beside him. When the last lug came loose, he yanked the tire off and rolled it to the back. Sitting down he wiped the sweat running down his face and into his eyes. When he turned, Ani was standing beside him with a towel and a bottle of water.

"You need to hydrate," she said.

"Thanks," he said, taking the bottle and drinking most of it down.

Wiping his head, he looked up at her.

"I never had a chance to ask you," he started cautiously before sipping some more water. "Does your boyfriend or husband know you came out here with me?"

"No." She laughed. "I don't either one of them. Does that surprise you?"

"Well, sort of."

"I'll take that as a compliment."

"It was," he said, tossing the empty water bottle away.

"I'm still looking for that...Mr. Right," she said before looking at him. "How about you...do you have a wife or girlfriend?"

"No," he said, positioning the new tire on the axle. "Never really went looking and figured, when the time was right, she would just show up, so I guess you could say I'm still also looking."

"There will be a time," she said.

Thinking about what she said, he tightened the lugs on the tire and dropped the Rover on the ground. Tossing the jack into the back, he struggled to get the old tire up to the roof and, finally positioning it, tightened the lugs. Finished, he tossed the lug wrench to the ground and sat on the other tire. Trying to catch his breath, she walked over and looked up at him, shading her eyes from the sun.

"So are you done?" she asked. "It's getting really hot."

"Yes," he said smugly, "and might I just say thanks for all your help."

"Good, then can we go?"

"Sure, oh great master." He grinned. "Is there anything else?"

"Yeah, some air flowing over me from moving would be nice."

"Your wish is my command," he said with a flip of his hand.

"Then move it, mister." She laughed.

Making sure everything was back in the Rover, he got in and, wiping the sweat away, started the engine. Looking over at her, she turned and just started laughing as they pulled back out onto the trail. Looking at the GPS, they still had a couple of hours to get to the position he had marked. Driving along in silence, he wondered what they would actually find once they got there.

Following the trail and watching the sun set behind them in the mirror, he just wanted to get to the spot and stop. Going through some deep sand, the GPS began to beep, indicating that they had arrived. Stopping on a flat area, he got out and looked around. Ani opened her door and stood up on the door jam. They both looked all around them before looking at each other.

"A perfect garden spot," Ani said with a sigh.

"Maybe," he said, glancing behind them. "But that might need to wait until tomorrow with the sun going down. We need to set up the camp."

"How about we set up over there by those rocks?"

"Yeah," he said, looking at the spot she was pointing to. It was only a couple of hundred yards away. "It might protect us from that storm heading our way."

"Let's go," she said, climbing back into the Rover.

Reaching the spot, he turned the Rover to act like a block to help protect the tent from the wind. By the time he had set up the tent and got everything organized, the sun was behind the horizon and the light was fading. Checking the ropes on the tent, Ani came around the edge and over to him.

"I'll get some food started for us before it gets too dark," she said, digging into the rover. "Want to start a fire?"

"It's next on my list."

She was quick when she said she would have food for them. The fire was barely started when she had a pot of food going against it. Within ten minutes, she was beginning to serve a plate of food to him. He was impressed that she could do that so quickly. Thanking her, he started to eat. She laughed, knowing it was only some beans and bread. He was starving, so anything would have tasted good.

After eating, they both sat around the small fire, enjoying the warmth as the air started to chill. He had also found a bottle of Ouzo in one of the backpacks, which, after the long ride, made it even more relaxing. The air was now starting to get cool from the desert breeze. In the distance, he could see the outline of the horizon highlighted by the big moon. He knew that would all change once the coming storm hit them in the next few hours. Turning, all the stars behind them were hidden, making the sky black as it approached. When the wind picked up, he knew they would have to take cover. Sitting beside the fire, they both stared ahead watching the flickering flames at their feet. It seemed to be very casual, but Johnny enjoyed the simple conversation.

For most of his life, he had never really just sat down and talked to a woman that he wasn't thinking of sex. Inside, he laughed, knowing that he had never been in any circumstance like this before to even have a casual conversation. Either he was coming on to them or they were. Looking over at Ani, she had her arms wrapped around her knees and held the cup in one hand. Every so often, she would lift it up and take a sip. Finally finishing it, she sat it down in the sand beside her.

"Do you want some more?" he asked, holding up the bottle.

"No, I think I'm good for now."

"Suit yourself," he said, pouring some more in his cup.

"Gog, this stuff is going right through me," she said, standing up.

Walking over to the edge of the tent, she leaned over and grabbed a small camp shovel with a roll of toilet paper slid down the handle. It was one of the first things they prepared just to be ready.

"Don't get lost out there." He laughed.

She ignored him and, swinging the shovel in her hand, walked away.

"It's a desert," she yelled out.

"That's what I'm afraid of," he mumbled.

Once she disappeared behind the Rover, he poured some more Ouzo in his cup and, leaning back, looked out into the distance. As he took a sip, he saw something at the edge of the light and sat up. Focusing, he saw it again and recognized it as a set of red eyes. Watching, several more sets of eyes appeared and they were moving. He knew that seeing them wouldn't be good, and some type of animal had come out of the desert. They may be heading for the camp in search of food. Standing up he had to get Ani back to the safety of the fire. Just then he heard her scream out in the darkness.

"Ani!" he yelled back in panic.

When he started to head toward the sound of her scream, he immediately froze as he saw several hyenas walking toward him and the fire. Thinking of possible options, one ran quickly past him with one of the open backpacks locked in its jaws. Several others joined it, investigating the contents of the pack.

Watching them, Ani then came racing around the corner of the tent. Clutching the top of her shorts she had barely pulled them up before running. After another step, a shape come from behind her and knocked her down before it stopped and twisted, jumping back at her slightly. It was another hyena but was much larger than the others.

"No!" Ani screamed in panic, bracing for it to attack. "Johnny!"

Hearing his name, his heart began to race. He could see the teeth as it began to whine and growl, saliva dripping from the corner of its mouth. Ani barely moved, watching and preparing for the eventual confrontation. The animal's teeth were ominous as it opened further as it stocked her. She dug her feet into the sand to help push her back away. He could see that the animal's eyes were keyed directly on Ani, paying him no attention. Johnny's eyes bounced back and forth between Ani and the rest of the pack. Before he could move, another one came from around the tent and walked slowly between them and prevented him from coming over to her rescue. He cursed under his breath.

"Try not to move," Johnny yelled out.

"You see me moving!" she screamed.

Once she screamed out, the hyena lunged quickly at her. As its mouth opened wide and tried to bite her, she reached up and grabbed it just under the jaws. The force of the animal along with its weight pressed her into the sand. Holding it tightly she tried desperately to prevent it from biting down on either her face or neck. The hyena was strong and the force was weakening Ani's arms and the sharp teeth were snapping at her. Several times, the hyena snapped and caught her flesh. She screamed in pain as it ripped open several wounds in long bloody lines. Johnny's jaws tightened as he saw all the blood on her, which the smell of fresh blood made the animal increase its struggle against her. The fight between them frightened the one animal stopping him from helping and it raced away to join the rest of the pack.

This might be my only chance, he thought.

He had already pulled out the knife from the scabbard on his hip and slowly turned it in his hand. When the one animal was far enough away, he took a quick step and tackled the animal on top of Ani. Rolling off her they continued to roll as it fought to turn and bite him. As he came to rest above it, he quickly jammed the sharp blade of the knife into the hyena's side. When the animal struggled to escape and yelled, he twisted the blade harshly. He didn't remember how many times he plunged the knife into its side, but he continued until it stopped moving.

"Son of a bitch," he gasped, pushing the dead animal away with his foot.

Knowing there were more, he jumped to his feet, prepared for the next attack. The other hyenas were pacing around but not attacking. Slipping the knife in the scabbard, he leaned over and grabbed the back legs of the dead hyena. Taking a step forward, he began to swing the carcass around before releasing it to sail out into the darkness toward the others. There was then a large commotion as they attacked it in a frenzy and dragged it away into the desert. Leaning over onto his knees, he tried to gather his breath. He then heard Ani moaning behind him.

Turning, he saw that she was now sitting up and holding her arm. He raced over to her side and, kneeling, examined her wounds. As he looked at each one, she began to sob and could see long trails of tears running down her face.

"Are you all right?"

"Yes, I think so," she said, still sobbing. "Where the hell did they come from?"

"Probably smelled our food on the breeze."

Checking her wounds, he wiped the blood away carefully with his handkerchief as to not hurt her. As he did, he looked up and saw that she was smiling at him. There was a glow in her eyes as she stared at him.

"What's the matter?" he asked, thinking something else was wrong.

"Nothing…just thank you," she said, curling her lips, "for saving my life."

"Hey, no problem," he commented with a grin.

"We need to get you cleaned up before this gets infected."

Looking at her, she produced a weak smile but didn't say anything. After a moment, she reached up and, taking his face, leaned over and kissed him deeply. It surprised him, but he wasn't going to turn down a reward for his bravery and returned her kiss. The kiss was deep and filled with passion. After a moment, she broke their kiss and looked at him with the same sly smile. A wicked thought passed through his mind and he laughed.

"What is it?"

"So…I take it that you're not going to go back and get the shovel?"

She immediately slapped his shoulder playfully.

"Not a chance in hell."

The wind was starting to pick up and he knew the storm was going to be there at any moment. Turning, he could see the flames of the fire flickering wildly in the breeze. Even in the meager light, he could see that she was cut almost everywhere on her body from the claws of the hyena. Almost all of them looked to be very superficial except for the one gash on her arm. It was the worse one and seemed deep enough to allow blood to continue to flow. He had to get her into the tent and out of the blowing sand to clean it up. There was also the issue of the coming storm and making sure nothing gets blown away, including them.

When it rains, it pours, he thought.

"I'm fine, really," she said, noticing his concern.

"Probably but let's just make sure, shall we?"

Standing up, he held his hand out to her. Reaching up and taking it, he pulled her up onto her feet. She was a little wobbly, and he held by the waist to steady her. With a long exhale, she turned and went into the tent. Once inside, she sat down on one of the sleeping bags. He didn't follow her all the way inside but only stuck his head inside.

"Let me make sure everything is tied down and I'll be right back."

"I don't think I'm going anywhere." She smiled, turning on the small light.

Closing the flap, he looked around the camp and couldn't see anything moving. He figured that between him killing the one hyena and the coming storm, they wouldn't be bothered anymore. Getting into the Rover, he pulled out another bag and the first aid kit from under the seat. He never for a moment thought he would have to use it, and whatever was in there, it would just have to do. Walking around the tent he inspected the ropes and made sure they were secure. Tossing some sand on the fire to put it out he turned and saw the Ouzo bottle still sticking up proudly in the sand. With a smile, he picked it up along with a cup and entered the tent.

"You doing all right?" he asked closing the flap.

"I guess so," she said.

He saw that she was sitting, examining her arm, and slowly looked up at him. He could now see that her shirt was all ripped up and blood covered most of it. Tossing the bags to the corner, he came over and sat down beside her. Opening the first-aid kit, he examined the contents and saw that there wasn't much in it as he began to dig through it. At least he noticed that there were several rolls of clean bandages and some antibiotic ointment.

"Want to take that shirt off while I clean you up?"

"Yes, doctor." She giggled unbuttoning the front.

"Easy girl." He laughed.

Pressing her lips together in a disappointed pout from his comment, she stripped her shirt off and laid it beside her. Since there was nothing to help clean it off, he stripped off his tattered T-shirt off and began to rip portions to clean the wounds. Taking the bottle of alcohol, he tipped the bottle against them and slowly cleaned all the blood away. When it was as clean as he could get it, he took the ointment and spread it along the cuts, covering as much as he could. He then grabbed a roll and began wrapping it around her arm until it was completely covered. There was at least a roll of tape and he secured the ends. She sat and watched him through the whole process. When he was done, he sat back and examined his work.

"I think that will do for now," he said, "at least until we get back to the city."

"You did a really great job," she said, flexing her arm in the air. "I don't think it's going anywhere no matter what I do."

"Glad to hear that," he said, picking up the bottle and taking a deep swallow.

"Oh my god," she then gasped.

"What?" he said quickly, turning and looking to the front flap, thinking something was trying to get inside.

"Your leg is bleeding."

Looking down, his pants were ripped in several spots, and blood was covering the material in one place. He gently pulled it to the side and saw there was a long cut in his skin that was still bleeding. It must have happened when he was struggling with the hyena, and the claws of his back feet must have caught him. Through it all, he hadn't noticed and there wasn't any pain to let him know.

"It's nothing," he said, shrugging.

"I'll be the judge of that," she said, pushing him to his back. "Your pants—off!"

With her hands on her hips, she stared down at him, waiting for him to comply with her request. He didn't think the cut was all that bad, but from the look on her face, she was going to be the one that determined the severity. Reaching down, he unbuckled his belt and slowly slid his pants down his legs. As he pushed them to his knees she obviously thought he was taking too long and, grabbing the edges, pulled them the rest of the way down. Once they were past his feet, she tossed them to the side and, picking up the lantern, examined his leg.

As her fingers pressed gently along the length of his leg next by the cut, he could feel the warmth of her breath on his skin as she exhaled. Trapped beneath her and not able to really move, he tried to contain himself, but as she persisted, he found he couldn't. Instinctively, he began to rise to the stimulation. He knew that she couldn't have not noticed his excitement and was beginning to be embarrassed by his growing arousal. Each long breath she took excited him, and after a moment, she finally sat back up and smiled.

"You were right," she said, setting the lantern down. "It's really not all that bad."

"I'm glad you concur."

Sitting beside him, suddenly there was silence and they only stared at each other. He started to lift up, but she reached over and stopped him with her hand. As he lay back, her hand followed the curves of his chest before softly stroking his stomach. All he could do was watch her face as their eyes were locked to one another. Wondering what she was up to, there was a look of desire and singular purpose showing across it. After pausing on his stomach, her hand then slowly began to move even lower, touching the top of his shorts. Her fingers never stopped as they slowly pressed beneath the edge. Each finger playfully twisted in the hair until her hand moved low enough to grasp him. The warm touch of her fingers cause him to jerk slightly, and he let out a small gasp as she then squeezed her prize.

"Are you sure?" he then asked her. "I mean really sure?"

"Oh yes," she said with a nod. "I'm absolutely sure."

Releasing him, she got to her knees and swung her leg over the top of him, settling on his stomach. Placing her hands for a moment on his chest, she slowly began to grind her hips against his pelvis. He could then feel the growing wetness coming from her as she slid back and forth against him. After a few moments, she stopped and, leaning back, reached down and pulled her halter over her head. Taking the tie from her hair, she shook her head from side to side, allowing it to become free and expand. The sight of her now naked and on top of him drove his excitement further into heightened ecstasy. Her firm breasts quivered against her rising chest as she felt his eyes burning into her skin. She beamed, feeling him now beginning to pulse over and over between her legs.

"I have to confess," she said softly while slowly leaning forward, "that I've had so many dreams about this particular moment since the first day I met you."

"I can only hope it won't be disappointing afterward."

"Not a chance." She grinned.

Now leaned over and pressed against him, she kissed him deeply as he wrapped his arms around her waist. Holding her tightly, she became limp in his arms, molding to him as she eagerly awaited anything he would do to her. Twisting her to the side, they changed positions as she folded beneath him but never broke their kiss. As his hands came up her side, she stopped him and pushed him away so she could see his face.

"I have to confess something else before we start."

"You can tell me anything," he said, seeing the sudden panic in her face.

"I've...I've never been with a man before," she told him cautiously, watching his face for any sign it bothered him. "Not like this anyway."

"Really?" he said with wide eyes.

"You will be...my first."

Letting her comment sink in for a moment, he then let out a long sigh.

"Will...does that make any difference?" she asked, afraid he might reject her.

"No." He grinned. "Not to me anyway."

Pleased by his response, she grabbed his face and pulled him hard toward her, kissing him deeply. Locked in their kiss, her hands released his face as he steadied his body above her. It allowed her now free hands to move down the length of his body. They once again took hold of his manhood, urging it. Instead of accommodating her request, he broke their kiss and slowly began to kiss and nibble at her ears and neck. Each delicate kiss brought him lower and away from her face.

As he moved, her hands released him and, taking the side of his head, tried to guide his direction as his lips delicately examined the surface of her skin. Circling lower to her breasts, he never took them like she urged but playfully nudged each mass with the tip of his nose while his tongue pressed into the creases. Teasing them into full hardness, he finally let his tongue trace slowly up the side of one mass before reaching the top and quickly taking the tip between his lips, sucking it into his mouth.

"Oh shit," she gasped.

While suckling her like a newborn, his hands moved in between her legs. They were wet with excitement as he traced the sensitive folds. Slowly, his fingers began to probe her depths, causing her to shake and shudder beneath him. Each time he entered her, she would moan with delight and rise against him. Glancing up, he saw a thin film of sweat beginning to cover her body, shimmering in the dim light.

"Yes…oh yes," Ani said, grabbing the top of his head.

Lifting his eyes, he could see her face was becoming flush while her back arched into the air. Knowing that she wanted more, he released her breast and continued down across the flat of her stomach. He could feel her hands tremble and release their grip on him. Feeling the tickle of hair on his chin, he slid between her legs and buried his face. She let out a small gasp as he flicked his tongue into the wetness to enjoy the fluid of her rising desire. Several times, her legs clinched his head, keeping him from moving. While trapped, his fingers continued their assault, diving within her. Feeling her begin to shudder violently again and again and cover his face, he lifted his head and looked at her.

"Please…no more," she begged weakly. "I want you now, inside me!"

Her hair looked wild and her closed eyes were tight. He could feel her fingers clutching frantically in his hair, begging him to rise back above her. Knowing she was almost at her limit, he obeyed her wishes and made his way back above her. Her legs quickly tightened around his waist, helping to position him. As he got in position, she reached down and, with shaking hands, tried to guide him. It was obvious that she couldn't wait any longer as she held him and rose up to try and help him enter her.

Even with her urging, he tried to lower himself into her very slowly. He wanted to make sure there was little pain since this was her first time. Once he was partially inside, she released him and bucked her hips quickly, driving him into her completely. She gasped once he was inside and, holding him into position, did not move as her muscles began to slowly accept him within her. He could feel her nails dig into the flesh of his back as she pressed her face against his shoulder and moaned. After a few moments, she released him and settled back against the ground, raising her legs. Wrapping his arms beneath them, he started a slow thrust, entering and pulling out. Ani screamed out in a passionate delight on each of his thrusts.

"Faster…oh please, faster," she yelled out, trying to match his thrusts.

Time faded away as he followed her lead and continued plunging within her. Every so often, she would explode, and fluid would flow from her. Their timing would be thrown off, and he tried to sync them up again. Each explosion was instantly followed by a low groan, along with several shudders before she would again match each of his thrusts. As he continued, he could feel the sweat dripping from his forehead and saw it dripping down onto her. She never noticed and, with her eyes closed, reveled in her feeling.

After what seemed like hours and more explosions within her than he could count, he could slowly begin to feel her legs becoming limp on his arms and try to fall off to the side. It was now obvious she was completely spent but, oblivious to her condition, still enjoying every moment. As he began to feel his own body begin to stiffen, he shuddered and slowed his pace, completely out of energy. Sensing he was close to his own release, she tightened around him with his final thrust, holding him tightly against her chest. As he continued to shudder, she tried desperately to hold him within her.

Finally spent, he rolled over weakly and, as she released him, flopped onto his back and, holding his chest, tried to catch his breath. She never moved and in the silence listened to her coo softly beside him. After a moment, she rolled over and laid her head on his chest. Wrapping his arm around her, she snuggled against him.

"That was absolutely wonderful, Johnny," she said, kissing his chest.

"Glad you enjoyed it," he said weakly. "But I thought you said that you've never done this before."

"That's very true, but I've read a lot of books," she said, lifting her head and grinning at him, "very…very dirty books."

He began to laugh at her comment.

"Let's do it again," she asked him, rubbing his chest, "please."

"I don't know," he said, wiping his face, "maybe once I get my strength back."

"Okay," she said, kissing his chest again. "I want more, so maybe this will help."

Never touching him, she slid down his chest, kissing him delicately. As she moved lower, he waited in anticipation. Her lips moved down the inside of his thighs and then circled back to go down the other one. She tantalizingly teased him and figured it was only fair considering he had done the same thing. With his eyes closed, he played with her long hair trailing her head and watched her within his mind.

Settling into a trance, feeling her lips slide against his skin, she paused and, twisting her head, suddenly dropped and took him. The deep warmth of her mouth as it surrounded him caused a gasp of delight to escape him as he enjoyed the feeling. She quickly lowered her head to then take all of him, tightening her jaws around him. The tightness made his legs shiver as she held him within her, wetting him fully with her tongue. He then felt her hand begin to massage him as she began to slide up and down on him.

"Holy crap, girl," he gasped.

Hearing him, all she did was moan and continue. From her professional action, she was determined to continue the night according to her plan. As he felt himself beginning to respond to her action and urging, he figured she was on a mission and nothing was going to stop her from accomplishing it. Letting his head relax, he enjoyed the pleasure she was providing and hoped it would not end until he was ready. From what she was doing, he didn't know if that would be possible.

For the next few hours, they took turns enjoying the other's body, and the night slowly faded away. Even the rising storm outside could not deter them from the pleasures awaiting the other. Neither of them worried about anything, the fluttering sides of the tent in the wind or the constant sound of the sand peppering the sides. Finally, they could not perform or give any more pleasure to the other and, curling up together, faded off to sleep.

CHAPTER 18

O BLIVIOUS FOR MOST of the night until they fell asleep in each other's arms, they never heard the sandstorm as it raged all around them. Trying to sleep, several times the fierce wind made him raise his head to make sure it wouldn't blow the vehicle over on top of them. Waiting, the vehicle remained steady and never did allowing him to fall back to sleep.

Waking up, the tent material glowed, and Johnny knew the morning sun had finally come up. The tent wasn't moving as the wind had calmed. He could hear the flaps of the tent gently fluttering in the calm breeze. Sitting up, he looked over and saw that Ani was curled up in the blanket on her side still sound asleep. Stretching, he got up and quietly slipped his clothes on before heading outside to see what damage the storm might have produced. When he unzipped the flap and stepped out, it was already warm, but the light breeze cooled him. Taking a deep breath, he looked around and stopped, shaking his head.

"Son of a..." he cursed lightly.

The whole side of the vehicle and one side of the tent was buried in over three feet of sand. It had blocked the wind but acted as a wind break, allowing the sand to pile up. If they were planning on going anywhere, he would first have to dig it all away.

He had to relieve himself, and walking to the other side of the Rover, he started to pee into the sand. As he did, he looked out and started to laugh. About thirty feet away, he saw the handle of the shovel she had taken out last night before the hyenas attacked. When he was done, he kicked some sand on the wet spot and walking out to pull the shovel from the sand. The roll of toilet paper was covered in sand, and shaking it, he tried to get off as much as he could.

When he turned to walk back, something caught his eye. It stood out against the brown sand. Looking closer, he saw that it looked like a hand sticking high out of the sand but were bleached white and nothing but bone.

"Son of a..."

Staring at it, he suddenly remembered the dream. He had to check it out.

Walking over to it, he knelt down and studied the hand wondering if there was more of the body still buried in the sand. Using the shovel, he careful began to clear the sand away before he came to the top of a skull. The smooth surface had a large gash across it as if it had been struck with something hard. He really didn't want to disturb it but was curious if there was some item that might identify when he had died. After a moment, a necklace began to appear around the figure's neck. Placing the shovel in the sand, he carefully pulled it up to examine it.

"It can't be," he said.

From what he could tell, it was really old. It looked like nothing from the early Egyptian period and had to predate that time. That would mean that this poor guy had died thousands of years ago. Looking around, he wondered what would bring him out into the middle of nowhere and who would kill him. Returning the necklace back around the figure's neck, he covered it back up with sand. Standing over the spot, he looked at the sand.

"Sleep in peace," he said softly. "Someone knows you are here."

Picking up the shovel, he walked back to the camp and wondered if anything else from his dream would come true. Opening the back of the Rover, he pulled out the big sand shovel and went around to the other side. He stopped, noting something else out of the corner of his eye. Focusing his eyes against the sun, they widened.

The small mound of rocks they parked beside for protection was now visible, showing a taller outcropping of stone. It had been the only rise of rock for miles. Some of the stone pieces were exposed and quite large. Beneath one almost-horizontal stone, it looked like an opening or entrance had appeared but was still partially blocked by a mound of remaining sand. There was darkness beneath it, indicating there might be an entrance or cave. Searching the horizon in every direction, there was nothing, not a stick, tree, or bush anywhere, just the never-ending sand. Before he could think about it further, he heard a voice.

"Hi there," she said, stretching her arms above her. "Good morning."

"Well, it's a morning," he said, walking over to the other side.

"Holy crap," she said then noticing all the sand.

"You forgot this in the sand, remember?" he said, holding up the shovel.

"Oh great," she said, "because I really have to go."

"Wouldn't want to help me, would you?" he asked, shoving the shovel in the sand. "It would go a whole lot quicker."

"I have a better idea," she smiled. "After I go, how about I get us some coffee going instead while you save us…again?"

"Oh, I see how this is going to go," he commented, beginning to flip sand away.

"Did you think it would go any other way? Besides, I'm wounded here, remember?" she said, holding up her bandaged arm to him.

"Yeah, I remember, but can you at least add some breakfast? I'll be starving after I dig all this sand away…by myself."

"Oh sure, I can do that." She laughed, bouncing to the back of the vehicle.

It took him about thirty minutes to clear the sand away so he could at least drive the vehicle out of the remaining sand. He had cleared most of the sand away from the tent so he could break it down after they were finished. The whole time he could smell the coffee and then the smell of something she was cooking. Whatever it was, it had his stomach growling. Wiping his forehead, he tossed the shovel into the sand and walked over to the small fire she had going, plopping down beside her with a groan.

"All done," she asked him.

"As much as it's going to be," he told her, wiping the sweat away.

"That's a good boy." She laughed, handing him a cup of coffee.

"I really don't know about this situation," he said, leaning back on his elbow. Sipping the hot fluid, he looked at her. There was a big grin on her face as she was filling up a plate with the food she had cooked.

"You'll get used to it I think."

Taking the plate, he sat up and looked to see what she had prepared. It was a plate of hot beans, and on the side, she had placed a piece of flat bread. When he looked at her, she still had the big smile on her face. Seeing his face, she produced a small laugh and looked at him.

"It's not like you packed any gourmet food for this trip you know," she smirked. "I had to do the best I could given the circumstances."

"Looks wonderful." He shrugged.

He remembered that Jorge had said he had packed some food in the back for the trip but never bothered to inspect it before he left. All he remembered was that there was enough for several days. Considering the climate, he didn't expect very much but still wanted to give her a hard time.

"Just eat it," she said, sitting back with her own plate.

"I'll try and get it down." He laughed.

"Just smile and chew as if you like it," she said, slapping his shoulder, "please."

"That's better," he commented, producing moans of pleasure with each bite.

"Okay, now you're overdoing it—stop."

"Sorry," he said, leaning back into the sand.

Looking over at the pile of rocks, it appeared that a dark stone slab that was covering the entrance fell off to the side. He didn't know if it had fallen from the storm or if the ground supporting it had eroded away. If it hadn't fallen, they might never have found the entrance or what might be behind it. Finishing his food, he turned and looked at the sun rising higher in the distance.

"Well, we better get going and see what's in that place," he said, tossing his plate over near the fire pit. "I'll grab the gear."

"And I'll clean up the breakfast," Ani said, grabbing up the plates.

"We might be able to check it out and still have time once we're done to close the distance back to the oasis."

Checking the supplies in the backpack, he picked it up and adjusted the straps. He glanced over at Ani as he checked to make sure the canteen was full. Putting it back into the cover, he slid the two covers over and snapped them into place. Ani wasn't having much luck with the pack and finally dropped it to the ground and looked at him.

"It's too heavy for me," she said, putting on the canteen belt.

"It's all right," he said, tossing it into the back of the Rover. "We'll do with what we have with us."

"Let's go," she said.

He shook his head as they headed off for the pile of rocks. It was only about a hundred yards to the entrance and, as they got closer, realized the entrance was larger than he expected it to be. Standing at the entrance, he looked it over before stepping through the loose sand and into the opening. On the other side of the small dune of sand, he turned and saw that Ani hadn't moved.

"So you coming?" he asked.

"There might be snakes inside," she told him, looking all around.

"Suit yourself," he said, turning, "but I'm going in."

"Wait," she yelled, causing him to stop.

"Yes?" He smiled.

"I'm coming but don't get too far ahead."

"I won't. Now come on."

Heading inside the opening of the tunnel, it became very narrow as earth tremors had caused rocks to come loose and fall. The deeper they entered, the more it became extremely treacherous. After only a few feet, the floor dropped steeply into the earth. Small pads of flat rock were the only thing keeping them from plunging down into the bottom. It appeared that they were placed strategically along the floor of the tunnel, allowing for better footing.

After a few feet, Johnny would turn to see if Ani was behind him. She was watching his every move to make sure she didn't fall or that there weren't any snakes coming out of the rocks near them. The tunnel became so narrow in spots they had to turn just to squeeze through. On the other side, he would help Ani wiggle through the unmoving rock.

On the other side, Johnny held up his lantern to check the pathway ahead of them. Ani was walking up to him and, when she looked up, took a step and fell on the slippery floor. With her scream, Johnny jumped back and caught her. Holding her in his arms, he waited until she caught her footing.

"Are you all right?" he asked.

"Yeah," she said, shaking her head. "I'll have to watch where I'm going and not on you."

"That might be a good idea in this place. Let's keep moving."

Finally, the tunnel leveled out and ended, opening up into a chamber. On the far wall was a huge statue carved in the form of a beaked head of a bird. Holding the lantern up high, Johnny instantly recognized it as the Egyptian deity Amun-Ra as the gold surfaces began to shimmer in the light. Seeing it, he walked into the middle of the room and paused.

"It *is* Amun-Ra," he gasped.

Moving the lantern, it allowed the light to highlight the structure. As he moved from side to side, shadows would dance across the sculpted surface, making the figure appear more imposing, almost ghostly. The large eyes were perfectly round and dark black. Lifting the light toward one of them, there was no reflection as if it simply absorbed the light.

"Why is this place even here?" Johnny asked.

Ani had walked over and swirled her hand in the water of the pool. He could see that she was looking all around and figured she was simply looking for snakes to appear as she sat on the edge. Coming over to her, he looked up and saw two figures looking at the other, which were delicately carved in the stone wall. He didn't recognize any of the figures, but none had gold or jewels adorning them. In their outstretched hands were water goblets being poured, and water flowed out to the pool below. Over to the side, the wall dipped away and the overflow disappeared into an opening to go back into the rock.

"This water is so cool," she said, continuing to swirl her hand in it. "Sure would feel good to take a swim in it after the heat of the desert."

"Maybe we can take a dip later…all right?"

"All right," she said, standing up and wiping her wet hand on her pants.

On the opposite wall was what looked to be a large rectangular stone altar. It was set on a piece of beautiful marble that was at least eight feet long and four feet wide. From the height of about two feet, he figured it had to weigh over a ton. Remembering the tunnel, he wondered how they could have gotten it down here. Mounted on either side of it were several torches placed strategically in the wall. He assumed from the position of the pieces in the chamber that it was used during some form of ceremony to prepare and purify the offerings that people were bringing to the god or gods.

"We need to keep going and check it all out."

"Sure." She smiled. "Maybe later we can take a dip when we come back out."

"Yeah, maybe," he told her, taking her arm.

They walked back to the mouth of the statue and looked at the smooth stone steps leading up inside. Holding the lantern down to one of the steps, he tried to read the inscription on the edge of each step.

"Do you know what they say?" she asked.

"Something about fearing the power of Ra," he said, moving to the steps and pointing, "and another passage about his servant Osiris, shepherd of souls in the underworld."

"I don't know about this," Ani told him.

"Hey, we've come this far, and listen"—he smiled—"no snakes so far."

"Yeah," she commented, looking around, "that's one good thing."

Going over and taking Ani's arm, they climbed up the steps together and entered the statue's mouth. Walking through the tunnel on the other side, the walls were smooth, carved down by thousands of hours of human work. He could just make out the marks from the tools they used. The tunnel ran for another hundred feet before they stepped out into another inner chamber several times larger than the previous one. Johnny and Ani stopped as they entered, frozen by the sight.

"I don't believe this," Johnny said, amazed.

Objects in the room began to glow as the light from the lanterns hit the crystals covering the interior walls and ceiling. He slowly walked out into the middle and, staring up, saw the entire ceiling light up. It was almost like looking up into the sky. The sight caused him to softly moan. This was something he had never seen and wanted to understand the principle of how it worked. Taking Ani's hand again, he pulled her close to his side.

"The ancients couldn't have known how to build something like this," he told her. "Even today, I don't think we could do it."

"Yet here it is," she said, looking at him.

"You're right. Here it is."

Walking out in the room, he slowly examined every pile he came to. He pressed his hand into one pile and grabbed a handful of jewels. Holding them in his hand, he could see that they were diamonds, rubies, and emeralds of all sizes. Tossing them back, he walked over to another pile containing coins and bars of gold. Looking at one of the gold coins, he didn't recognize the figure that had been pressed onto the surface. He saw that there were several large statues near one side of the room, all golden and standing in repose. Stepping up close, he slid his hands gently over the surface.

At the very back of the chamber, beyond all the piles was a small podium with a throne in the middle. It was made out of solid gold, and even from where he stood, he noticed that it was covered in glimmering jewels that artisans had mounted in every crevice. Walking over to it, he turned and plopped his body into the seat, throwing his leg over the armrest. Ani saw him and began to laugh.

"All hail the king," she said.

"I could probably get used to it but—"

"Are you saying it's really not you?"

"No, it's a little much," he said, standing back up. "Probably too much responsibility."

"Still," she said, coming over to him, "you looked good sitting there."

Turning, there was a spot behind the throne that caught his eye. Stepping behind it, he saw that there was another pedestal with delicate crystal panels swirling around it. Along the edges of the panels were layers of gold, highlighting each one, making them look almost like they were caressing the center portion.

As he walked up to it, the base began to pulse softly like a heartbeat creating subtle blues and greens. There was a small opening between the panels in the front that looked to be big enough for a person to access into the center. On each side of the opening near the base were small rectangular panels with strange writing on it. Kneeling beside one of them, he saw delicate writing that seemed to change as he looked at it. Over on the other panel was a specific depression as if something was supposed to be placed in it.

That must be what Dad sent me in the package, Johnny thought.

As it continued to pulse and change colors, Johnny stood up and stepped away. The pulses began to diminish as he moved away. Turning, he saw that Ani was not watching and examining a pile of raw jewels. Walking over to her, she had probably twenty cupped in her hand watching as they changed colors and sparkled when she moved.

"I think we need to leave," he told her.

"Who is going to believe this?" she asked, tossing the gems back on the pile.

"I really don't know," he said, looking around.

Over on one of the piles of coins were several small golden statues. Walking over to them, he picked one of them up and examined it. Placing it back in the pile, he picked up another one and smiled. The next one had writing on it near the base. Smiling, he opened his backpack and slid it inside and closed it up.

"Do you think that is wise?" she asked, watching him.

"Even if we never get a chance to come back, we need something," he told her, placing the pack over his shoulder. "We probably need to get going."

When they came out of the tunnel and back to the desert, he noticed that it was already starting to get dark. Grumbling that there wouldn't be enough time to pack up and make it back to the oasis, he let out a sigh. Making their way back to the camp, he looked over at her.

"It's gotten too late so we'll leave first thing in the morning," Johnny said, adjusting the pack and turning off the lantern. "If we start early, we should make good time heading back to town."

"So," she said, producing a devilish grin, "one more night in the desert, huh?"

Johnny just looked at her and smiled.

"Are you afraid to be with me one more night?"

"I was going to ask you the same question."

CHAPTER 19

JORGE HAD A terrible feeling in the pit of his stomach all the way to the hotel and was worried that Ani hadn't called since she left. That was several days ago, and he knew it wasn't like her not to at least call to let him know where she was or if she was going to be late just to settle his mind. With no call, he was afraid that something terrible might have happened to her. Walking into the hotel lobby, all he could think about and picture in his mind was her lying out in the hot desert, hurt or, worse, dying.

She should have called… She always calls, he thought.

Deciding he would go straight to Johnny's room, he bypassed the desk and thought he would get his frustration out by taking the stairs up to the third floor. All the way there, he couldn't shake the sickening feeling as it slowly overwhelmed him. Until he heard from her, he would not be able to shake it.

Reaching the top of the stairs, he stopped and leaned against the wall, glancing back and forth to see which way Johnny's room was located. The signs on the wall indicated they were to his right, and once his breathing calmed, he stepping toward the room. He began to grin as he walked, realizing the effort of climbing all those stairs and how he had almost raced up them to the top.

Seeing the room door, he noticed that it wasn't closed and was cracked open slightly. It didn't appear there were any lights on inside. Placing his hand against it, he slowly pushed it open and knocked.

"Hello," he said. "Is there anyone here?"

There was no answer, and he took a few steps farther inside. He could see a lamp across the room lying on the floor occasionally flickering on and off. All the cushions from the couch were pulled from it and leaning against the small table. Pictures, papers, and various items were scattered all over. It looked like someone had come in and ransacked the place.

Before he could move or think further, a figure came out from the side and tackled him to the ground. He didn't know what they wanted or why, but the blows hitting the side of his head indicated they wanted to hurt him.

Blocking a punch, Jorge swiftly lifted his knee and struck him in the groin. The blow caused the figure to pause and allowed him to get in a few punches of his own. One caused the figure to roll to the side, but he had a hold of his shirt, causing him to roll over with him. As he did, the figure was able to get his foot beneath him and shoved him away, crashing into the wall. The figure jumped up and rushed him.

Locked together, each fought to get the upper hand on the other. The dark figure slammed Jorge's head against the wall and then wrapped his arm around his neck. Trying to break his grip, the figure twisted and drove him into the wall head-first. He could feel blood across his face as the fall had created a gash in his forehead. The figure tightened his hold around his neck, choking him. Gasping for air, he tried desperately to slap at the figure's face but could feel the energy to fight further slipping from him. Blinking his eyes, his arms slowly became limp. Before he went unconscious, the figure released him and pushed him to the side.

Lying on his side, he held his throat and coughed trying to get air into his lungs. Knowing the figure might still be in the room, he rolled over to his back and looked around. The figure was standing only a few feet from him, pointing something at him.

"Why are you doing this?" he asked.

"Because," he said simply.

The shot was almost silent to his ears as Jorge instantly felt the burning when the bullet entered his body. Wanting to scream out, the pain flooded through him, stopping his throat from saying any words. Clutching his heaving chest, he could feel the warmth of his blood as it escaped his body from the wound.

Watching, the figure came over and, inspecting his work, kicked him violently in the side forcing all the remaining air in his lungs to be purged. Now he lay unable to breathe and wounded. His strength was gone, and he found he couldn't move. His eyes watched as the figure walked over the door and, glancing outside, disappeared. Raising his hand, the door clicked shut, and the room became dark.

"Oh, Ani," he moaned. "Where are you?"

Closing his eyes, he waited for the end to come, knowing there was no help.

CHAPTER 20

"**O**H MY GOD," she said, leaning over to the console. "What is it?" Johnny asked, seeing her frantic search. Digging through the items, she pulled out her cell phone.

"With everything going on, I completely forgot. My father is such a worrier, so I better let him know I'm all right and we'll be home soon."

Turning on the phone, she cursed softly, wondering why she had turned it off. She knew that she had earlier just to save power and knowing that there wouldn't be any service. Holding the phone up, the string of bars appeared and she sighed in relief. Ani then saw that there were several messages from her father on her phone

Dialing the number, she looked over at Johnny and smiled. Ringing several times, a different voice of a man she didn't recognize answered the phone.

"Hello," the voice answered quickly.

"Hello, who is this?" she asked, confused before looking at the screen to see if she had dialed the right number. The numbers were correct, and placing the phone back to her ear, she listened to the voice.

"This is Officer Dural with the Cairo police department, and who is this?"

"I'm Ani, Jorge's daughter," she said softly. "Where is my father, and why are you answering his phone?"

"I'm sorry, ma'am, but I have to inform you that he was shot earlier today."

"Uh, is he all right?" she said, straightening up in the seat. "Where is he?"

"Yes, he is alive and resting comfortably at the hospital, but I really have no other information than that."

"Thank you," she said. "I'll be there as soon as I can."

Hanging up the phone, she looked at Johnny.

"What's wrong?" he asked.

"My father has been shot and is in the hospital," she said, almost breaking down.

"I'll get you there as fast as I can drive."

"Thanks," she said, leaning back onto the window edge.

Walking out of the elevator, Carmen saw the nurse's station up ahead and went over to the counter. There were several nurses sitting behind it, doing paperwork in charts before one noticed her standing there and looked up.

"Can you tell me what room is Jorge in?" she asked.

The nurse checked the charts and, standing up, pointed down the hallway.

"He's down in room 234, on the right."

"Thank you." She smiled, heading for the room.

"I think that there are people inside with him," she indicated as she walked away.

"Okay, I won't bother them," she said.

As she got near the doorway, she began to hear voices inside and paused before slowly peeking around the corner. Inside, she saw Johnny and Ani with their backs to her and standing beside the bed. Wondering if she should go inside and disturb them, she heard Johnny say something that changed her mind.

"Ani, I don't think him getting shot was a coincidence, especially when it happened at my room. I don't know how, but it just has to be linked to what my father gave me. They must have been looking for it in my room, and he came in and they panicked."

"This…thing you have from your father," Ani asked, "did you tell anyone about it?"

"I don't think so," he said, trying to remember. "No…I'm sure I didn't."

"Then how could they even know?"

"Well, it might be just a guess on their part."

"So where is this thing?" Ani asked.

"When I got here, I didn't want to drag it with me so I placed it in the safe deposit boxes at the hotel."

"What is it that could be so important?"

"I don't know, but I'm going to find out."

As Carmen listened intently to their conversation, her eyes constantly scanned the area to see if anyone might approach and see her standing by the doorway. Hearing their voices beginning to get lower, she leaned closer to the edge of the doorway to hear clearer. When she did, out of the corner of her eye, she then saw Detective Deniko come around the corner from the other hallway. She quickly took several steps across the hallway near an empty room just to get away from the door. Rummaging around in her purse, she tried to act like she was looking for something.

"Carmen," Deniko said, surprised to see her.

"Oh, Detective." She smiled, looking up at him.

"What are you doing here?" he asked softly, looking around.

"I heard about Jorge and just thought I would come and see him."

"Really?" he said, surprised. "Did you see him?"

"No, I haven't because his daughter and some others are in there with him."

He took her into the empty patient room, sweeping her quickly into his arms. Holding her, he kicked the door closed and kissed her deeply. As he did, her arms folded against his chest and her body molded to him.

"I just can't take this anymore," she said, holding her hands against his chest and almost breaking down into sobs. "I think he might suspect about us and with the denials and secret rendezvous as we slip around… If I get caught, he'll kill me. Or worse, send me back to that awful place."

"That won't happen, and besides, it won't be much long…I promise."

"You keep saying that."

"This time it's different," he said, lifting her chin with his hand. "I finally heard from a friend of mine, and he has gotten me a job that is far away from this place."

"How far can we go that he can't reach us?"

"It's a job in England." He grinned. "How's that sound?"

"I…I don't know," she said with a blank expression. "I've never really been to England before. Is it a nice place?"

"You'll like it, and if you don't, we'll just go somewhere else."

"Okay." She smiled as he pulled her close and kissed her.

"I need to go see Jorge and check on his condition. I'll meet up you later. Just call me later and I'll tell you all about it."

Nodding, he kissed her once more and stepped out of the room. Watching him disappear into the room, she took a deep breath and left the hospital. Getting outside, she walked down the sidewalk and around the corner. Parked next to the curb was the black limousine. As she approached it, the driver got out and, coming around, opened the back door. Settling in the seat, he looked over at her.

"Well, did they say anything?"

"He indicated that he had something locked in the hotel safe and that it was sent to him by his father. From what I could hear, he suspects that Jorge getting shot was caused by someone looking for it."

"That is exactly what I expect from you," he said, squeezing her chin. "Information I can use."

"He also indicated that he brought back something from the desert."

"Really?" he said as his eyes widened.

"How will you get it from him?" she asked cautiously.

"Don't worry about that. I have a perfect plan in mind." He smiled to her while holding out his glass. "Freshen up my drink and, since you were so good, make one for yourself."

Taking the glass from his hand, she slid forward to the bar and poured some liquor in his glass. Turning, she handed it back to him before fixing her own drink. Moving back beside him, he hand placed his glass in the console beside him and had the phone up to his ear. Settling back his hand came over and rested on top of her thigh, pushing her dress away.

"Yes," he barked into the phone. "I have a job for you and it needs to be done now."

Sipping her drink, she listened to him command the people on the phone as he gave them instructions. It appeared they did not say a word and only listened. When he was done, he paused to hear what they had to say.

"I know the risks and your fee will be doubled, but it has to be now," he told them before hanging up. Tossing the phone down, he picked up his glass and looked toward the front.

"Hades, I believe we have a little time and I'm hungry. Once you drop us off at the restaurant, I need you to go back and check out the vehicle they were driving. Maybe they left what they found inside it. I need to know exactly what they found in the desert."

"Yes, sir," he said.

"Then when you're done, come back pick us up."

"It will be done."

Widdal smiled and then looked over at Carmen. "Now then…"

She didn't like the look on his face or what he might have in mind but smiled back.

"Yes," she said, sipping her drink.

There was now only the silence and the road noise as he stared over at her.

Now what? she thought, looking at his eyes.

CHAPTER 21

JOHNNY WAS SITTING in the chair near the window and watched Ani standing vigilantly beside the bed. Her eyes were focused on Jorge, looking for any sign that he was all right as they waited for the doctor. He watched Ani tenderly stroke his arm while holding his hand. It was such a helpless feeling knowing all they could do was wait and listen to the beeping monitors in the room.

When they heard footsteps nearing the doorway, they both looked and saw that it was only Deniko entering the room. He smiled to them and saw the disappointment in their faces as they produced a sigh while he walked to the end of the bed. In the silence, his eyes scanned over the machines hooked up to Jorge on either side of the bed.

"So is he all right?" he finally asked them.

"We don't really know for sure," Ani said. "All the nurses would tell us is that the surgery went well, but there are still some complications. We're waiting for the doctor to come in from his rounds and talk to us."

With nothing further, the silence returned. He watched as Ani adjusted the chair beside the bed and, leaning over on the edge, picked up his hand and kissed it. Knowing that there wasn't much he could do or say, he turned and motioned with his head for Johnny to step outside with him. Nodding, he got up and started to follow him outside the room before stopping.

"I'll be right outside if you need anything," Johnny told her.

"That's fine," she said meekly, never turning her head.

When they left the room, Ani turned around to see exactly where they were. She got up and peeked around the edge of the doorway and saw that they had walked down near the nurse's station halfway down the hallway. Returning to the bed, she looked down at Jorge and caressed his cheek.

"It will be fine." She smiled. "I will make sure."

Knowing she had very little time, she placed her hand out flat just above his chest and closed her eyes. Her hand began to glow, and Jorge started to moan. Within seconds, her hand was a bright yellow and pulsed. A moment later, she clinched her hand and the glow quickly faded. Opening her eyes, she looked down at him and smiled.

"We're all done," she whispered. "Go to sleep and heal."

Turning her hand over, she opened it and saw the gray fragments of the bullet that were inside him lying in her palm. Looking over to the table, there was a cup, and reaching over, she let the small pieces drop inside. Wiping her hand on her pants, she returned her hand to his chest and felt his chest rise and fall as he breathed. It appeared normal to her and she smiled. Hearing a noise, she turned and saw a doctor wearing a white smock walking into the room holding a chart in his hand.

"Excuse me, but are you the daughter?" he asked, looking at the chart.

"Yes, I'm Ani."

"It might be better if, as I explain his condition to you, I show you his charts and his chest x-rays on a monitor. Will you come with me?"

"Certainly," she said, stepping toward him.

Exiting the room, she paused and looked down the hallway but didn't see Johnny or Deniko to tell them that the doctor had finally come. Thinking they would find out later, she followed the doctor as he led her down the hallway the other way and to a small room around the corner.

"We can speak in here," he told her, opening the door.

Walking inside, she saw that another technician was near the back of the room folding sheets on a gurney. The room wasn't that large but didn't see any monitors. It looked more like a simple holding room after someone had a procedure done. When she began to turn to ask what was going on, a hand clamped tightly across her mouth. The man behind her held her tightly as she began to struggle and grab his hand trying to scream out. She then saw the other man begin to walk toward her and frantically began kicking at him.

"Don't struggle and make this harder," she heard one of them say to her.

Instantly, she felt a sharp stab in her neck as something sharp penetrated the skin. She then saw the syringe as he tossed it to the floor. The room began to spin, and she could feel her body becoming weak. Her struggle became slower, and finally, her arms dropped and became limp. Picking her up, the man carried her over to the gurney and laid her down. She could see but couldn't resist against them.

"It is only a strong sedative," the man told her looking at her face.

They adjusted her arms and legs before strapping her down. Taking one of the sheets they covered her so only her head was showing. Placing a netting over her head, they then put a mask over her mouth. She found she couldn't keep her eyes open, and the room was spinning wildly. As they turned the gurney to take her out, the room slowly went dark as she faded away into a deep sleep.

Johnny and Deniko walked back into Jorge's room and saw that Ani wasn't there. He figured that she might have just gone to the bathroom or gone to get something to drink. He figured he would just wait until she returned. After about a half hour and she hadn't returned, he was getting anxious. When he stood up, a doctor came into the room. Johnny knew that this is what she was waiting for, and now his concern grew larger.

"Are you the patient's relatives?" the doctor asked.

"No, sir," Johnny said. "I'm just a friend and this is Detective Deniko."

"Oh," the doctor said somewhat, surprised. "Are any of them around?"

"His daughter is here, but she seems to have stepped out."

"Well, since she's not here and I have to see other patients, I'll just swing back later."

"Thank you, Doctor," Johnny told him. "I know she wants to know exactly how her father is doing. I'm sure she won't be long."

The doctor walked over beside the bed and checked Jorge. When he was done, he pressed a few buttons on the monitors before scribbling some notes in his chart. Smiling, he turned and left. When he left the room, he looked over at Deniko.

"I wonder where she went to," Johnny asked.

"Beats me."

"I'm going to go look for her. Will you stay here in case she returns?"

"Most certainly," he said, sitting down in the chair. "I'll let her know you're looking for her if she comes back."

"Thanks," Johnny said, heading out of the room.

Checking with the nurse's station, he asked if any of them had seen her. When they indicated they hadn't, he began to search the entire floor. Walking up and down the hallways, he looked in every room to see if she might have stopped to visit someone. Checking the entire floor, he then thought that she might have gone outside to get some air. Taking the elevator to the ground floor, he went through the lobby and looked in the various shops. Not seeing her, he went outside and looked around. Looking up and down the street, he didn't see her standing around. Now he didn't know what to think. It wasn't like her to simply disappear.

Standing near the front doors, he rubbed his chin trying to think of where she would go or somewhere he might have missed. With people passing him, he knew he was in the way and stepped over to the side next to the building. Standing and thinking, his eyes scanned the people, hoping to get a glance of her. In the back of his mind, the only place he didn't check thoroughly was the cafeteria. He figured he would start there and check the hospital one more time. As he moved, a hand grasped his arm, and he turned to see who it was.

"Carmen," he said, shocked to see her, "what are you doing here?"

"They told me to find you," she said almost in tears.

"What's going on?"

He noticed that there was a bruise under her eye as if she had been struck.

"Several men grabbed me off the street and said they are watching me. Their instructions were that I come here and give you this to you," she said, holding out her trembling hand. There was a slip of paper clutched in her fingers. When he took it and opened it to read it, she began to cry and fell against him.

"Oh my god," he gasped, reading the slip of paper.

"They said they would kill me," she said between the cries.

"Why would they do this?" he said, looking around.

"I heard one of the men say they wanted something…something you have."

Listening to her matched the instructions on the note.

Bring the package to the warehouse 42 in the storage district and she lives.

"I have to go," he told her, pushing her away. She clung to him and won't let him go.

"I'm coming with you," she said, holding tightly to his arm.

"No, Carmen, it's too dangerous."

"But they could come back for me," she said, looking at him, pleading, "and kill me."

"All right," he said, relenting and believing that she might be next on their list. "But when we get there, you have to stay back and hidden."

"I will, I promise, but just don't leave me alone."

"Fine, let's go," he said grudgingly

Taking her hand, they walked to the parking lot and, finding his Rover, got in. It was only about twenty minutes, and he pulled up to the front of the hotel and, parking, told her to stay put and he'd be right back. Leaving it running he got out and headed through the front doors. The doorman stopped him.

"You can't park here," he told him.

"I just have to get something from the desk clerk and then I'll be gone," he told him. "Five minutes at the very most, all right?"

"If not, they will tow it away even with someone in it."

"Five minutes," he said, holding up his hand with five fingers. "Tops!"

Heading inside, he quickly went up to the counter and told the attendant behind it that he needed to get into his security box. Telling her his name and handing her his key card, he stood impatiently by the counter. He watched as she checked the computer and turning, unlocked the box door and slid out the container inside. Placing it on the counter, Johnny quickly flipped it open and grabbed his package. Thanking her, he turned and briskly walked to the doors. Seeing the doorman, he checked his watch and grinned.

"Four minutes," he told him, never stopping until he reached the Rover door.

Starting to drive away, he suddenly turned and began to rummage through the console before slamming it shut and cursing.

"What's wrong?" Carmen asked him.

"I don't know where this place is located and I don't have my GPS."

"I know where it is," she said, looking at the streets.

"Tell me then," he said angrily. "We don't have much time."

"Turn right up here at the next light."

Hoping she actually knew where to go, he did as she indicated, following her instructions down the avenues and business streets. The whole time he drove, he would check his watch and knew that time was slipping by and he had to hurry. Several times he swerved to miss a slow car, jumping into the other lane to avoid hitting them before coming back into his lane. Each time Carmen would just look at him and hold on. Finally, they came to several old warehouses, and she pointed to a street on the left.

"Turn in here," she told him. "I think it is the building down on the right."

Pulling up, the building looked run-down and no one had been there in years. Parking in front of a side door, they got out and looked around. He didn't see any other cars parked nearby, and there wasn't any noise, just the wind whistling through the buildings and broken glass windows.

"Are you sure this is the place?"

"I'm almost sure it is," she said, looking at the building.

"All right," he said, getting out. Leaning in, he grabbed the package from the seat and shut the door. "Just stay behind me, and if and when I tell you, I want you to find a hiding spot, got it?"

Heading for a door near them, Carmen followed close with her hand on his back. Checking the door, he found it unlocked and, turning the doorknob, slowly pushed it open, trying to be quiet. He didn't know who was inside waiting and didn't want to give them a hint they were there until he figured out the situation.

Once inside, there was machinery of all types all over the place that were covered almost completely in a layer of dirt. Patches of white spider webs hung from every bar and created barriers he had to knock down to get through. Seeing the long strands intact meant that no one had passed through them recently. He hoped seeing the intact strands meant he could possibly surprise the people waiting for him.

Moving past a large tank, he looked over and saw Ani tied in a chair in the middle of a large area. Stopping Carmen, he indicated that he wanted her to stay where she was while he checked out the area. She nodded that she understood and slid against the side of tank. He smiled and walked to the side behind another tank. Glancing back at Carmen, she was still crouched beside the tank and was watching him.

When he reached the end, he looked around and couldn't see anybody and focused over at Ani. She was tired to a chair and he could see a wide piece of tape covering her mouth. Her head hung forward, but it seemed she was all right and could see her breathing. That simple fact relieved him. Figuring it had to be now or never, he took a deep breath, stood up, and rushed over to her. Reaching her, he took her face and lifted it before looking around the area.

"Ani," he said softly, "Ani, it's me Johnny."

She didn't answer but did produce a low moan. Carefully peeling the piece of tape away from her mouth and tossing to the floor, he watched her breathe deeply. Reaching down, he started to hurriedly begin to untie the ropes binding her legs to the chair. Struggling with the ropes, he then heard steps behind and then a voice.

"Ah, Mr. Cortez," the voice stated, "glad you made it on time."

Turning around, he recognized the man. It was Widdal. He had several other men with him including his bodyguard. Struggling in the arms of one of the men was Carmen. She hadn't hidden herself as well as he told her. Reaching him and Ani, they stopped and looked at the two of them.

"Figures all this was a result of your doing," Johnny stated.

"Come now," he said, walking over to Ani. "Do you really think that I don't know things, especially concerning your activities?"

"Did you shoot Ani's father?"

Ani was now becoming awake and making noises as her head began to roll around and blink her eyes. Reaching over, Widdal grabbed her chin and twisted it toward him. Her eyes widened, seeing him and tried to pull away. Feeling her arms and legs tied she, struggled still trying.

"That minor incident is behind us now," he laughed, releasing her face. She looked over and saw Johnny standing near her. "We have much more important business between us to attend to."

"Is this what you did all this for?" he asked, holding up the package.

"That is only part of this process."

Walking over to him, one of the men followed him as he reached out for the package in Johnny's hands. The gun in his hands kept him from trying anything and he handed it over to him. Walking away, Widdal carefully took the wrapping covering the package and produced a soft moan of pleasure when he saw it. He then nodded to the men who came over and began to tie his hands behind his back.

"You got what you wanted, now let us go," he told him.

"Not just yet," he said, stepping over and taking Carmen by the back of the neck, pulled her close, and kissed her.

"Carmen," Johnny said, surprised.

She ignored him and wrapped her arms around his waist, accepting the kiss as his hand began to caress her body. When he was done, he stepped to the side, allowing her to look over at him.

"I'm sorry, Johnny," she said, walking over to him. "This would have been so simple if you just would have mentioned what you had and where it was when we were together. I sort of enjoyed it when we got together."

"I'm glad someone did," he said, watching Widdal and the others behind her.

"Oh, come on, I know you enjoyed it," she said, looking over at Ani while she reached down and grabbed him. Rubbing him, she grinned. "Especially what I did for you the other night in your hotel."

"I knew what you were up to the whole time."

"Sure, you did." She laughed, licking his cheek. With a grin to Ani, she stepped back and walked over to Widdal's side.

Looking at Widdal, she could see that there was only a small smile across his face. She wasn't sure why he had made the face but knew she had done exactly like he asked. Kissing her cheek, he reached up and gently stroked her face.

"I'm so disappointed in you," he told her.

"I did everything you asked," she said, confused.

"And then some."

"Carmen," Johnny asked, "why?"

"Because, Johnny, it's what he wanted me to do," she said softly. "He owns me and I obey all his wishes."

"That's a very obedient slave." Widdal chuckled.

Stepping back, he pulled the gun from his waist just as she turned and looked at Johnny. He lifted it quickly to her temple and he pulled the trigger. Ani screamed out in horror, watching her head fold to the side with the impact of the bullet as it tore through her skull. Her body leaned to the side, and she fell limply to the floor in a heap. Watching her fall, he watched and just shook his head.

"That was such a shame," Widdal said, kneeling beside her.

"You are such an evil bastard," he told him, struggling against the man holding him. "I suppose now you're going to do the same thing to us now that you got what you wanted."

"Carmen had served out her usefulness, and besides, there are so many others out there who are more than willing to step in and take her place," Widdal said while stroking her cheek. "This had to happen because she was having feelings about you, and it kept her from doing her job properly. I'm strictly a businessman, and I can't have that."

"What do you really want, Widdal?"

"I want you to take me to the spot in the desert you visited."

"But we didn't find anything," he told him, lying.

"For your sake, I hope you're wrong because if there isn't anything, then that is where you will both die. I know from what your father told me and what you've been doing since you have arrived, there is something fantastic out there. You will not keep me from it."

"And if there is something out there?"

"Then I might feel gracious and let you live," he said. "It's time to go."

He then instructed the men to clean up any evidence they were there. When they asked about Carmen, he began to laugh.

"Once we've left, place a call to the police and tell them that there was a shooting. Let them come out and take care of the mess. Just make sure they can't tie it back to us."

"Yes, sir," they said.

One of the men untied Ani's arms and legs. Once they were free, he quickly bound them behind her back and pushed her forward. Widdal's bodyguard grabbed them by the arm and pushed them, indicating they should begin to follow him outside. Passing Carmen on the floor, they could see the large pool of blood surrounding her head. Ani looked over at Johnny, and he knew what she was thinking.

I just hope that isn't us later out on the desert sand.

"It's time to go, people," Widdal indicated, raising his hand.

CHAPTER 22

OUTSIDE THE BUILDING, they got into the back of the limousine and headed for the small airport. With Widdal beside Ani and him on the other, Hades sat in front of them with the gun ready for any movement they may try. Slowly struggling against his bonds behind his back, there was nothing he could do to break them. Glancing over to Ani, he could see the fear growing on her face.

"It'll be all right," he leaned over and told her softly.

"I know it will," she said, producing a weak smile.

God, I have to think of something to get us out of this, he thought.

When they finally stopped and got out of the back, he could see a helicopter several few feet away that was waiting and beginning to warm up. Standing beside the door, Johnny saw Widdal walk quickly over to the other side and get in next to the pilot. Feeling a hard push from behind, he glanced back as Hades smiled and pointed. He then jabbed the gun hard into the small of his back to insist. His other hand pushed Ani ahead of him. With their hands tied, it was hard to climb into the back. After sitting down, Hades strapped the harnesses around them and took his seat, holding the gun toward them. Widdal turned in his seat to them.

"Now then," Widdal said sternly, "the coordinates of the spot if you please."

Johnny saw him pointing his pistol at Ani and knew he had no choice.

"It's in my left shirt pocket," Johnny said, motioning with his head.

Hades reached over and pulled out the small paper and handed over his shoulder to Widdal. Taking it, he quickly read it and, smiling, gave it to the pilot before turning back to them.

"This is going to be a great day." He grinned. "For all of us."

"The location is only about forty minutes away," the pilot told him.

"Excellent," he told him with a slap. "Shall we go?"

The drone of the swirling blades increased, and the helicopter lifted into the air. Widdal turned and placed his headsets on so he could talk to the pilot. Leaning his head back against the seat he watched as they headed out over the desert and to the site. He wondered what would happen once they got there and if they would be allowed to live.

Looking out the window, Johnny noticed that they were flying very low, maybe only a couple of hundred feet above the sand. It was obvious that they didn't want to be shown on any of the radar sites around the area. With only a glance at the foot in his chest, he concentrated on the bland landscape.

Speeding along for about a half an hour, he then began to notice a long caravan of what he thought were wandering camels growing larger in the distance. From what he could tell, there had to be at least a few hundred people with camels loaded down with all of their belongings and livestock. Many of them walked beside the animals, and when they flew over, it appeared to startle many of the animals. Watching them scatter in all directions, Widdal let out a laugh and slapped the pilot on the shoulder as they continued on.

After almost another twenty minutes of silence, the helicopter began to circle, and Widdal pointed over to the ground. The pilot nodded and slowly sat the helicopter on the ground. Johnny instantly recognized the formation of rocks and could see the small entrance as the blades began to slow. The side door slid open, and Widdal stood beside it with his weapon.

"Time to show me the rest of what you found," he said, waving the pistol and motioning for him to get out.

Hades reached over and unbuckled his harness. As he twisted and stepped out onto the sand, the heat hit him in the face. He then turned and saw that he was also unbuckling Ani from her seat. After she was free, he then motioned for her to get out. Once she was out and standing beside Johnny, they began to slowly walk toward the entrance. Near the opening, he stopped hearing the helicopter, take off.

"No need to worry." Widdal grinned. "He's just going a short distance but will be back in thirty minutes or when I tell him. Keep going."

"Fine, but once we're inside, it's not that easy and there are several tunnels. In the dark, we could slip and fall," he told him, turning his body as the helicopter began to disappear in the distance. "We'll need our hands to keep our balance and hold the lantern."

"Fine," he said, nodding over to Hades, "but she stays tied up."

Once Johnny's ropes were cut, he rubbed his wrists and looked at the black shape getting smaller. Turning, he took a lantern from Hades and headed for the entrance. Heading inside, the tunnel was extremely treacherous and, after only a few feet, dropped steeply into the earth. Small pads of flat rock were the only thing keeping them from plunging down into the bottom. Johnny would turn and see that Widdal watched his every move to make sure he was leading them correctly. The tunnel was so narrow in spots they had to squeeze through the small openings in the solid rock.

Johnny held up one lantern as he led them along, and Widdal was near the back holding up another. Ani was walking behind him and fell several times on the slippery floor. Johnny would hear her scream out and catching her, helped her up. Hades would then motion for them to keep going.

Finally, the tunnel leveled out and ended, opening up into the first chamber. On the far wall was the huge statue, the beaked head of a bird. Even from the back, Widdal instantly recognized it as the Egyptian deity Amun-Ra as the gold surfaces began to shimmer in the increasing light. Seeing it, he quickly pushed past them before holding up his lantern and pausing.

"Amun-Ra," he gasped.

Moving the lantern, it allowed the light to highlight the structure. As he moved from side to side, shadows would dance across the sculpted surface, making the figure appear more imposing, almost ghostly. The large eyes were perfectly round and dark black. Lifting the light toward one of them, there was no reflection as if it simply absorbed the light.

"Magnificent," Widdal gasped, examining the eyes, "absolutely magnificent."

Walking over to the pool, he swirled his hand in the cool water and saw the figures carved in the stone above it. He didn't recognize any of the figures, but none had gold or jewels adorning them. Surveying the wall, he noticed that in several places water flowed out and into the pool below before the overflow drained out and back into the rocks near him. He then walked back to the mouth and looked at the stone steps.

"What do they say?" he asked.

"Well, the loose translation of the inscription is," he said, moving to the steps and pointing, "'all fear the mighty wrath of Ra, he who is the giver of life and master of Osiris, shepherd of souls in the underworld.'"

"Fear," he scoffed. "I fear nothing that has been dead for thousands of years."

"It is a loose translation I said."

"Let's move on," he said, waving his pistol.

Going over and taking Ani's arm, they climbed up the steps and entered the statue's mouth. Walking through the smoothly carve tunnel for another hundred feet, they came out into another more inner chamber several times larger than the previous one. Johnny led Ani to the side and allowed Widdal to enter.

"Well, this is it," Johnny said, waving his hand around. "Hope it's what you thought."

"Oh yes," Widdal gasped as the room began to light up, "and more."

The room began to glow as the light from the lanterns hit the crystals covering the interior walls. He walked out into the middle and moaned from glee. Hades pushed them farther into the room so he could watch them. Taking Ani's arm again, he held her close to his side.

Widdal looked like he was a kid in a candy shop, bouncing from pile to pile, examining everything around him. He began by grabbing handfuls of jewels and, looking at them in the light, tossed them into the air before going to another pile. Near one side of the room, he stepped over to a large golden statue, stroking the surface gently with his hand.

"This has to be almost as good as finding King Solomon's mines!"

"If you believe all the legends it might be," Johnny said.

Watching him walk around, he suddenly stopped, standing in front of the portal.

"Yes, this has to be it," he yelled out before turning to them. "Isn't it?"

"Has to be what?" Johnny asked, seeing the glow in his eyes.

"This has to be the doorway your father mentioned," he told him, "the one that leads to the greatest of all treasures. It has to be it."

Widdal walked over to him and took out the amulet in his pocket. Flipping the cloth covering away, he handed it over to him while pointing the weapon at his head. The look in his eyes indicated that operating the portal was his whole focus.

"I said…make it work," he commanded still staring at it.

"I don't know how it works," he said, watching him, "I swear."

"I won't ask again."

"Really, I don't know—"

Widdal didn't wait for him to finish and, turning slightly and without saying another word, fired his weapon. The bullet struck Ani in the upper chest, and she screamed out in pain. Watching her face contort, Johnny could see the blood beginning to soak the material of her shirt as she crumpled to the ground near his feet. Grabbing her before she hit the ground, he cradled her head and held her delicately in his arms.

"Ani," he said, looking at her, "stay with me, please."

"I'll…I'll try," she said softly as blood dripped from the corner of her mouth.

"You bastard," Johnny turned and screamed angrily.

"If you want to save her, you'll do as I ask. Once you have operated the portal, you can then get her the help she needs…perhaps even in time."

Johnny turned back to Ani and, reaching down, ripped a big strip of his undershirt away, packing the wound to try and stop the bleeding. She moaned as he slipped it beneath her shirt and pressed it against her skin. From her expression, he knew she was in a great deal of pain but couldn't do anything more to help her. His hand from beneath her was covered in blood and thought that the bullet had passed straight through her body. He knew that she really needed a doctor.

"She needs a doctor," he then told him.

"Probably, but right now, you're wasting your precious time being stubborn," he said, becoming frustrated. Stepping back, he motioned for him to leave her and go to the machine. "Now activate the machine!"

Johnny stared down at Ani and wondered what to do. Holding her, Widdal bellowed behind him and knew time was running out. He had to do something or she would die here in the chamber. Turning, he saw him moving closer to the portal, inspecting every inch probably trying to figure out how he could salvage all the precious material. His eyes were big and his mouth hung open at the thought of more gold and riches. He was a man totally possessed and wouldn't stand for anything other than what was in his mind. The next question from him was obvious.

"I've given you enough time," he said, turning to him. "Make it work."

"If I can I'll try."

"Do you know how it works?"

"The only thing I can think of it's a machine that is older than humanity. It bends space so the traveler can go to another location."

"Yes, go on," Widdal said, never taking his eyes off the golden blades. Several times he would glance back at Johnny.

"The platform is where the person travelling would stand and the panels would create a field to stop time before bending space and prepare the traveler to go to another place."

Widdal stepped around the golden blades into the center of the platform. He looked around before lifting the gun and pointing at him.

"This is your last chance," he stressed. "Make it work or you will both die and I'll find another way to get it to operate."

"Are you willing to do this on a guess?"

Widdal remained on the platform still pointing the gun at Johnny.

"Yes."

"Even if I were to get it operating, I don't know if there is even oxygen to breathe in the place it will take you."

Widdal didn't look affected or worried at all by his comment. Johnny continued. "You could die as soon as you got there and then what? Even if you see this treasure you think is there, you couldn't bring any of it back."

"I'll find a way," he stressed.

"I think this is only for people and the magnetic field won't allow any type of metal to be transferred back and forth."

"This," he said, waving his hand around the chamber, "didn't all come from here. There has to be even more on the other side."

"I just wanted to make you aware of the dangers and—"

"I don't care about any of your scientific ramblings. This portal made it to our planet without any troubles, and if there are riches from where this machine came from, then there will be plenty of gold for me. I'll be rich beyond anyone on Earth. So are you going to do as I say or just let me kill you where you sit?"

Widdal stepped from the platform and pointed the gun barrel to his temple. Looking at his eyes, he pressed harder against his head.

"Okay," Johnny said, "I'll make you a deal."

"A deal." He laughed. "I have a gun and hold all the cards."

"But you don't have the gold…yet."

Widdal pulled the gun slowly away from his head.

"I'm listening, go ahead."

"If I get the machine to run, you'll let Ani and I go free."

Johnny waited for him to reply

"First of all, I don't care how you start, but you need to just do it. If you can make it work and it sends me to the land of riches, then who cares about your pathetic lives? You can't make me any money anyways! This is a deal."

Widdal lowered his gun and stepped back. He stood with his arms crossed, waiting to see what Johnny was going to do.

Johnny walked over to the portal and kneeled down to one of the panels. He turned and reached out with his hand, wanting the package he had taken from him. Pulling the wrap from his pack, he handed it to him. Unwrapping it, he looked at it.

Dad, I sure hope you sent me the key.

Johnny looked up as though he was talking to something in space and then looked down. He took out the object and placed it on the ground. The package was a small plastic container with something silver inside. Johnny took the plastic apart and opened it. It was a round silver-type ornament with designs on the surface. On one side was a picture of a planet and on the other side was a golden sun. He smiled, noticing that the ornament was the same size as the depression on the panel and then looked back at him.

"You have to come and stand on the platform."

Widdal walked over to the platform and, holding the gun at him, carefully stood in the middle between the golden blades. Johnny noticed that the platform wasn't pulsing as it had when he first discovered it. Glancing up, Widdal had spread his feet as a rod materialized behind him, allowing him to rest his back against it. He didn't take his eyes from Johnny, watching every move he performed as he adjusted his position.

Johnny knew he had to get it operating before he could do anything for Ani. He didn't know exactly what he was doing, but it looked like it was beginning to operate. Deep inside his gut, something guided him while he fought back the anger within him. He had to have a clear mind to do this.

"Once I start this, there is no going back," he told him. "There really isn't an 'off' switch that I'm aware of."

"Just do it," he said in anticipation.

"It will take you...somewhere."

"No worries since in moments, I'll be rich beyond belief. Hurry, get me to my gold."

Johnny inserted the silver object into the spot, and the platform began to pulse and produce the green and blue colors he had noticed before. Once he did, the blades began to vibrate, causing a tone to fill the room. Widdal appeared a bit scared at first and in fear but never moved. Reaching over, he placed his hand on the other box that had risen from the floor to almost the height of his waist and glowed brightly. Pulling his hand back, he took several steps away and watched. Between the blades, small bursts of light appeared and swirled around Widdal. As the number of lights increased, a wind swirled around the platform, blowing leaves and sand around. He saw Widdal start to move.

"Stay on the platform and don't move," Johnny shouted.

Johnny saw him lifting his gun up toward him.

"You bastard," he grimaced. "You tricked me."

"No, just be patient and let the machine operate."

Johnny took another few steps slowly away and Widdal noticed it. As he pointed his gun at him, it suddenly flipped from his hand into the air and landed on the ground about ten feet from him. Then, in a few moments, the air became normal and the blades glowed constantly. A glowing cloud of sparkling light surrounded Widdal, and in a burst of light, he was gone. Walking over, Johnny removed the amulet from the panel and stuck in his pocket. Grabbing the gun, he ran back over to Ani.

"We have to get you out of here and to a doctor," Johnny said, picking her up in his arms.

CHAPTER 23

RIVING BACK TO the hospital from the police station, Deniko's thought about everything in the file. They had come up with nothing except elusive leads that led nowhere. Even his sources could provide nothing in the way of evidence to charge Widdal with anything. He pounded on the edge of the steering wheel several times in frustration. Just then, the radio began to crackle and a voice came on. Trying not to hit the swerving cars all around him, he listened to the voice coming over the speaker. It indicated they had a report of a shooting at one of the riverfront warehouses and they have a body. They are requesting the nearest detective to respond. Gritting his teeth, he picked up the mic.

"This is car 17, Detective Deniko," he told them. "I'm five minutes from the location and responding."

"All units," the voice indicated, "car 17 responding. Supervisor is on the way."

Making a left at the next light, he headed for the location of the shooting. He knew Jorge and Ani were good people and just didn't understand why Widdal would involve them in his dealings or for that matter have Jorge shot. There were no witnesses and no evidence, but one way or the other, he was going to find out.

Dammit, I have to get this guy, he thought.

The warehouse district appeared on his left, and he pulled down one of the streets. He could now see several police cars with lights flashing up ahead parked beside one of the buildings. Pulling up beside them, he stopped and got out. Walking toward the doorway, he saw several officers talking. Coming up to them, they turned to him.

"So," he said, pausing, "what do we have here?"

"A single white female," one of them said. "It looks like she might have come here for some reason and then shot. There is no sign of a struggle, which means she probably knew her attacker."

"Do we have any idea of who she is?" he asked, stepping past them.

"Not yet, sir, we're still checking."

"What about any witnesses?"

"There are a half-dozen men checking the surrounding area."

Walking inside, there were several more officers standing beside a cover that they had placed over the body. Nearing it, he could see a pool of blood on the floor, and the cover had soaked some of it up into the material. Kneeling beside it, he looked at the legs sticking out from the edge and shook his head. Grabbing the edge, he pulled it back to look at her. When her face appeared, he gasped and almost fell backward. One of the officers saw him and grabbed him by the arm.

"Do you know her, sir?" he asked.

"Yeah, I know her," he said, almost breaking down into tears.

Looking at her, he remembered the first time he had seen her. It was at Widdal's home when he went to ask him some questions. She was walking down the winding staircase wearing a beautiful and silky red dress. He didn't remember what he said to him as his eyes were focused on her coming over to him as he listened to her heels click on the hard tile floor. In his eyes, she was the most beautiful woman he had ever seen, attractive and young. During his early years, there we others he had feelings for, but nothing compared to her.

He remembered how the dress she wore accented every curve of her body, and he found he could not keep his eyes from looking at her. Everything she wore from her heels, nails, and lipstick were a bright cherry red. Walking up to him, she shook his hand, and he finally felt the smoothness of her skin. All he could remember was his heart began to melt and race holding her warm hand. No other woman had affected him the way she did during that first meeting, and seeing her this way saw all his plans smashed and crumble into pieces.

"Oh, Carmen," he moaned. "What did you do?"

With her laying on the hard concrete, his jaws began to tighten in rage. He knew that Widdal had something to do with her death and he had to get him no— no matter what or who might get into the way! Anything else in his life didn't matter any longer, not even his job. Pulling the cover back over her, he stood up and simply stare at the form.

Walking out to his car, he pulled his mike out. Speaking on the radio, he issued a command to use every available means to locate Widdal and any of his associates. Tossing the mike back onto the seat, he leaned his head against the roof and closed his eyes, his mind flooded with the thought of Carmen.

"Sir," an officer said.

"Yes?"

When he turned, an officer was almost beside him, along with two other officers approaching him with a man between them. Even from a distance, he could tell that he was probably a vagrant that may have been living in some part of the warehouses around the area. He was extremely dirty with torn clothes and looked like he hadn't shaved in years. When they got up to him, there was a strong stench surrounding him.

"Who's this?" he asked, examining him.

"We found him over in an alley near here. From what he told us, he saw the people from the warehouse."

"Really," he said, stepping up to him. "What is your name?"

"It is Linnar," he told him, never looking up.

"This officer said you saw some people here earlier?"

"Maybe," he said softly.

Deniko was not in the mood to play games. Infuriated, he struck him with the back of his hand across his face. The blow almost knocked him down, but the two officers held his arms to hold him up.

"Who did you see in this building?"

"It was a big black car," he told him while looking to see if he would hit him again.

"A limousine?"

"I don't know about cars, but it was big and very shiny."

"Okay, how many people were in it, and what did they look like?"

"I saw three men and a woman," he said. "They came out of the building and got into the back and drove away."

"What did they look like?" Deniko asked, grabbing his shirt.

"Like any other person except for the one."

"Why was he so different?"

"He turned and looked in my direction and his mouth…well, it was strange."

"Strange…how?"

"It was all shiny, like he had gold all over."

"Perfect," Deniko said with a smile. "Take him downtown and question him more."

"Yes, sir," they said, dragging him away.

It was unusual that Widdal would be so sloppy and leave any clue or a witness. That must mean he didn't care or has a plan that would put into question everything and perhaps get him off no matter what sort of evidence he had on him. He can place him at the scene and has a body. With a touch more digging, he could build a case—enough to put him away.

I got you, bastard, he thought.

He didn't know how long he leaned against the car, but he heard another vehicle drive up and stop. Lifting his head, he saw that it was the coroner's van. Spinning, he watched as several officers came out of the building with a gurney and a black bag strapped down on top. His heart skipped, knowing she was inside. As they loaded the gurney, the radio began to crackle and he heard his name.

"This is Detective Deniko. What have you got?"

"Sir, we found out that a private helicopter left from a small airport northwest of the city several hours ago. There was no flight plan recorded in the system. Financial records indicate it was paid for by a company owned by Mr. Widdal."

"What about a direction? Did they show it on the airport radar?"

"The airport indicated they headed almost due west into the desert and then they dropped altitude and disappeared. The controllers figured they dropped down low enough and under the radar to avoid detection."

That was exactly what he wanted to hear.

"Have a helicopter standing by for me to arrive," he barked.

"Yes, sir," the voice indicated.

He wouldn't go out there for nothing. If they went out into the desert, then that's where I'm going, he thought, jumping into his car.

All the way to the airport, his mind raced at chasing Widdal and seeing Carmen lying in a pool of blood. With each scene popping into his mind, he found his foot pressing harder against the accelerator. He wanted desperately to put his hands around the man's throat for what he had done. It was less than an hour before he pulled into the airport.

Pulling up next to a service hangar, he saw several police cars with their lights flashing surrounding a helicopter. There were at least a dozen men gathered around another man in a flight suit. Getting out, he went over to see if there was an issue.

"What's going on?" he asked, showing his badge.

"This is the pilot that took the suspects into the desert, sir."

"Really," Deniko said, looking at the man. "Who did you take out there?"

"It was Mr. Widdal and three others. They wanted to be taken to a particular spot and then I was supposed to bring them back. His associate came out and told me that they had other transportation and I could leave, which I did. The spot was close to my range limit."

He could see the man was nervous and didn't understand what was going on.

"Where in the desert did you take them?"

"Here are the coordinates," he said, holding out his logbook.

"What was out there when you dropped them off?"

"There was nothing but sand everywhere as far as I could tell," he said, looking at the other officers. "I wouldn't have gone out there and especially on foot, but that was what he wanted."

Looking over to the other end of the parking area, he could see the long-range police helicopter near the edge of the hangar. Taking his notebook out of his pocket, he scribbled down the coordinates in the logbook and handed it back to him. Turning, he began to head for the helicopter.

"Sir," one of the officers said. "How many officers are you taking with you?"

"None," he said without turning around. "This one is only for me."

"But, sir," he yelled, watching him walk away. "It could be very dangerous."

Maybe for him, Deniko thought as he reached the helicopter.

CHAPTER 24

HOLDING HER GENTLY in his arms, pressed against his chest, he took her out into the other chamber. She began to groan, and he stopped, placing her on the ground. Checking her wound, he could see that it was still bleeding heavily. Opening her eyes, she looked up at him.

"Place me in the pool, Johnny," she told him.

"Why?" he asked, confused. "You need a doctor. I have to get you out of here."

"We have to do this before the temple keepers come."

"The temple keepers, who are they?"

"They must not know," she said in pain, "that we have returned."

"Returned? Who has returned and who are the *we*?"

"The pool…please," she begged.

Lifting her, he took a step toward the pool but heard noises behind them. Turning he saw Hades had entered the chamber and was smiling at him. He pulled a large knife from under his tunic and swirled it in his hand. Placing her down on the ground, he pulled the gun out and, pointing, smiled.

"I see you brought a knife to a gun fight…okay then."

Squeezing the trigger, nothing happened. Looking at it, all the gun parts appeared to be fused from when Widdal held it in the portal.

"Oh crap," he said, throwing it at him.

Dodging it easily, he began to step toward him. From his walk, he wasn't going after him but heading for Ani. Holding the knife toward Johnny, he reached out for her and tried to grab her neck. Knowing she was in no condition to fight back, he lunged at Hades and caught him off guard.

Tackling him at the waist, he at least avoided the knife in his hand. He held desperately onto the wrist that was grasping the knife, squeezing it as hard as he could. Johnny didn't know where this was going to end, but he knew he had to do everything he could to keep him from reaching her. Johnny rolled over and tried to pound his hand against the ground, hoping to loosen the knife from his grip. Hades quickly rolled and tossed him away.

As Johnny got to his knees and looked, he saw him walk over to the knife. Johnny froze, trying to figure out what to do next. His adrenaline began to rise as he glanced over at Ani. He rushed over to put himself in between her and Hades and waited for him to make his next move. Watching, he saw Hades pause and smile. It bothered him and then saw him toss the knife to the ground.

"I will enjoy this more using just my hands…on both of you."

"Over my dead body," Johnny told him.

"So be it." Hades grinned.

Walking over to Johnny, he took a swing as he reached him, catching him squarely on the chin. The blow barely fazed him, and he slowly looked back at him. Before he could swing again, Hades reached over and grabbed him by the neck. Squeezing tightly, he lifted him from the ground, allowing his feet to dangle. Kicking wildly, he tried to breathe but the grip was slowly closing off his wind pipe. Finally, he jammed his knee into his crotch as hard as he could. When his knee struck him, his grip loosened slightly, giving him an opportunity to get free.

When his feet hit the ground, he rolled and took Hades feet from under him. Hitting the ground on his back, Johnny struck him in the middle of his chest with his elbow. The blow took the wind from him and he struck him again as he tried to get the upper hand. Again Hades grabbed him by the throat and dragged him over to the pool. Shoving his head below the surface, he was trying to drown him. Feeling the air slip into bubbles within the water, he saw a shard of glass on the bottom of the pool. Grabbing it, he stabbed him several times in the hands. The water began to turn red from the flow of blood.

Hades released him, and Johnny quickly lifted his head from the water. Turning, he could see Hades trying to stop the bleeding from his cut wrists. Johnny came over and began punching him in the head over and over until he saw him begin to stagger. When he did, he grabbed his tunic and began pounding his head into the ledge of the pool. He didn't know how many times he had done it but, after a few moments, felt Hade's body become limp.

This will be my only shot, he thought.

Releasing him, he ran over and grabbed the knife he had dropped. Coming back over to Hades, he held the knife to his throat but never moved. He looked up at him and began to laugh.

"You don't have the balls, boy," Hades said. "If you don't, I'll finish what I started."

"Wrong answer," Johnny said.

He was amazed how easily the knife slid through the skin and how deep as he brought it across his throat. Blood instantly began to squirt from the cut veins as he stood over him holding the knife. As he began to gurgle from chocking on the blood filling his air pipe, he couldn't stand it any longer. Placing the tip of the knife in the middle of his chest, he plunged it into him. He watched Hades try to take one last gasp and his head rolled to the side as the life escaped him.

Standing up, he stood near his feet and could only stare down at him. He had killed him, and oddly, it didn't bother him. It was a strange sensation filling him, and glancing down, he saw the blood covering his hands. Before he could think about it further, he heard Ani cough and moan. He rushed over to her.

"Ani," he said, picking her up into his arms.

"Place me into the pool," she said softly.

"Into the pool?" he asked, confused. "Why?"

"Yes," she said, looking up at him. "It's the only way."

Lifting her from the ground, he obeyed her wishes and stepped over the ledge and walked over to the middle of the pool. Kneeling, he lowered her into the water. As he held her head just above the water, he looked around as the water began to change color. Looking up at the figures on the wall, they also began to change colors. The water around them began to glow and turn white as they remained in the center. He could only watch as the water changed and was more interested in her.

"Place me under the water," she begged.

Doing as she asked, the water became so bright he couldn't look at it. Even with his eyes closed, he could see the light. A moment later, the light disappeared, and when he opened them, he brought her back up against him. Checking her, she suddenly gasped and sat up. She turned and looked at him. Smiling, she leaned over and wrapped her arms around his neck, kissing him deeply. Breaking their kiss, she just grinned and looked at him.

"What the heck is going on, Ani?" he asked her.

"Something that had to be done," she said, stroking his cheek.

"I don't understand any of this," he told her. "Now what?"

"Come with me," she said, taking his hand.

He followed her back into the other chamber and to the portal. As they reached it, he looked at her even more confused. Standing before it, the pedestal began to pulse, and the colors from before started to appear. Still holding his hand, she led him onto the pedestal.

"We're going to use this?" he asked her.

"It's the only way you'll get your answers."

"And where are we going?"

"We are going to my home." She smiled, taking his hand. "Please be patient and all will be explained…I promise. Once you see, I think you'll understand better and I'll answer any question you might have."

"I'm sure I'll have a bunch." He smiled not knowing what was coming.

"Tell me one thing," she asked as the glowing lights began to surround them.

"Anything," he said, watching.

"Do you really love me?"

Without answering her, he pulled her over and kissed her deeply. After a moment, he released her and looked into her eyes.

"What does that tell you?"

"Exactly what I needed to know." She smiled.

Feeling his skin begin to tingle, he closed his eyes and waited.

CHAPTER 25

Not knowing what to expect, Johnny had his eyes forced shut. His skin tingled as if on fire, causing his muscles to contract. The pronounced ringing in his ears from the machine also slowly faded. Finally feeling that he could breathe, he took a deep breath and slowly opened his eyes, looking around. He found himself standing on a wide stone platform with the machine surrounding him. All the colors had faded away, and it returned to its normal color. At first, his mind swirled, not focusing, while it tried to figure out exactly where they had gone. He then felt a warm hand on his arm and, turning, saw Ani standing beside him with a big smile.

"Where are we?" he asked.

"This is my home…Stix's," she said, glancing around and breathing in the air. "Isn't it beautiful? I haven't been back here in what seems like forever."

"We're on another planet?" he asked, stunned. "Where is it located?"

"It's in what you call Orion's Belt."

"Oh my god," he gasped.

The surface of the planet was a dull gray and didn't appear to be dirt but had the consistency of stone. Looking up, the sky was filled with brilliant streaks of yellow and red stretching across the heavens. From what he could tell from the light, it was either almost sunrise or sunset. With no reference of time, he thought it had to one or the other. Across the landscape was strange vegetation with trees that looked like they folded over on themselves. Some of the plants seemed to have big beautiful bulbs with wide leaves supported by long stems. The air around them had no movement feeling perfectly still.

"What do you think?" she asked softly, afraid of what he might say.

"This place is…is awesome!"

"The city is right there," Ani said, pointing to the horizon.

Johnny didn't hear much of what she said and looked to where she pointed. He was dumbfounded by all the wondrous sights around him. Nothing in his wildest imagination could compare to this place. In the distance, he saw the golden glow of a city that didn't seem to have buildings, but he could see structures with a large pulsing halo surrounding it. Off to the side stretched out a large black ocean going out to the horizon. There were no waves that he could see and nothing floating on it. In front of him, scattered along each side of the pathway were several smaller structures. They almost looked like small homes, but in this world, he couldn't be sure.

"I've never seen anything like this," he said.

Ani held onto Johnny's hand and let him immerse into the wonders of her world. She didn't want to be quick in introducing him to more than he could absorb. As he stepped forward, she tried to lead him down the path toward the city. His legs were still wobbly from the trip and she tried to support him until his strength returned.

I'm really on another world, he thought, still amazed.

Walking slowly toward the city, it never occurred to him how advanced civilizations might actually live, only how they might look. Nothing looked like the stories of what was portrayed in television. He grinned, thinking that was a good thing as he thought about little green men. Walking along the path to the city, he began to laugh at the thought and turned and looked behind him. The pad and the machine were located on the side of a hill and was surrounded by a structure resembling a temple. From the position in the area, it was a place of great prominence.

Coming up to one of the first buildings beside the road, people were outside and greeted them as they passed. Now that he was closer, there were fields of the strange plants lined behind the buildings resembling plantings for harvest. One of the people came over and offered their crop to them, a large bluish bulb. Accepting it from them, he thanked them and continued. The object looked like it might be a strange fruit of some sort. Watching him examine it in his hands, Ani began to laugh.

"It is called a Fam and is very sweet," she said, taking it from him.

Pressing her thumbs deep into the skin, she pulled it to the side and broke it apart, handing him half of it. She began to eat around the seeds at the center, only eating the green flesh inside while watching him. He lifted it to his nose and sniffed it first before taking a small bite. Chewing it carefully, he turned to her and began to smile as he swallowed.

"This is delicious," he told her, taking another bite.

"I knew you would like it."

Continuing to walk toward the main entrance of the city, he still couldn't believe what he was seeing. He could now see the high walls surrounding the city, which had a green glow about them. It was a different color than the golden glow above the city. Nearing them, his skin began to tingle once again and turned to Ani.

"Ani," he asked, "is there some form of shield around the city?"

"Yes." She laughed, noticing him rubbing his arms. "It is there to protect the citizens."

"From what?"

"Anything." She grinned.

Entering the city, the streets were a dull yellow as though they're made from solid gold. It was everywhere. The sky behind them began to change, and he realized that it was going to be sunrise. Looking up at the sky above the city, it was changing into a bright red with blues and greens highlighting it. When he turned around, he saw the crescent shape of the sun rising slowly above the far hills.

"This is just so unreal," Johnny said.

"Mother," Ani yelled out.

When he turned, he saw Ani rushing down the pathway toward a figure dressed in white coming toward them. As they reached each other, they both jumped into each other's arms, kissing each other. He walked up to them as they still held onto their embrace. It was a moment later that the woman looked over at him.

"So is this the man from Earth we have heard so much about," she asked her. "Please, daughter, introduce me to him."

"Yes, Mother," Ani told her, stepping to the side. "This is Johnny Cortez and, Johnny, this is my mother, Osiris."

"Very glad to meet you," Johnny said, shaking her outstretched hand.

"All the rumors I've heard do not do you justice, Mr. Cortez." She grinned.

"How so?" Johnny asked, confused before looking over at Ani.

"Yes, definitely more handsome," Osiris said before turning to her. "Well done. Your father will be very pleased."

"I do hope so," Ani said, reaching over and taking his hand.

"Come," Osiris told him. "There is someone waiting to see you."

As they followed her into a chamber near them, Johnny's mind raced thinking of what had happened. All the names were similar to those of Egypt and wondered if there was any direct connection between them. Walking up a set of stairs, it opened up into a gathering area with several tables. There were probably a dozen people sitting around, talking and enjoying what looked like drinks. Osiris stopped and pointed over to a table.

"I think you might know these people," she indicated the couple sitting at it.

An older woman turned and, seeing them, stood up and rushed over to them. She was dressed in the same white robes as everyone else. Pausing before him, she began to cry and hugged him. Johnny didn't know what to think or what to do as he simply placed his arms around her. He looked at the others with a blank expression, not knowing why this woman was hugging him. With her face cradled against his shoulder, Osiris came over and rubbed her back.

"This is my dearest friend, Tulare," she indicated, looking at her, "and your mother."

"My what?" he gasped.

He had never known his mother since she left them when he was very young. Pushing her away slightly, he looked at her. There was nothing about her, hair facial features or anything, that he recognized. When she smiled at him and stroked his cheek, his heart did skip a beat and something inside him said it was her.

"Mother," he said, now completely confused.

"And there is someone else," Ani said.

"What else could it be?" Johnny asked, still staring at the woman is his arms.

"Hello, son," a man's voice said.

The voice he instantly recognized and, turning, his eyes lit up.

"Father?"

His mother released as they then hugged. Ani looked at them and began to cry from seeing the emotion between them.

"What are you doing here?" Johnny asked him. "And Mother?"

"It's a very long story." He smiled. "Let's all sit down and I'll tell you what I can remember."

Leading over into the seating area, Johnny was now totally confused by the whole situation and could feel his head swimming. Here was his missing father that he thought was dead and the mother he never knew all in the same place. A place other than where they should be. He didn't know if he could wrap his head around it all and hoped the explanation would help resolve many of the questions he had in his mind.

Once they were all settled in the couches, a woman servant came out from the side wall and sat drinks down on the table before leaving them alone. Osiris poured him and Ani a drink before sitting back in the couch to listen.

"Well, it's the weirdest thing," Manny started. "I don't really remember anything except waking up and your mother sitting beside me."

Johnny watched as he squeezed her hand.

"In my thoughts, there was only this dream of a vast desert and I seemed to be lost and couldn't find my way out. I only remember bits and pieces, but the only real memories I have are of you and your mother."

"I got the package you sent me and your message," he said, leaning over to him. "When the police came to my hotel, they only said you were missing. I could only think that you were dead. That was the reason I jumped on a plane and came to Egypt… I had to look for you."

"And we are so glad you did," his mother stated. "We have now a chance to see you and talk to you."

"But that doesn't explain how you ended up here, either of you."

Before they could answer, there was a soft set of tones in the air. Everyone around them stood up and looked over to the entrance. When Johnny stood and looked, an elderly man was walking toward them. Even though he appeared old, his figure was imposing as if he was only in his thirties. He greeted people as he came up to them.

"Johnny," Osiris said, "I'd like to introduce the leader of our society."

"Greetings," the man quickly stated.

Johnny noticed that there was no smile on his face, but it also wasn't anger either. It was more of indifference to them.

"This is Ra-is, my husband and father to Ani."

Oh crap, Johnny thought, looking over at Ani. She just shrugged her shoulders.

He stood very tall with a definite air of confident. There wasn't much difference in him from any of the other people except that he was probably a head higher than anyone. Johnny's first impression was that he could be a player in for a basketball team with his height. His eyes were black and slightly slanted as if there were some Asian influence. Even his long brow indicated strength beyond others.

"Please sit and continue your discussion," he indicated.

As he spoke, it was almost like a command, which everyone, including those in the other couches, obeyed. Once they were seated, he spoke again.

"I hope their comfort has been attended to," he turned and asked Osiris.

"Yes, husband," she told him.

"Good," he said, looking back to them. "I know there are many questions in your mind and hope I may answer them."

Johnny spoke up immediately.

"Why Earth, and why us?"

"If you have noticed, this is much different than the world you come from. Some time ago, our scientists detected a change in our sun. It was producing a type of energy that our science could not protect us from. We were only aware of the dire problem when our birth rate began to fall dramatically, jeopardizing our civilization. Our science was finally able to protect us, but by that time, the damage had already been done."

"You were dying," Johnny asked.

"Yes, in a manner of speaking. We reached out and searched through the heavens with many worlds but found nothing. That was until we found your world. It was backward and primitive at the time, but we found that the human hosts occupying it were very similar to ours."

"When was that?"

"That was almost twelve thousand years ago."

Johnny sat back, realizing the implications of his statement.

"Our only option was to try and integrate our two people together."

"Was it the women of your world or the men that were affected?"

"It was a mixture, and each individual was affected differently. Many were simply sterile and others were still fertile. Unfortunately, we propagate our species on a very long cycle other than that of humans. For our children, it is close to one thousand years before they are born. At that rate, our way of life would have perished in the blink of an eye."

"Has it worked?" Johnny asked.

"Yes." He smiled slightly. "You are one of the products of those unions. Many of the people you see around are from those interactions."

"Me," he said quickly, turning to his parents. "I'm part alien?"

"Your mother Tulare was from our world, and your father was born from yours. That selected union produced you."

"May I speak, Father," Ani asked him.

"Speak child."

"I've thought long and hard as you know for my other and I feel it has ended. Speaking with Mother, she has agreed to my decision. This is the man who I've chosen," she said, taking Johnny's hand.

"I'm what?" he said, surprised.

"I know he is, child, and I give you my blessings," he said, watching her reaction. She straightened up and smiled widely. "But know that he cannot be allowed to stay for much longer. He has not been processed properly when he arrived."

"Thank you, Father," she said, coming over to him and kissing his cheek.

"We will meet another time," he told them, saying his goodbyes.

Watching him walk away, Johnny could only sit and stare after him. What had happened boggled his mind, and all the information he told him was too much to process. All he could do was simply shake his head in disbelief. Ani came over and, sitting down beside him, gently kissed his cheek.

"He approves of you and gave his blessing." She grinned. "Isn't that wonderful?"

Ani's mother was sitting, grinning from ear to ear as she got up and came over to her.

"I'm so happy for you," she said, kissing her. "Now, let's step away and give them some time before he has to leave. I'm sure they have much to talk about...as do we, daughter."

"Yes, Mother," she said, standing up and looking at Johnny and his parents. "I'll be back in a while and then we will go."

Kissing him once more, her mother took her arm, and they walked over to the other side of the room. He then turned to his parents and didn't know where to start. Tulare took his hand and smiled to try and reassure him.

After what seemed like hours of talking, Johnny saw Ani and her mother now walking back, which indicated that it was time to leave. Seeing them approach, they all stood up and began hugging each of them. As he held his mother, Johnny found that he was having a hard leaving them. Finally, he sighed and, with Ani taking his arm, started to walk away. With each step, he would turn around and look back. He could see them wave to him. Noticing his anxiety, she held tightly to his arm.

"Don't feel bad, Johnny. You'll see them again," she told him.

"Why do I feel that I won't?"

"Because my father told me you would," she said, looking into his eyes.

The walk back to the portal was slower than when they arrived, and she could tell by his look that he was trying to visualize everything around him. It seemed he was determined to remember all the sights and smells before they left. Reaching the portal, they stood on the pedestal and looked across the valley and the city.

"Are you ready?" she asked him.

"Yeah, I'm ready," he groaned.

"Remember that it's much easier if you close your eyes."

Closing his eyes, in his ears he could hear the machine start up and the low whining sound grew louder while his skin began to tingle. Before the machine could do what it was designed for and transport them back and his mind faded into darkness, he had one thought he tried to press into his memory.

I'll be back again, Father and Mother...no matter what.

At the end of his thought, his mind went blank and the world faded to black.

CHAPTER 26

HIS FIRST SENSATION was that he was on fire and he began to scream. Even with the scream, there didn't seem to be any pain but a strange sensation. Opening his eyes, he looked at his arms, and they looked like steam was coming off them and the rest of his body. Feeling his skin, there was nothing and he didn't look to be burned.

What the hell happened?

Looking around him, he saw that he was in the treasure chamber. He was lying on the ground near the pedestal and, turning, saw Ani was standing beside him looking down. There was a panicked look on her face.

"Johnny," Ani asked, kneeling down beside him, "are you all right?"

Blinking his eyes, Johnny looked at her and could still see concern across her face. He didn't understand her concern as he slowly began to stand up beside her. She helped him up and held onto his arm. His legs were a little wobbly.

"What the hell happened?" he said, rubbing his forehead.

"We walked off the platform and a giant bolt came out of the machine. It struck you and you dropped to the ground. I thought it killed you."

"I don't remember that part," he said still looking around the chamber. "I just remember walking onto the platform to examine it and then waking up here on the ground."

"At least you're all right."

"I guess so," he told her, still not sure of what had happened.

"We have to go," she said, beginning to pull on his arm.

"Why?" he asked, wondering why the rush.

"It's the keepers," she commented, pulling him step by step. "They will be coming and we have to go before they get here."

"Who are these…keepers," he asked but still following her.

"I'll explain it to you later," she said still pulling him. "Please, we have to hurry."

Walking in to the outer chamber and out of the mouth, they froze as they saw six men standing on the other side by the exit. They stood in a row and never moved, just watching them. From their appearance, Johnny thought they were perhaps the Bedouins they had come across in the desert flying to this place. Each brushed their robes back, revealing the swords in their belts. Did they follow them inside to rob them? All the riches they needed were in the other room. Telling them might keep them from getting killed. Before he could say anything, one of the men stepped forward toward them.

"Why have you come and defiled this sacred place?" the one man asked.

"It's not that…" Johnny began before Ani broke in.

"Please, keepers, we mean no harm to this place or to you," Ani told them before kneeling and crossing her arms across her chest. Johnny saw her and followed her example. "We did not know it was sacred and came in by mistake… You must believe us."

"You have seen the sacred temple and the contents not meant for people of this world. You must be punished by law and the punishment is death," he said.

He motioned with a sweep of his hand and several of the men behind him began to step forward. Before the men could take several steps to them, the ground in the chamber began to tremble, causing everyone to look around. When Johnny looked over at Ani, her head was back slightly and her eyes were closed.

Wondering what was happening, he then heard the men begin to gasp and all of them quickly knelt, burying their faces to the ground. Turning, he saw a cloud of gray mist growing within the mouth of the statue before a figure materialized and walked to the edge of the steps near them. The figure paused and looked around the room.

"Crap...Ra," Johnny gasped. "No, it just can't be."

"Oh great and holy one," all the men began to chant.

The figure was just like he stepped out of the history books. His head was that of a falcon or some predatory bird. Long colored feathers hung from the side if it's head. Its eyes were the same as the statue, pitch-black with no reflection. Even though the body was that of a man, it appeared more powerful than an average human. Muscles rippled across its chest and arms as it stood before them. Around the waist was an ancient Egyptian skirt with gold and colors along the edges. Johnny could imagine that a figure within his books had jumped off the pages and come to life.

"Why have you come and entered this place?" the figure proclaimed loudly, stretching out its arms. "Temple keepers, explain the intrusion."

"Oh great one, as guardians we only come to purge the holy temple of those that come to defile it," the leader said never looking up. "That is our sworn and sacred duty in life."

"What is this? Blood has been spilled in my temple."

Again the ground began to tremble.

"Not by our hands, oh great one," the man said.

"The stench of the unholy dead within my temple fills my senses," he said as the ground began to quiet. "Take this form from my sight and place it in the desert that it might provide a warning for all who might seek to enter this place."

"Yes, great lord," the man said, waving back to the others.

Two men quickly came over and grabbed Hades by the head and shoulders and carried him from the chamber. When they had disappeared into the tunnel, the man turned his attention back to Johnny and Ani.

"And what of these others?" he asked the figure. "They have also entered, desecrating this place. What shall we do with them?"

Ra looked down at Johnny and Ani and began to laugh. The sound made Johnny nervous as if he had different plans for them.

"These are my servants, and no harm must come to them. You will take them and tend to them as your own until you have returned them to the civilization of this world. Until that time, you must protect them with your lives."

"But, lord, they have found this sacred temple."

"That is not your concern. It will be buried once again, never to be found until the appropriate time. Continue to guard it as faithful servants until that time."

"Yes, great one," the leader said.

"Leave us," he commanded. "I will speak with them alone."

"We obey," he said, ushering the others from the chamber.

The figure stood motionless until they had gone. Johnny didn't like the feeling he had now that they were alone with the figure. He did like the part about "no harm," but from what he could tell, this figure was not to be messed with. Not knowing if he should stand or stay where he was, he waited.

After a moment, the figure once again laughed but never moved. Finally, it turned and walked away into the rising mist and simply vanished into thin air. Standing, he still couldn't believe his eyes at what he had seen. He then heard Ani take a deep breath and stood up beside him.

"I don't believe what just happened," Johnny told her.

"That was amazing, and something no one will ever believe."

"I hardly believe it myself."

Staring at her, he watched as she began stripping her clothes off.

"What the hell are you doing?" he asked.

"If I have to spend all those days packed into a caravan all the way back to the city, then I'm going to go for a swim."

"Unbelievable," Johnny said, watching as the last piece of clothing hit the ground. "What about the men waiting outside?"

"I guess they will wait…won't they?" she said with a smile, stepping into the pool. "You going to join me?"

"I guess I will," he said, shaking his head.

Stripping off his clothes, he joined her in the water. It felt cool and wonderful against his skin as he came over to her. Swirling around him, she waited until he had lowered himself in the water before coming over and wrapping her arms around him. Without a word, he pulled her close and kissed her as they dropped below the surface. In his mind, he could only think of one thing.

No one is ever going to believe this.

After almost an hour, they finished their swim and got dressed. Outside the tunnel, they saw that several camels were already near the opening and waiting for them. Several men came over and helped them up onto each animal. When they were ready, the men then mounted the other camels, and they headed away from the tunnel and out into the desert. Johnny looked over at Ani and could see a large smile on her face. He could tell that she had never ridden a camel, and for that matter, neither had he. Seeing her bounce between the humps of the camel made him begin to laugh. The man riding beside him looked at him curiously. He shrugged his shoulders and looked ahead, wondering what would come next.

CHAPTER 27

WITH HIS EYES still shut, he felt the machine beginning to stop, and almost by instinct, Widdal took a cautious step forward. In his mind, the first thing he noticed was strange sounds and, finally opening his eyes, turned and looked behind him. The sounds were coming from the portal machine as it sizzled in the surrounding air.

I actually made it, he thought.

Looking around the crackling sound came from moisture in the air evaporating from the massive power of the portal. Taking a deep breath, he suddenly began to cough and gag as the air burned at his lungs. Still coughing, he turned and looked at what was before him.

What the hell?

He didn't see the piles of gold, jewels, or riches that he had imagined would be waiting when he first entered the portal. Off in the distance he could see multitudes of volcanoes gushing pillars of black clouds up into the deep orange sky. Down almost every slope of the volcanoes were bright rivers of red lava flowing into the valleys below them to fill burning lakes of fire. In front of him, he saw a pathway leading down to the edge of a cliff. Near the edge was a pile of gold.

That's it? It can't be?

Widdal ran toward the mound and stopped in front of it. The air burned his lungs even more as he tried to catch his breath, leaning over his knees. Struggling for air, he again looked at the horizon and noticed a giant red sun was beginning to rise above the horizon. In the back of his mind, he envisioned this world would be similar to Earth and filled beyond imagination with riches. His urge of riches beyond imagination overrode his ability to think of anything else or understand any perceived dangers.

Still leaned over his knees, he couldn't breathe and held his chest. Suddenly, he heard a loud boom and crackle off to his right. He looked and saw a huge volcano only a few miles away explode and bellow dark clouds high into the air. Glowing lava was beginning to flow from deep cracks down the slopes of the dark landscape. He noticed the layer of sweat began to drip from his forehead and, reaching up, quickly wiped it away.

No one can live in this hell.

He had a second thought in between his exhales for more oxygen. There had to be another place that contained the riches that he sought. They wouldn't just be sitting out in the open. Struggling to breathe, he turned and the pile of gold was changing. The heat was making it begin to melt and flow over the edge into the valley below.

There has to be another place.

Looking around he saw up on the slope beside the portal a structure almost like a castle but was old, and many of the stones within its walls were missing. From the shape, it was built right into the side of the mountain. With nothing else around, he knew it had to contain the riches he wanted.

Knowing he had to get there and out of the heat, he turned and walked down another pathway toward the structure. Watching it grow larger, it seemed in his mind to take longer than he would expect since it appeared so close. Finally reaching the entrance, he felt his heart racing as it tried to pump oxygen into his body. After a few moments, a little strength returned to his legs and he walked inside.

On the other side of the entrance, he began to look around. It was definitely old and thought it might contain something. The inside of the building was completely different from what he expected. There were metal chairs almost as good as modern Earth and scattered around the room. Broken glass was everywhere along with plates, eating utensils, and other objects. He ignored them and kept looking. There was a set of large doors, broken away from their hinges and hanging loosely from the supports on just one corner.

Entering, he saw a throne on the far wall with two doors on either side. He knew that it must be close. On the floor was a golden strip and as it reached the throne split and led to the two doors. His heart raced knowing he must be close and he picked up his pace. Nearing the throne, he wondered which path to check out first. Pausing he chose the one on the right and raced to the opening. As he entered, he stopped and gasped.

"Oh yes, this is what I'm talking about," he said.

Before him was a large room that appeared to be a cavern that was filled with gold as far as he could see in every direction. The steps in front of him led down to the golden surface and then disappeared beneath it. Leaning against the edge of the doorway he marveled at just how much gold was contained in the room.

I wonder what's in the other room.

Without waiting and knowing the treasure wasn't going anywhere, he turned and headed for the other door. As he passed the throne, he saw a huge plaque on the wall behind it. It was something he hadn't realized when he came in. There were two blackish serpents surrounding a vertical sword. Each of them looked very imposing, and he wondered where they got the idea of the snakes.

Knowing that he had not seen any living thing since he got there, even a blade of grass, he figured that everything in this world was dead and gone. Reaching the doorway, he paused to let his heart calm before entering. He knew it had to be just as good as the other chamber. With a breath, he walked in and stopped.

The room was filled with every imaginable jewel but one object kept his focus and made him sigh. On the far side of the room was a diamond that was huge. Even from where he stood, he figured that it had to be at least the size of three men tall and produced a glow even in the dim light. Just the sight of it made his heart pound wildly. Stepping inside, there were piles of jewels that made the treasure chamber on Earth seem insignificant. In one pile, he picked up an emerald that had to be the size of a watermelon. He twisted it in his hands before the weight of it made him put it back. Glancing around the piles, rubies and diamonds were everywhere. This room was almost as big as the other.

Moving to the large diamond in the back, he looked at each of the mounds of jewels. Nearing one pile he saw something out of the corner of his eye and, looking, jumped away. It was the skeleton of a man stretched onto the side of the pile. He looked like he was caressing the pile and had died against it. Moving one, he then saw several other skeletons around other piles. By the time he had reached the large diamond, he had counted over ten of them lying beside the various piles.

Before he could think, the floor began to shake and small pieces of stone fell from the ceiling. As quick as it started, it stopped. His mind raced on how he would get any of this back to the safety of Earth, including him. The portal machine must work enough to allow him to return without the key to operate it. Walking slowly back to the doorway, he picked up the emerald he held before and took it with him.

If I can just make it back to the portal, I'll return and make Johnny come back with me and we can retrieve all this.

Holding the jewel against his chest, he moved back through the rooms and to the entrance to the building. Once outside, he could see that the air was now filled with black soot floating in the air as it belched from the tops of the surrounding mountains. As he tried to walk toward the portal, he was struggling to breathe, and finally, he couldn't walk any farther. With all his energy gone, he slumped to his knees and held the emerald in his lap, gasping for air. He could see the portal but knew he couldn't reach it.

In front of him, the ground began to crack and rise in several spots. Watching, a section of the ground flipped to the side and two serpents rose up from the earth. They were huge and looked to be the same as in the plaque behind the throne. Each had wings on the side of their heads, and their eyes glowed a fiery red just like the lava around them. Slowly, they came completely out of the ground and began to circle him. He figured they had to be over thirty feet long as they surveyed him.

"Oh crap," he moaned, watching them.

Letting go of the emerald, it rolled from his lap several feet away. One of the serpents curled around it and pulled it away as if guarding it from him. The other came in front of him and curling rose up high above him, his head tilting down at him. All he could see was its tongue darting in and out of its mouth before slowly opening it to reveal rows of sharp teeth. Seeing it begin to move its head back, he knew he was about to strike.

"Cortez," he yelled out, watching, "you bastard!"

On his last word, the serpent struck, swallowing his head.

CHAPTER 28

EVEN THE AIR coming through the small door window did nothing to cool him. The pilot had tried to adjust the internal air, but it wasn't enough to keep him from sweating in his suit. He wanted to take it off but was strapped to the seat and really didn't like flying. Looking out the window at the miles of hot desert sand and nothing else, he wondered what could be so damn important to come out here. The pilot tapped him on the shoulder and pointed up ahead.

In the distance, he could see the black shapes of buzzards circling over a spot in the desert. They were either waiting for something to die or waiting their turn to feast on something that had already perished. Several miles to the east of the buzzards, they could see a giant sand tornado swirling high into the sky. The bellowing cloud at the top seemed to act like an umbrella, allowing the rising sand to arch back to the ground. From the enormous size, it was throwing sand everywhere, and they didn't want to be caught in it. The pilot hovered for a moment and indicated it was moving away, and they would be all right.

Reaching the spot where the buzzards were circling, they saw that there were at least twenty or thirty birds attacking an object. The noise of the helicopter landed near them scared the birds away. Once on the ground, Deniko got out and, taking off his jacket, tossed it onto the seat. Walking over to the spot, he stopped and shook his head.

"Jesus," he said, looking around at the carnage. "Hades."

He was strapped to a set of poles in a cross, allowing the birds to pick their meal from anywhere. As he got closer, he saw that he wasn't just tied up but had been cut up. His legs and arms had been severed from his torso, and on a separate pole behind it, his head had been speared above the rest of him. From a distance, he looked intact, but he could see where the birds had been feasting. His stomach had been ripped away, and his intestines were dangling almost to the ground. He could see where the birds had chewed into them. Dark blood covered the sand below him.

And so where the hell is Widdal? he wondered. *These two are never separated.*

Seeing Hades hanging dead in the sand changed everything about his thoughts. All the way out here he wanted vengeance, and now that he was here, there was nothing to hate, and his mind would only let it fester inside him. Kicking the sand angrily, he wandered around the area, cursing, groaning, and slapping his head. Deep inside, he felt he just couldn't let it go that easily. He might have been able if it wasn't for the fact about Carmen dying. With nothing left, he slowly walked back toward the helicopter and climbed in.

"We're not taking that bloody mess back with us, are we?" the pilot asked.

"No," he said with a sigh, adjusting his straps. "The desert can claim another life like it has done for thousands of years… He stays. You're a witness that we found the corpse of Hades, Widdal's bodyguard."

"Thanks," the pilot said. "Ready to head back?"

"Yes," he said, leaning his head back. "Take me home."

All the way home, he wondered how he was going to write all this up in his report. No one was going to believe a word of it. He hadn't found Johnny's father, he had a body, and the main suspects went out into the desert and are lost except for one. The chief was going to go crazy. Thinking about it, he began to laugh.

After the helicopter ride and the slow drive back to his apartment, all he could think about was sitting down and relaxing. His emotions were all over the place, and he found he couldn't get a handle on them. They would go from anger to sadness and then back again. Pulling up to his parking spot, he thought of only one thing.

I really need a drink.

Trudging slowly up the steps to his door, he placed his keys in the lock and, turning it, pushed the door open. As soon as it opened, he saw that there were lights on, and he could smell food cooking in the kitchen. His heart raced as he pulled out his weapon, expecting an intruder in his place. Hearing some dishes rattle, he slowly walked over to the kitchen entrance and stepped in, holding the gun ready. Pausing, his mouth dropped open.

"Mica?"

Hearing her name, she turned around and smiled at him. She was only wearing a small wrap around her body, and she was busily cooking food on the stove, humming some song. He walked over and sat down at the table and placed his gun beside him. Stirring the food, she twisted her head and looked at him.

"I thought all this work would go cold if you didn't come soon," she said, starting to serve it on a plate. Walking over to him, she placed it in front of him. "I hate reheated food, don't you?"

"Yes," he said, looking at the plate. "What are you doing here?'

She didn't answer and, grabbing a bottle from the cabinet and a glass, came over and poured it almost half full. Setting the bottle down, she fixed her a plate and, coming over, sat down beside him.

"I was lonely and figured that you might be also," she said, taking a bite of food.

"No, how did you get in here?"

"The superintendent was so sweet… He let me in."

"I'll get him for that," he commented, picking up his glass and taking a drink.

"Don't be too hard on him." She smiled. "It's not like he hadn't seen me here before."

"That was a long time ago, Mica."

"Things change you know."

Watching her eat, he felt her foot come over to his leg beneath the table and begin to caress his calf with her toes. There was a smile growing on her face as she sat in silence eating but never looking at him. Picking up his fork, he stuffed some of the food in his mouth and tasted it. Instantly, the early days came flooding back.

Could she take some of the pain away? he thought, staring at her.

CHAPTER 29

I T WAS NEARING sunset, and the Bedouin caravan had stopped in a small valley to set up their camp. Johnny and Ani had been placed in one of the Bedouins tents and not allowed to do anything, which for Johnny was fine considering the heat. Lying on a carpet spread out on the floor of the tent along with pillows, the noise of a passing helicopter passing over them scared the camels near the tents. They all began to cry and rustle around, pulling at their ropes. Hearing it, he started to get up, but Ani quickly grabbed his arm.

"They won't land," she told him.

"Why is that?"

"It's just the way of the desert, and they are left alone."

Several women came in and placed food and drink on the floor near them before bowing and quickly retreating. He sat up and looked at the food and poured a drink from the bottle beside the plate. After a quick sniff, he took a swallow and, licking his lips, smiled and looked over at Ani.

"All I could think about was a nice stiff drink to settle my nerves," he said, pouring her a glass. "And they bring this, a wine that is fantastic. I don't know where they get this, but I'm not going to question them."

As they sipped their drinks and began eating, Ani looked over at him.

"I'm sorry we didn't find your father, Johnny," she said.

"Thanks," he told her, looking out the flap of the tent. "But you know, deep down I think he's not dead but is fine. I don't know why I feel that way, but I just do."

"You'll see him again," she said, moving over closer to him.

"People always say that when a person loses someone close to them, but I don't know," he said, shaking his head, "but I think it'll be…well, different. I just have this nagging feeling that he isn't really dead, and I'll see him soon. That thought is comforting oddly enough."

"Does that bother you or what?"

"Well," he said, leaning back on his elbow, "I think it'll all work out just fine in the end. It seems to have been good so far."

"Good." She smiled. "So no more searching the desert?"

"All I see in my mind is him smiling at me so…no, no more searching."

For several minutes they sat and eat the food that they had been given while watching the people move around outside the tent. The quietness slowly relieved the stress that was in them from all the nightmares that had happened in the last few days. Finally, Ani shifted and looked at him.

"I really have to ask you something."

"Ask me anything," he said, noticing her face.

"Does your earlier comment to me still hold true?" Ani said cautiously.

"Which comment is that?"

"The one where you said you loved me."

He started laughing, and his outburst made her angry. She began slapping his arm.

"I never thought I would ever say those words," he said, grabbing her wrist. "But once I came here and saw you, I can't picture never saying them."

"Really?" she said as her eyes began to sparkle.

"Of course I love you and that hasn't changed since I said it."

"Oh, Johnny," she sighed.

Jumping into his arms, she began to kiss him. Her weight knocked him over onto his back and he wrapped his arms around her. She didn't just kiss him but moved all around his face, kissing his nose, eyes, chin—everywhere. After a moment, she sat up and looked down at him, grinning ear to ear.

"I want babies, Johnny—lots of babies," she told him, almost giddy.

"Uh, you mean more than one?"

"Well, at least one at a time."

"If I have to support all these kids, then I need a dowry."

Reaching into his pocket, he pulled out his hand and showed her. There were six large jewels that he had taken from the treasure chamber. Her eyes widened seeing them and quickly turned and looked outside the tent.

"You weren't supposed to remove anything from the chamber," she said softly.

"I think that the gods of the temple can consider it a wedding gift to us, don't you think?"

"A wedding gift?"

"You really can't have all those babies without a wedding, right? They aren't cheap."

"Never thought of it that way."

"Well, seems by that comment someone in this relationship has to."

"Yes, master." She grinned.

Laughing, he leaned up and took her in his arms, pressing her against him before rolling her over to her back. Before he kissed her, he produced a large smile.

"That's a very good answer…Mrs. Cortez."

"Just shut up and kiss me," she moaned, pulling him down.

As he obeyed her command, only one wonderful thought flashed through her mind.

Mrs. Cortez…

ABOUT THE AUTHOR

ANTHONY GOODRUM GREW up and was raised in Colp, Illinois. It was a town of only 250 people but they were supportive of his life and childhood. His parents, Tony and Grace are married over fifty years, and he has been happily married to his wife, Pamela, for over twenty-five years. He graduated from Colorado State University where he met a great author of children's books—Carol Beckman, *Channels to Children*. *Dunes of Fire* is his finest work and first of two novels he is writing. He and his wife have two beautiful daughters. Anthony teaches basketball and referees high school basketball as a hobby. He enjoys people of all ages and watching fantasy movies.

Enjoy his book *Dunes of Fire* and see if you can figure out what happened to Dr. Cortez.